Jekyll & Hyde Inc.

To purchase Baen titles in e-book form, please go to www.baen.com.

Jekyll & Hyde Inc.

Simon R. Green

A Baen Books Original

Baen Publishing Enterprises
P.O. Box 1403
Riverdale, NY 10471
www.baen.com

ISBN: 978-1-9821-2528-8

Cover art by Todd Lockwood

First printing, September 2021

Distributed by Simon & Schuster
1230 Avenue of the Americas
New York, NY 10020

Library of Congress Cataloging-in-Publication Data

Names: Green, Simon R., 1955- author.
Title: Jekyll & Hyde Inc. / by Simon Green.
Other titles: Jekyll and Hyde Inc.
Description: Riverdale, NY : Baen Books, [2021]
Identifiers: LCCN 2021029297 | ISBN 9781982125288 (hardcover)
Subjects: GSAFD: Horror fiction. | LCGFT: Paranormal fiction.
Classification: LCC PR6107.R44 J43 2021 | DDC 823/.92--dc23
LC record available at https://lccn.loc.gov/2021029297

Printed in the United States of America

10 9 8 7 6 5 4 3 2 1

Jekyll & Hyde Inc.

✤ ✤ ✤

Whatever happened to all the monsters?

For as long as there have been people, there have been creatures who preyed on them. Lurking in the least-traveled parts of the forest, or hanging around on street corners in the worst parts of town; watching for the weak and the vulnerable, with hungry eyes . . . The drinkers of blood and the tearers of flesh, the things that reek of the tomb but aren't nearly dead enough, the hunters and the liers in wait.

The really wild things, without conscience or limits.

Everyone knows the names: vampires, werewolves, ghouls. Monsters who preyed on Humanity for centuries, striking from the shadows and then disappearing back into the night . . . But as first gas and then electricity filled the world with light, shadows became harder to find and the night concealed less and less.

By the end of the nineteenth century, it had become clear to the monsters that they couldn't hope to survive the sharp clear light of the scientific age. Growing mass communications meant everyone knew about garlic and wolfsbane, wooden stakes and silver bullets. So the monsters went underground, disappearing into the underworld of crime; civilization's shadow. Looking for new ways to prey upon the weak and the vulnerable.

And everyone forgot that monsters had ever been real.

In the white-hot glare of the twenty-first century, no one believes in monsters any more. But they're still here, more dangerous and more powerful than ever. Someone has to save us.

It takes a thief to catch a thief . . . And a monster to kill a monster.

✤ ✤ ✤

Chapter One
THE CHOP SHOP

✢ ✢ ✢

LATE-NIGHT CAFÉS STAND ALONE, like campfires holding out against the fall of night. Offering solace to their customers, from endless empty evenings and mean rooms no one ever visits. Daniel Carter, tall and lanky, dark-haired and dark-eyed, sat alone at his table in a café in old Soho. Outside it was cold, inside it was warm; but that was really all you could say in its favor. Daniel hadn't been there long, and already he was wishing he were somewhere else.

He glanced casually round the café. This late in the evening there were only a handful of customers, all of them quietly intent on their own business. Daniel sipped some more coffee he didn't want, and shifted uncomfortably inside his suit. He hadn't been in plainclothes long, and he was still getting used to it.

He had thought ditching his uniform, and moving up in rank would mean he finally got to work the kind of cases that mattered, but all he did was sit behind a desk, moving papers from one pile to another. Not at all what he'd had in mind, when he first made the decision to join the police.

Daniel allowed himself another quick glance at his watch. He'd arrived early, because he'd been too impatient not to, but someone should have joined him by now. For want of anything better to do, he studied the two waitresses in their shocking pink uniforms. Angels of mercy, sisters of the night, dispensing cups of coffee in place of benedictions. The senior waitress was leaning heavily on the counter, defiantly smoking her cigarette right under the THANK YOU FOR NOT SMOKING sign, while the junior waitress darted in and out of the tables, doing all the real work.

Daniel looked round sharply as the door opened, and was surprised to see Paul Mayer, of all people. Easygoing, lazily handsome, and always that little bit overweight, Paul had never been known to give a damn about anything. He looked quickly round the café, dismissed everyone but Daniel, and sat down opposite him. They barely had time to nod to each other before the young waitress came bustling over with her jug of steaming coffee and a new cup.

"Black," said Paul.

"Like your heart?" said Daniel.

"Maybe not that black," said Paul. He waited till his cup was full, and then slapped a handful of change on the table. "Don't hurry back, love."

The waitress scooped up the money and retreated to the counter. She knew a lost cause when she heard one. Paul tried the coffee, pulled a face, and put the cup down.

"So, Danny boy, it's been a while since we last got together. I take it you're also here for the highly secret briefing?"

"You don't think I'm drinking this stuff by choice, do you?" said Daniel.

"Why did we have to meet in this dump?" said Paul. "I feel like I'm raising the tone just by being here—and that isn't like me."

"I was told this operation would be very definitely off the books and under the radar," said Daniel. "Which of course isn't at all worrying."

"Someone is going to want us to volunteer," Paul said gloomily. "To do something risky, to benefit someone else."

"But something that just might be in our best interests, if we can pull it off," said Daniel. "That's how our betters always bait the hook."

The two young men nodded slowly, contemplating the way of the world.

"That is some suit you're wearing," said Paul. "Was it on sale?"

"At least I look respectable," said Daniel. "You look like you stole yours off a homeless person."

"He didn't put up much of a struggle," said Paul. He looked thoughtfully at Daniel. "It's been what . . . three years? Since we started out in training together?"

Daniel nodded. "Where does the time go, when your career's going nowhere?"

"You too?" said Paul. "Hard to believe we were the high fliers; the ones who were going to make our mark in record time. But, you can't fight the system . . ."

"I thought we were supposed to be fighting the bad guys," said Daniel.

Paul started to raise his cup, remembered, and put it down again. "Why did you want to be a copper, originally?"

"To help people," said Daniel. "To protect them from all the scumbags who prey on the vulnerable. To fight monsters. You?"

"I just thought it would better to be one of those giving the orders, than those who had to take them," said Paul.

"You do surprise me," said Daniel. "I thought you were only in it for the money."

"Well, that too," said Paul.

They laughed quietly together, and then looked round quickly as the door swung open and two more familiar faces entered the café. Oscar Marsh was a large, sturdy type in a heavy fur coat, while Nigel Rutherford was a tall, slender aristocrat in a very expensive suit. They both smiled at Daniel and Paul, and pulled up chairs to join them.

"It's the Bear!" said Paul. "I can't believe you're still wearing that same old animal pelt, Oscar."

"Fur never goes out of style," said Oscar, in his deep rumble of a voice.

"Still visiting the old family tailor?" Daniel said to Nigel.

"Money never goes out of fashion," Nigel murmured. "I have to say . . . it does my heart good to see you chaps again, but I'm not sure I like this. What are the odds that four ambitious types who started out together would be selected for the same clandestine meeting?"

He broke off as the young waitress showed up with her coffee jug, only to retreat again in the face of clear disinterest. She hurried back behind the counter to be comforted by the older waitress, who knew plainclothes cops when she saw them.

"I take it you two received the same mysterious summons we did?" said Daniel.

"And that your careers aren't everything you thought they were going to be?" said Paul.

"Got it in one," said Oscar.

"The word 'promotion' was mentioned," Nigel said diffidently.

"I just want work that matters," said Daniel.

"Still the Boy Scout," said Paul, not unkindly.

"Somebody has to be," said Daniel.

"But why you?" said Nigel.

"Because people who choose to be monsters, when they could be people, offend the hell out of me," said Daniel. "Life is hard enough without the bad guys making it worse."

They glanced round one last time as the door banged open, and then they all sat up straight. Alicia Gill was the youngest police commissioner ever—a short, blond powerhouse packed full of authority and ambition, with a face that might have been attractive if she ever smiled. She was out of uniform too, though wearing something too expensive to be properly anonymous. The four police officers started to rise to their feet in the presence of a superior officer, but Gill glared them into quickly sitting down again. She hauled a chair across from the next table, dropped into it, and set her briefcase down beside her. The young waitress started forward hopefully, but Gill stopped her with a look.

Paul fixed Gill with an equally hard stare. "So. Why are we here, Commissioner?"

"Call me Gill," she said sharply. "And keep your voice down, because officially I am not here and this meeting never happened. Now pay attention; I have a job for you."

"How can we help someone like you?" said Nigel. "We don't even breathe the same air."

"Right," said Oscar.

"I have hit the glass ceiling, and discovered it's made of bulletproof glass," said Gill. "No more promotions and no way forward—unless I can pull off something really impressive, on my own initiative. I need someone useful to take care of the heavy lifting, so I chose you four because you're all new to plainclothes."

"But still—why us?" said Daniel.

"What he said, only louder," said Paul.

"None of you have any experience in undercover work, so I can be sure no one knows about you," Gill said steadily. "On the street, or in the force."

All four of them sat up and took notice. Gill leaned forward across the table.

"This operation is strictly volunteers only, but it's guaranteed promotions all round, if you can bring this off."

"I'm sensing a difficulty in our near future," said Nigel. "Some built-in drawbacks, to place obstacles in our path."

"What's the catch?" said Paul.

"You'll be taking on an established firm, with a reputation for extreme violence when it comes to protecting its assets," said Gill. "Is that going to be a problem?"

Oscar grinned. "Sounds like fun. I like solving problems."

He cracked his knuckles loudly, and his three friends looked somewhere else for a moment. The Bear had his own reputation for violence.

"Is this mission something worth doing?" said Daniel. It bothered him, that he was the only one at the table to ask that.

"Of course," said Gill.

"I'm in," said Paul. The others nodded their agreement, and Daniel went along, because he knew this was going to happen with or without him. And he really was tired of shuffling papers.

"Who's the target?" he said.

"An underground surgical organization," said Gill. "There's a branch just a few streets from here, hidden away behind a secondhand bookshop."

"And that's why we're meeting here," said Paul.

Gill allowed herself a small smile. "I certainly didn't choose this place for its ambience."

"I doubt anyone here could even spell that," said Nigel.

"Snob," said Oscar.

"You say that like it's a bad thing," said Nigel.

"The firm in question calls itself The Cutting Edge," said Gill. "They specialize in unauthorized transplants, unsafe cosmetic procedures, and the kind of really unpleasant fetish work that never gets talked up in the glossy magazines."

Daniel frowned. "Black-market organs means big money . . . and high-up protection."

"They're all going down," Gill said flatly. "But you can go up, if you've got the balls to grab for the golden ring."

"I'm in," said Oscar.

"Of course you are, o Bear of little brain," said Nigel.

"Don't you want this?" said Oscar.

"Of course I want it," said Nigel. "I'm just debating whether the reward is worth the risk."

"You can always stay where you are," said Gill. "Who knows? You might get another promotion. In ten years or so."

"Hell with that," said Oscar. "I'm in."

Nigel sighed. "And so am I."

"What kind of security will we be facing?" said Paul.

"Just basic muscle," said Gill.

"I'm still having trouble seeing the moral high ground in this," said Daniel. "Who exactly will we be protecting, if we take down these Cutting Edge people?"

Gill looked at him impatiently. "Many of the patients involved are simply ordinary people driven to desperate measures by long waiting lists, or because traditional hospitals won't help them. But if anything goes wrong, they just get dumped by the roadside. And if anyone tries to complain, well...dead patients tell no tales. Is that good enough for you?"

Daniel subsided. He could tell the others were getting impatient with him.

"I want this Cutting Edge stamped on hard," said Gill, looking steadily round the table. "I need you to get in, hold everyone, and gather evidence. Then call me for backup."

"So this will be official, eventually?" said Daniel.

"Of course," said Gill. "Understand me, all of you: screw this up and I never heard of you, and certainly never authorized anything. But get it right, and I'll take you all the way up the promotions ladder with me."

"Fair enough," said Paul. And everyone else nodded.

Gill slapped a card on the table. "Here's the address for the bookshop. And..." She gestured at the briefcase by her feet. "I brought you a few toys to play with. Four sets of Tasers, and some extendable batons. Don't say I never give you anything."

"No guns?" said Oscar.

"You're only going after a few backstreet surgeons and their hired muscle," said Gill. "Give me half an hour to put some space between us, and then you're on."

She got up and left the café. The four men looked at one another.

"Does she really believe she can just walk away from this, if it should turn pear-shaped?" said Daniel.

"It would be our word against hers," said Paul. "And she's somebody, while we're not. You can bet there won't be any paper trail connecting her to us—and that's all a Board of Inquiry would care about."

"Any of you heard of these Cutting Edge people?" said Daniel. There was a general shaking of heads. "Don't you think we should have, if the firm is as big as she says?"

"Why would we?" said Paul. "This isn't our territory."

"You can bet good money the lady will get a lot more out of this than we will," said Nigel.

"But we'll get enough to make it worthwhile," said Paul.

"Right," said Oscar.

"I'm still concerned that we're missing something," said Nigel. "You know what they say: If you can't see the patsy in the deal, it's you."

"Are we going to do this or not?" said Paul. "It's make-up-your-mind time, people . . . This is our chance to bring down some big league bad guys, and acquire major brownie points in the process."

"It's a way out of jobs we hate," said Oscar.

"And . . . we get to do some good," said Daniel.

"All for one, and all against one!" said Nigel. "Let us venture forth into the night and stick it to the bad guys!"

"Right," said Oscar. He cracked his knuckles again, and everyone winced.

The four of them ended up loitering casually on a street corner, in an area that had never even heard of gentrification. The bookshop was a shabby affair, the only window painted over in thick swirls so no one could see in. The sign above the window said simply SECONDHAND BOOKSHOP.

"Not even a name?" said Paul. "They could have made an effort."

Daniel looked up and down the street, checking out the long gloomy stretches punctuated by pools of lamplight. Like spotlights on an empty stage, and a play no one wanted to be in.

"Where is everybody?"

"It's late," said Paul.

"Not for Soho," said Daniel. "There's usually someone around, selling things they shouldn't. And the odd punter looking to do something unwise."

"Unless the local population knows something we don't," said Nigel.

"There's no muscle guarding the door," said Oscar.

"Try not to sound so disappointed," said Paul. "Remember, Bear: unconscious people can't answer questions."

"They can't give you any trouble either," Oscar said reasonably.

They all took a moment, to check that the Tasers and batons they'd stowed about their persons were ready to hand.

"Ah, memories . . ." said Oscar.

Daniel looked at him, but said nothing. Every plan of action needs someone like Oscar.

"Can't help feeling we'd be better off with proper guns," said Nigel.

"It's just a backstreet chop shop," said Paul. "A Taser will take down anyone, no matter how big they are. It's very democratic."

"How do we want to do this?" said Oscar.

"Keep it simple," said Daniel. "Less to go wrong that way. We walk in, flash our IDs around, and arrest everything that moves. Oscar, you can flatten any muscle who objects, just to show we mean business. Then we tear the place apart until we find some useful paperwork . . . and perhaps even some computer records, if anyone's been stupid enough to use an obvious password. Once we're done we can just sit on everything, call the commissioner, and wait for backup."

"Assuming everything goes smoothly," said Nigel. "And we don't have to lay down the law in an assertive fashion."

"Best part," said Oscar. He cracked his knuckles loudly, and everyone found a reason to look somewhere else.

"Paul, you can take the front door, with me," said Daniel. "Nigel, Oscar: nip round the back. Just in case anyone rabbits."

"Since when are you the commanding officer?" said Nigel.

"Do you have a better plan?" said Daniel.

"That's not the point," said Nigel.

"It sort of is," said Paul.

"Let's get this show on the road!" said Oscar.

He strode off, heading determinedly for the narrow alley beside the shop, and Nigel went after him.

"If you crack your knuckles one more time, Bear..."

Paul grinned at Daniel. "It does feel good, to be doing something that matters."

"This is what I joined up for," said Daniel. "To be the man in the white hat, riding to the rescue. Do you think anyone in there is going to give us a hard time?"

"Why should they?" said Paul. "Makes more sense for them to just sit quietly, and wait for the firm's lawyers to break them loose."

"Then let's go fight some monsters," said Daniel.

"I take it back," said Paul. "You're not a Boy Scout, you're a knight in shining armor."

"Somebody has to be," said Daniel.

Inside the shop, the walls were covered in shelves packed with cheap paperbacks, while a bored-looking teenage girl stood slumped over the counter, concentrating on her phone. A tall, gangling sort with spiky hair, a white T-shirt, and black leather trousers, she made a big thing out of ignoring the new arrivals while still being very aware of their presence. Daniel moved forward to confront her, while Paul drifted casually into position to block the way to the rear door. The receptionist looked up from her phone, her eyes quietly alert while her face gave nothing away.

"See anything you fancy, gents? Got some nice Agatha Christies."

"We're not here for books," said Daniel.

"Didn't think so. Do you have an appointment, gents?"

Daniel showed her his warrant card. She just sniffed.

"We're paid up. You want anything special, your bosses will have to talk to my bosses. Not my department."

"Cut the crap," said Paul. "We're shutting you down."

The teenage girl stood up straight. It was hard to tell whether she looked more surprised, or outraged. "Like hell you are. I told you: we're all paid up!"

"We heard you," said Daniel. "We don't care. You're under arrest."

She didn't even try to bluff him, just bolted for the rear door. Paul was ready for that, but she lowered her shoulder and slammed right through him, sending him crashing into a bookshelf. She was already through the door and gone by the time he got his feet under him again. Daniel shook his head.

"You have spent far too long behind a desk."

"She must be on something," said Paul, with what dignity he had left. "She punted me out of the way like a runaway truck."

"She won't get far," said Daniel. "Nigel and Oscar must have blocked off the rear by now, and if she tries that trick on Oscar she'll just bounce right off him."

"Well, no more mister nice guy," said Paul. He drew his Taser. "From now on, anyone who even looks at me funny is going to dance the funny dance."

Daniel nodded, and drew his own Taser. "She's probably already on her phone to someone higher up, to ask for instructions."

"Let her," said Paul. "It's time to bring the hammer down."

The back room turned out to be just an open space, its gloom only partly pushed back by light spilling through from the shop. No furniture, no stock, nothing but another door on the far side of the room. Which crashed open suddenly as Oscar barged through, with Nigel right behind him.

"Thought it had been quiet a bit too long," said Nigel. "So I had the Bear announce us. He's so useful to have around; our very own human battering ram."

"Next time I'll use *you* as a battering ram," said Oscar, massaging his shoulder.

"Did a teenage girl just run past you?" said Paul.

Nigel raised an eyebrow. "Hardly."

"Where is everybody?" said Oscar.

"There was only the one girl," said Daniel. "And she got away. But if she didn't leave through the back door . . ."

"Then there must be a hidden exit in here," said Paul.

It didn't take them long to discover the trapdoor in the floor. They got it open easily enough, revealing rough stone steps falling away, illuminated by a single hanging bulb. Daniel held his Taser out before him and started down, with the others following close behind. After a while, Daniel wrinkled his nose.

"Can you smell . . . blood?"

"Reminds me of the butcher shop my old uncle used to run," said Paul.

"We knew this was a chop shop," said Oscar.

"Even a backstreet surgery should smell of antiseptic, not offal," said Nigel.

"This is going to be a bad one," said Daniel.

Nobody argued with him.

The steps ended at a locked door. Daniel stood to one side, so Oscar could do the business. He charged down the steps and slammed the heavy door open, and they all rushed in, Tasers at the ready. The low-ceilinged cellar was bigger than the shop above, starkly illuminated by overhead fluorescent lights and packed from wall to wall with trestle tables bearing dozens of naked corpses, cut open so the organs could be removed. Blood-spattered rib cages had been levered back, over empty crimson caverns. Arms and legs had been sliced open, to get at the muscles and tendons. There were no eyes in the faces, no tongues in the gaping mouths. Even the skulls had been sawed open and emptied out. The harsh light was merciless in revealing every detail, and the stench of blood and death was almost unbearable.

The policemen huddled together, like children who'd found their way into an ogre's lair.

"This is no surgery," said Nigel. "This is a charnel house."

"A chop shop," said Oscar.

"This isn't what we came here for," said Paul.

Daniel didn't say anything. He was too sickened, and too angry.

At the back of the room, three figures in blood-soaked surgical gowns were bent over a patient on a table. Held in place by heavy leather straps, he still fought and heaved as the surgeons' hands disappeared into the hole they'd made in his torso; and bit by bit they took him apart. Scalpels cut and slashed, and gloved hands removed all the useful pieces, placing them carefully on waiting steel trays. The patient would have filled the cellar with his screams, if he hadn't been so thoroughly gagged.

Blood spurted, and steam rose from the opening into the chilly air of the cellar. Daniel stood frozen in place by shock and horror, as one of the surgeons put aside his scalpel and thrust both hands into the bloody opening. He pulled out the man's heart, and held it up so the other surgeons could admire it. The patient heaved against his restraints one last time, and then lay still. Blood spilled down his sides, and dripped off the table to splash on the floor.

Daniel knew there was nothing he could have done to save the man. Everything he'd seen had taken place in just a few moments. But for the rest of his life he would be tormented by the thought that he should have done something. He raised his voice.

"Get away from him, you bastards!"

The three surgeons straightened up and stared at the newcomers with wide, surprised eyes over their face masks. Blood dripped thickly from the instruments in their hands. Daniel raised his Taser and looked around for the missing teenage girl, but couldn't see her anywhere—which meant there had to be a hidden exit. He was surprised he could still think clearly, in the midst of so many atrocities. But perhaps he needed to, in order to stay sane.

Paul leveled his Taser at all three surgeons impartially.

"Police! You're under arrest!"

The surgeons looked at one another. One carefully lowered his bone saw, and stepped out from behind the bloody mess he'd been working on.

"But . . . we're paid up!"

"I am getting really tired of hearing that," said Daniel. "You can't bribe your way out of this."

"Damn right," said Oscar.

"What have you people been doing here?" said Nigel.

"Just the usual," said the surgeon. He looked to the other surgeons for support, but they were happy for him to serve as spokesman, so he turned reluctantly back again. "We take the bodies apart, and then ship everything off for transplants. It's all used up; nothing goes to waste."

"Where does it all go?" said Daniel.

The surgeon shrugged. "Not our department. Storage, somewhere. There are always orders waiting to be filled."

"This is sick," said Oscar.

"That's not the worst of it," said Daniel. He gestured angrily at the nearby trestle tables, his hand shaking with the strength of his emotions. "See the heavy restraints, at the wrists and the ankles? All of these people were strapped down, to stop them from struggling."

Paul looked at him sharply. "You mean . . . they were alive, when these bastards started cutting? Like the one they just butchered?"

Daniel glared at the surgeon. "Why would you do something like that?"

The surgeon shrugged. "Anaesthetics cost money..."

"You little shits," said Oscar.

"That's why they put the surgery this far down," said Daniel. "So no one would hear the screams."

"They were only homeless people!" the surgeon said quickly. "No one who'll be missed. At least this way they serve some useful purpose."

"Someone stop him talking," said Nigel.

"Love to," said Oscar.

"We're shutting this butcher's shop down," said Daniel.

"You can't!" said the surgeon. "This is a Frankenstein Clan operation! We're protected, by very high-up people!"

"They can go down with you," said Daniel.

His hand was suddenly entirely steady as he shot the surgeon with his Taser, and the man fell jerking to the floor, trying to force out a scream. Oscar charged forward, not bothering with his own Taser. He raised his baton and clubbed the other two surgeons to the floor, grunting happily with the effort he put into his blows. Blood flew on the air, and the surgeons soon stopped screaming, but Oscar just kept going. And after everything Daniel had seen, he didn't feel like intervening.

And then the spiky-haired teenage girl burst out of a concealed side door, along with two hulking figures in hospital whites. She stabbed a finger at the policemen, her voice shrill with outrage.

"Kill them! Kill them all!"

The two huge figures lurched forward. Big enough to be serious steroid abusers, their hands opened and closed menacingly as they advanced; but there was something odd in the way they moved, as though their muscles weren't connected properly, and they couldn't feel the floor beneath their feet. Most disturbing of all, their faces were completely empty, their eyes fixed and staring. Like dead men walking.

"They're on something!" said Paul.

Oscar smiled, and hefted his baton. Blood dripped thickly from the extended nightstick.

"Won't make any difference."

Paul tasered the nearest big man but he just kept coming, as though he hadn't felt anything. Oscar charged the other figure and hit him head-on. The man was actually bigger than Oscar, and the two of them grappled clumsily as they wrestled back and forth, crashing into trestle tables and overturning them. Paul dropped his Taser as the first figure advanced on him, and thrust his baton viciously in under the man's sternum, hard enough to paralyze the heart. The big man didn't even blink. Huge hands clamped down on Paul's shoulders, and he cried out in pain. Daniel moved quickly in beside Paul, raining blow after blow on the attacker's head with his baton, but no blood spurted, and the big man didn't even seem to notice. Paul was screaming now, as his collarbone shattered under the heavy hands.

The teenage girl advanced on Nigel, grinning nastily. He hesitated, not wanting to hurt a woman—until he saw the look in her eyes, and then he shot her at point-blank range with his Taser. Her grin widened and she surged forward, ignoring the drooping wires and the current they carried. She slapped the Taser right out of his hand. Nigel switched to his baton, and whipped it across her face. She didn't even flinch. Nigel backed away, and the girl went after him.

Oscar screamed shrilly. Daniel looked round just in time to see the huge figure take a firm hold on Oscar's head with both hands, and rip it clean off his shoulders. Blood fountained from the ragged neck, splashing against the overhead lights and dripping back again in a crimson rain. Oscar's body crumpled slowly to the floor.

Paul suddenly stopped screaming. Daniel looked back, to see the massive figure crushing Paul in a bear hug. There was an awful snapping sound as Paul's back broke, and then the big man just threw him away. Paul hit the ground hard, and didn't move again. Daniel threw himself at the huge figure, and hit him again and again with his baton, shouting helpless obscenities, and the man slowly turned his head to look at him. The eyes didn't see him at all. The scalp had been half torn away from the forehead, but there wasn't any blood. Daniel lowered his baton, and staggered backward.

He saw the teenage girl punch Nigel under the breastbone so hard that blood flew from his mouth, and the light went out of his eyes.

Daniel never knew who hit him from behind. As he fell to the floor, his last thought was, *We were set up.*

Chapter Two
BACK FROM THE DEAD
✤ ✤ ✤

IT WAS DARK when Daniel woke up. He pushed the bedsheets away and started to sit up, only to stop abruptly when the pain hit him. He gritted his teeth to keep from crying out. He had that much pride left. He dry-swallowed a handful of pills from the bedside table, breathed slowly and steadily until the pain died back to a bearable level, and then carefully swung his legs over the side of the bed.

It had to be heading out of night and into morning, because enough light made it past the closed curtains for him to make out his surroundings. Not that there was much worth looking at. His flat had only ever been somewhere to come back to, when he wasn't working. Daniel sighed, and decided he might as well get up. He knew he wouldn't be able to get back to sleep again.

His pajamas stank from the night's cold sweats, and he slowly stripped them off and let them drop to the floor. He had difficulty getting dressed, because of what had happened to him in that terrible cellar under the bookstore. Everyone at the hospital kept telling him he was lucky to be alive after so many serious injuries, but he found that hard to accept on days when he had so much difficulty just doing up his shirt buttons. His fingers were numb this morning, which was a good thing. On the really bad days it felt like his hands were on fire.

Daniel finally forced himself up onto his feet and shuffled out of the bedroom, heading for the kitchen. He didn't bother to turn on the lights. He preferred the gloom, so he wouldn't have to look at what his life had become. He moved slowly around the kitchen, getting out the mug and the tea bags and turning on the electric kettle. He found the ritual comforting, even though he wasn't sure he actually wanted any tea.

He'd been found in the wreckage of the cellar, more dead than alive. Not by police reinforcements, but by the local fire brigade responding to an anonymous call. The bookstore had been completely burned down, but the firemen dug Daniel out of the cellar in time to save his life. Daniel was still having trouble deciding whether that had been a kindness.

The investigating team found a few bits and pieces of Oscar, but no trace at all of Paul or Nigel. Daniel kept insisting that they were both dead, murdered by monstrous creatures... but no one believed him.

He was suspended without pay the moment he left hospital. Pending a Board of Inquiry that no one seemed too eager to set in motion. An unauthorized raid was bad enough, but an unsuccessful one? Best to let it just fade quietly away, and be forgotten. Commissioner Gill had also been suspended, for exceeding her authority. Or at least she would be, if anyone could find her.

The police review board interrogated Daniel over and over again. He told them everything that happened in that awful underground abattoir, but they couldn't accept any of it. Not about the homeless people being dissected alive, or the Frankenstein doctors (the board really didn't like it when he used that name), or the huge, hulking figures who'd shrugged off Tasers and took no harm from flailing batons.

They told Daniel the force had no record of a firm called The Cutting Edge. That there were no reports of missing homeless people in the area. And that there was definitely no such thing as a glass ceiling in the modern police force. They made it very clear they thought he was mad, or lying. They didn't believe a word he said.

Especially when he wouldn't shut up about the monsters.

So now his time in the police force was over. A cripple, and a disgrace. The man who only wanted to help others couldn't even help himself. Daniel looked at the cup of tea he'd made, and wondered what he was going to do with his day.

There was a knock at the front door. It took him a while to react. He didn't get visitors, these days. Friends and colleagues had been conspicuous by their absence, the media had stopped bothering him once he made it clear he was never going to talk to them, and his parents hadn't wanted anything to do with him from the moment he told them he was joining the police, instead of following the university course they'd mapped out for him. His father told him to his face that he'd broken his mother's heart.

He did phone his parents once, to let them know he was still alive. Daniel's father said he'd told him nothing good would come of choosing to work in the gutters, to help people who weren't worth saving. He said Daniel had brought it all on himself, by turning his back on the life his parents had sacrificed so much to make possible.

He wouldn't let Daniel talk to his mother. And he told Daniel never to call again.

While Daniel was still working his way through all of that, the knocking came again—louder, and more impatient. Whoever it was, they weren't giving up. Daniel made his way slowly through the flat to his front door, groaning quietly to himself as the pains came and went. It took him so long his unknown visitor knocked a third time, hard enough that the door jumped and rattled in its frame. Daniel hauled the door open and then stood very still, staring in shock. Wrapped in a long grubby coat, Paul looked like he'd lost a hell of a lot of weight. His face was gaunt, almost painfully bony, and the taut skin was so pale as to be almost colorless. His eyes had sunk back into the skull, and looked a lot darker than Daniel remembered. Paul smiled briefly at Dan, little more than a quirk of the lips.

"Hello, Danny boy. Been a while, hasn't it?"

"Paul...?" said Daniel.

"Well, you look like shit," said Paul. "Aren't you going to invite me in?"

"Why not?" said Daniel. "It's not like you're interrupting anything."

He stepped back, and Paul slipped quickly past him. He seemed to drift rather than walk, and his feet made no sound at all on the bare floorboards. That last thought struck Daniel suddenly, and he glared at Paul.

"How are you able to walk? I saw that creature snap your spine!"

"I got over it," said Paul.

There was something wrong with his voice, Daniel decided. It sounded harsh, painful...as though every word was an effort. He closed the door, and looked Paul over carefully. There wasn't much left of the man he used to know. The lazy, overweight Paul who breezed through life because he just couldn't be bothered had been replaced by an emaciated scarecrow. He didn't say anything, just fixed Daniel with an uncomfortably intent gaze until he felt obliged to say something.

"Where have you been, all this time?"

"Underground," said Paul. "Out of sight."

He looked around Daniel's flat, still mostly hidden in the gloom. Daniel reached for the light switch.

"No," said Paul. "Don't. Please."

Daniel looked at him sharply. He didn't think he'd ever heard Paul use that word before.

"Would you like some tea?" he said finally, for want of anything else to say.

The quick smile came and went again. There was no humor in it.

"I don't drink tea."

Daniel felt suddenly tired of the whole conversation. It wasn't like he'd wanted any company. But the return of a man who was supposed to be dead demanded he at least make an effort.

"What are you doing here?" he said, with as much politeness as he could manage.

Paul was suddenly standing right in front of him. Daniel blinked confusedly, and almost fell back a step. Up close, his old friend was unhealthily pale. His lips had no color, and his eyes were disturbingly sharp. His long coat was in foul condition, and spotted with stains. He smelled like recently disturbed earth.

"We need to talk," said Paul.

"All right," said Daniel, trying to pretend this was a normal conversation. "Let's start with: What are you doing up at this hour? You never used to be a morning person."

"I had to come while it was still dark."

"Dark as your heart?"

"It never gets that dark," said Paul.

"Where have you been hiding yourself?" said Daniel. "Everyone's been looking for you."

"I know," said Paul.

"Is Nigel with you?"

"He's with someone else now," said Paul. "We don't talk."

"Wait a minute," said Daniel. He closed his eyes for a moment, as a wave of weariness washed through him. He put out a hand to the nearest wall, to steady himself. "I need to sit down. I'm not a well man, these days."

He shuffled over to the nearest chair. It took a while, because every movement hurt. Paul waited patiently for Daniel to settle himself, and then sat down facing him.

"I can't stay long, Dan."

"What's the problem? Do you turn into a pumpkin when the sun comes up?"

"Something like that."

Daniel frowned. "Are you worried you might have been followed here?"

"No," said Paul. "I can't stay because it will be light soon. Please, Dan, shut the hell up and let me talk. I have so much to tell you."

Daniel shrugged, and then winced despite himself. "Get on with it, then. I'm not stopping you."

Paul sat very still in his chair, staring unwaveringly at Daniel. "You must know you were never supposed to survive. They left you for dead."

Daniel nodded slowly. "I did wonder why the surgeons didn't take my body with them, so they could harvest my organs. I thought that was what happened to you and Oscar and Nigel."

"They had other things in mind for me and Nigel," said Paul. "They left one body behind to show what happened to policemen who interfere."

"And then I had to go and spoil everything, by not dying after all," said Daniel. "And not keeping my mouth shut."

"The only reason you're still alive now," said Paul, "is because no one believed you when you talked about the monsters."

"It was all true!"

"Of course it was," said Paul.

"What were those oversized freakshows?" said Daniel.

"Creations of the Frankenstein Clan," said Paul. "And yes, you did hear that name correctly. Tell me, Dan, did you ever wonder what happened to all the monsters everyone used to believe in? The vampires, werewolves, and mummies..."

"They weren't real. And most of us grew out of fairy stories."

"They used to be real," said Paul. "Real as you and me. They just chose to reinvent themselves, to disappear into the underworld of crime. These days, the Frankenstein Clan deals in illegal surgeries. The Vampire Clan deals in all forms of seduction. The Clan of Mummies deals in drugs. The werewolves supply muscle and enforcement, for when the Clans don't want to do it themselves. All the shit work, basically. And the ghouls make sure the bodies are never found. Because they'll eat anything."

Daniel looked at Paul, lost for words. His first thought was that his friend had been driven out of his mind by his experiences, but that didn't explain how a man with a broken back could walk into his flat. And if there was a way for a broken body to be repaired... Daniel wanted to know about it.

"I was so sure you were dead," he said finally. "How are you still alive?"

"They wanted to know how we'd found out about them," said Paul. "And the best way to be sure I would tell them everything was to make me one of them."

"A criminal?" said Daniel.

"A vampire," said Paul.

"And they say I'm crazy," said Daniel.

Paul surged forward, grabbed Daniel by the shirtfront, and lifted him out of his chair as though he was weightless. Daniel's feet kicked helplessly above the floor. He grabbed Paul's wrist with both hands, and then snatched them away. The skin was horribly cold, like touching a dead man. Paul marched Daniel across the room and slammed him against the far wall. Daniel cried out at the pain, and Paul clapped his other hand over Daniel's mouth to silence him. The hand smelled like something dead, but Paul wouldn't let Daniel squirm away. He pushed his face right up against Daniel's, and then he smiled slowly, revealing jagged, pointed teeth. His breath stank of blood and death. And his eyes were full of all the darkness in the world. Paul eased up a little, and Daniel turned his head away. In the mirror hanging on the wall beside him he saw his reflection... and no one else. He seemed to be hanging unsupported in mid air.

His heart lurched painfully in his chest, and he made himself look back at Paul. The eyes boring into his were as inhuman as a shark's, and the smile was full of predator's teeth. For the first time, Daniel realized Paul wasn't breathing. They were so close Daniel should have been able to feel Paul's breath on his face, but there was nothing. His old friend stank of the grave, and things that had been dead too long. Daniel stared wide-eyed into the unblinking eyes before him, his mouth crushed under a dead man's hand, and wished he'd never survived to know such things were possible.

Paul slowly lowered Daniel to the floor, let go of him, and stepped away. Daniel breathed deeply, trying to get the dead man's smell out of his nostrils. He rubbed hard at his mouth with the back of his hand, trying to forget how the dead flesh had felt. He was shaking so much he had to lean back against the wall to steady himself. He glanced at the mirror again. Paul was standing right in front of it, but there was no trace of him anywhere in the reflection. Daniel made a sound, deep in his throat, and Paul laughed softly. He went back to his chair and sat down. Daniel watched him, until his heartbeat and breathing had returned to something like normal. And then he went back, and sat down opposite Paul again.

Because his world had just been changed forever, and he needed to know what the hell was going on.

"Sorry about that, Danny boy," said Paul. "But I needed you to believe me."

"All right," Daniel said steadily. "I'm convinced. You're a vampire. Is this what happened to Nigel?"

"No," said Paul. "He's something else now. Listen to me, Dan. This is important. Do you still want to help people? To defend them from monsters who prey on the weak and the vulnerable?"

"Yes," said Daniel. It was one of the few things he was still sure about. "But I can't be a cop anymore."

"You could be a hunter of monsters," said Paul.

"Of things like you?" said Daniel.

"I hate what I've been made into," said Paul. "Driven by a hunger that never ends, always at the beck and call of things worse than me. No one trusts me, so I get all the worst jobs. Like disappearing innocent people, when they get too close to the truth about how things really are."

"People like me?" said Daniel.

"You're not dangerous enough to be a problem to them," said Paul. "Though you could be, if you wanted."

"Have you . . . fed, yet?" said Daniel.

"Of course I have! I didn't have any choice. This is what I am now." Paul shook his head slowly. "The only chance I have for revenge on the monsters who did this to me, and all the others who make this world a living hell for everyone else . . . is you. That's why I risked everything to come here. You're the only one I can trust to do the right thing."

"Look at me!" Daniel said harshly. "It's all I can do to walk from one end of my flat to the other. How am I supposed to fight monsters?"

Paul produced a card from inside his coat. "This is the address for Jekyll & Hyde Incorporated."

Daniel couldn't help but smile. Paul didn't.

"You have got to be kidding . . ." said Daniel.

"I don't do that anymore," said Paul.

"But . . . Jekyll and Hyde? Really?"

Paul smiled, showing his teeth. "Set a thief to catch a thief. Or a monster to kill a monster. Go see them, Dan. They can tell you everything you need to know. And . . . they can put you back the way you used to be."

While Daniel was still struggling to get his head round that, Paul rose to his feet. He produced a book from inside his coat and thrust it into Daniel's hands. A battered old copy of *The Strange Case of Dr. Jekyll and Mister Hyde*, by Robert Louis Stevenson. Paul smiled.

"Do your homework before you go to see them."

"Aren't you going to give me *Dracula*, as well?" said Daniel.

"No," said Paul. "Stoker got it all wrong."

He drifted silently over to the front door.

"What about Commissioner Gill?" said Daniel. "Do you know what happened to her?"

Paul looked back at him. "*I* happened to her. The Clan sent me to shut her up, and after what she did to us . . . it was a pleasure. Listen to me, Danny boy: I can't help you directly in this, but I will be around. In the background."

"Is there anyone you'd like me to contact?" said Daniel. "There must be people who'd be glad to know you're back . . ."

"Let them think I'm dead," said Paul. "Because I am."

He left, closing the door quietly behind him. Daniel sat alone in the quiet of his empty flat, and looked at the address on the card.

Chapter Three
HYDE AND SEEK
✤ ✤ ✤

ALL THE WAY ACROSS LONDON on the Tube, no one sat next to Daniel. His permanent scowl had a lot to do with that. He needed a stick to walk any distance, and hated the way it made people look at him. But anger and stubbornness kept him going, and by late afternoon he was limping through an only slightly run-down business area. The pavements were so crowded he was sorely tempted to strike people down with his stick when they didn't get out of his way fast enough, and from the looks on some of their faces he thought they understood that. Daniel was not in the best of moods, but then, he rarely was.

The address Paul had given him turned out to be a pleasantly old-fashioned building, with a businesslike facade and tinted front windows, but no name on the door. Daniel shouldered it open and lurched into the lobby. The great open space was saved from a natural gloom by bright shafts of light streaming in through the higher windows. A gleaming parquet floor smelled as though it had been waxed extremely recently, and Daniel was careful to watch his footing as he slowly crossed the wide-open expanse. There was no reception desk, and no one to be seen anywhere. There wasn't even any background music. He ended up before a long list of company names, scrolling proudly down a wood-paneled wall, and right there at the top in dignified gold leaf was: JEKYLL & HYDE INC. There was nothing to indicate what the company's actual business might be . . . but it wasn't as though he had anywhere else to go.

Daniel took the elevator to the top floor, and wondered all the way up what he was getting himself into. How could Jekyll & Hyde Inc. possibly help him, when all the doctors had given up? Being offered hope again was almost worse than doing without. It hurt more. And what was he going to say to these people? That he'd been told to come and see them by a dead man? No, worse than that—by an undead man . . . The lift doors finally slid open to reveal a long, empty corridor, and Daniel limped stubbornly down it until he came to the door with the right name. He stopped for a moment, to get his breathing back under control, and then braced himself and knocked loudly. A polite voice called for him to enter, and he opened the door onto a comfortably welcoming reception area.

Thick carpeting, pleasant but uncontroversial art on the walls, and a middle-aged but determinedly glamorous secretary sitting behind a desk, intent on her computer. Daniel did his best to walk normally as he approached her, barely leaning on his stick at all, though the effort brought beads of sweat popping out on his forehead. The secretary in the ruffled blouse and very smart jacket looked up and smiled at Daniel as though there was nothing out of the ordinary about him; a small politeness for which he was quietly grateful.

"Daniel Carter," he said. "I believe I'm expected."

He waited for her to consult some long and impressive list of appointments, and then inform him politely but firmly that his name wasn't on it. And then he'd have no choice but to turn and walk away, back to his cold little flat and his life full of nothing. But the secretary didn't even consult her computer, just nodded immediately.

"Of course, Mister Carter. We weren't sure when we should expect you. Please go straight in. Mr. Hyde has been looking forward to meeting you."

Daniel wanted to raise an eyebrow at such a casual use of the name, but he kept his face carefully impassive. If they wanted to follow the joke all the way, let them. The secretary didn't even call through to announce him, just nodded at the door behind her and then returned to her work.

Daniel didn't knock this time, for his pride's sake. He just opened the door and strode in, banging his stick down hard as though to announce himself. The office was comfortably old-fashioned, designed to reassure a client that this was a place where professional work could be expected. Shelves were packed with leather-bound volumes, the usual flowers leaned resignedly in vases, and the gleaming mahogany desk was a definite antique. A single visitor's chair had been positioned invitingly in front of it. And then Daniel got his first shock, as the man behind the desk got up and came forward to greet him.

Mister Hyde didn't so much as stride as swagger, his every movement radiating vicious strength and brutal authority. Although he was barely medium height he had wide shoulders and a barrel chest, and his every movement put such a strain on his suit's expensive material that Daniel almost expected him to burst right out of it. Mister Hyde moved like a man ready to walk right through anything the world could put in his way. His face was unashamedly ugly, with a pronounced bone structure, a low brow, thick dark hair, and deep-set, ice-blue eyes.

Just looking at Mister Hyde made Daniel want to hit him. There was a cold and crafty menace to the man, of evil not just acknowledged but embraced, and barely held in check. Just the look in those awful feral eyes was enough to make Daniel's skin crawl. The look of a man who had done terrible things, and exulted in them. Something about him reminded Daniel of the hulking creatures he'd fought in the cellar underneath the bookstore—but Hyde was so much worse. Like something so vicious, so foul, it should never have been allowed to exist. As though Hyde bore proudly on his brow the mark of Cain—the Mark of the Beast.

He crashed to a halt before Daniel and grinned fiercely at him, recognizing everything Daniel was feeling and savoring it. He thrust out a huge hand and Daniel made himself shake it, even though he just knew Hyde could crush all the bones in his hand to splinters, if he felt like it. But the handshake turned out to be calculatedly brief, and when Daniel pulled his hand back, Hyde's eyes were full of a terrible silent laughter.

"I am Edward Hyde, founder and sole head of Jekyll & Hyde Inc. My name, for all the world to see. Because I'm a great believer in hiding in plain sight. Call me Edward. Now sit down before you fall down."

His voice was deep and harsh, and edged with a caustic mockery, as though everything in the world was only there for him to laugh at.

He turned away abruptly and stomped back to sit behind his desk again. Daniel lowered himself carefully into the visitor's chair, priding himself on not letting out a single groan.

"Edward Hyde?" he said finally, when he was sure he could trust his voice. "Like in the movies?"

"Exactly so," said Edward, grinning unpleasantly. "I am the monster inside every man; the face most people never dare to show the world. And I love it."

Daniel took a moment to think about that. Edward stared at him unblinkingly, and rather than meet that stare and perhaps fail to, Daniel gave all his attention to Edward's desk. There was nothing on it apart from two photos in old-fashioned silver frames. He expected to see the usual shots of wife and family, but instead they were faded images of two men in Victorian clothes, captured in the stiff unsmiling poses of the period.

"The scrawny fellow on the left is Dr. Jekyll," said Edward. "The one on the right is his friend and lawyer, Utterson."

Daniel looked at him sharply. "In the original version, Utterson was the narrator. Are you saying the story was based on real people?"

"Oh yes," said Edward. "Though of course the author found it necessary to change a lot of the details. To protect the guilty."

"So Dr. Jekyll's potion . . ."

"Was real."

"That part of the story never did make sense to me," said Daniel. "Why would the good and saintly Dr. Jekyll want to take a potion he knew would turn him into someone utterly evil?"

"That's the question, isn't it?" said Edward. "Perhaps he saw it as releasing the potential in him. To be strong, instead of weak."

"So, what relation are you, to the original Mr. Hyde?" Daniel said politely.

Edward's grin widened. "I *am* the original Mr. Hyde. I am what the potion created, still alive after all these years and stronger than ever. Now . . . if I told anyone else that, they'd think I was crazy. But you've already seen your fair share of monsters, haven't you?"

Daniel thought of Paul, and the horrors in the cellar, and nodded slowly.

"I've read your official file," said Edward. "Passed on to me by one of my contacts inside the force. I have people everywhere . . . Your story made for fascinating reading. Someone who'd been broken by contact with the underworld of monsters, but hadn't let that beat him."

"Are you sure about that?" said Daniel.

"Of course," said Edward. "Or you wouldn't be here."

"My friend Paul came to see me," said Daniel. "He's a vampire now. And that word didn't throw you at all, did it?"

"Not in the least," said Edward.

"He told me about the vampires, the werewolves, and the Frankenstein family." Daniel made himself say the incredible names steadily, not allowing himself to sound uncertain. "Paul proved to me that he was . . . undead. So I have to believe."

"Then let's start with the Frankenstein Clan," said Edward. "The gods of the living scalpel, the sculptors of flesh. Always on the cutting edge of medicine, and what it can do to people. Some of which you saw, during that ill-judged raid of yours."

"It wasn't my idea," said Daniel. "I had no idea of what I was getting into."

"What did Commissioner Gill think she was sending you into, I wonder?" said Edward. "I don't suppose it matters now. You've seen what the Frankenstein Clan does. To them, we're all just grist to their mill. But if you think they're bad, they're nothing compared to the Vampire Clan.

"Their elders are centuries old, steeped in blood and horror. They specialize in the more lucrative forms of seduction—everything from high-priced escorts to targeted honey traps. Because you only ever see what a vampire wants you to see, they can be anyone you ever dreamed of."

Daniel wondered if the Paul he saw was the real thing, or just a mask Paul allowed him to see. But then, why would Paul want to look that bad? Unless there was something even worse, underneath . . . He realized his thoughts were drifting, and made himself concentrate.

"Vampires can be your first love, or anyone you've ever lusted after from afar," said Edward. "Your wildest dream and most secret fantasy. But of course once they've fed on you, you're their slave forever. You'd be surprised how many powerful people bare their throat in secret. And then, there are the mummies . . ."

"Hold it," said Daniel. "You mean . . . actual mummies?"

"Of course," said Edward. "When those Victorian archaeologists started breaking into long-lost Egyptian tombs, some of them were astonished at what they found waiting beyond the locked doors. The mummies weren't supposed to survive what the priests did to them, but the drugs they'd already taken kept death at arm's length. So that when their tombs were finally opened, the mummies got out.

"And now the Clan of Mummies deals in drugs—everything from out-of-this-world highs to the promise of immortality." Edward shook his great head. "I'm not convinced by that last one. The mummies aren't immortal, just remarkably well preserved.

"The werewolf clan was pressed into service long ago, to provide protection for the other monsters. They're really just attack dogs on short leashes, used to keep peace between the Clans and deal with any outsider who might pose a threat. Second-class monsters, because sometimes they're only human.

"And finally, the ghouls are there to dispose of anything incriminating—including all the inconvenient corpses that inevitably pile up in the monsters' wake."

"What are ghouls, exactly?" said Daniel.

"Appalling creatures with revolting table manners," Edward said briskly. "Useful enough, but trust me when I say you wouldn't want to know them socially. Of course, they don't get out much."

He stopped and leaned back in his chair, still smiling his unpleasant smile, while he studied Daniel to see how he was taking all of this. Somewhat to his surprise, Daniel found he believed every word. Partly because of what he'd seen in Paul's face, but mostly because of what he'd discovered in the cellar. You have to believe in monsters, when they kill your friends and ruin your life.

"Where do you fit in?" Daniel said finally.

"I'm the only monster who wouldn't lower himself, to hide from the world inside organized crime," Edward said flatly. "For me, it was never about the money. I glory in being what I am. And now . . . I'm the only monster prepared to do it to his own kind. Just for the fun of it."

Daniel sat back in his chair, fighting hard not to wince as stabbing pains shot through him. He kept his gaze fixed steadily on Edward, his face calm even as beads of sweat appeared on his forehead. It seemed to Daniel that he was being asked to take an awful lot on trust, just because Edward Hyde said that was the way things were. All of Daniel's old policeman's instincts stirred at the back of his mind, reminding him that he was being told all of this by a man who repulsed him on every level. A man who claimed to be the incarnation of pure evil. Hardly a basis for trust... Daniel met Edward's sardonic gaze with his best hard look.

"You've been Edward Hyde for... how long now?"

Edward grinned. "I have seen London rise and fall, seen generations come and go, but I go on."

Daniel wasn't quite sure what to say to that, but felt he should say something.

"The world must have changed a lot since your day."

"The world changes, but I don't," said Edward, with a certain grim satisfaction. "I'm as perfect now as when I first escaped from the shadows of a lesser man."

Daniel pressed on, in search of a weak spot he thought he could sense, if not actually name.

"But... don't you feel lost, out of place, in a world that's so different from the one you were born into?"

Edward shrugged his heavy shoulders. "People are still people. They just have more toys. And the monsters are still monsters."

"But do you see yourself as a monster because you don't belong? Do you stay a monster because that's all you know?"

Edward's frown lowered, becoming threatening. "Don't think this little chat we're having is in any way personal, boy. We're not here to get to know each other. I'm just offering you a chance to become so much more than you are, so you can get your revenge. Because I have a use for a man like that."

"And I have to decide whether I trust you enough to take that offer," Daniel said flatly.

Edward smiled, though it didn't even come close to touching his eyes. "What's trust got to do with it? You'll take Dr. Jekyll's marvelous Elixir because it's in your best interests to do so. Unless you want to stay a cripple all your life... while the people who did this to you get away with it."

Daniel winced, just a little, at the word *cripple*, though he couldn't deny it. All the muscles in his back, and in his legs, were screaming at him for having sat still for so long. He wasn't even sure he'd be able to get up out of the chair without having to ask for help. If the Elixir really could do everything Edward said it could, then it was everything he needed, an answer to all his problems and all his prayers. And yet, still he hesitated. Because the man offering him a hand out of hell made his skin crawl every time their eyes met. A man who boasted of being evil. And Daniel knew what happened to people who made a deal with the devil.

He thought hard, letting Edward wait. Why would a man like that offer a second chance at life to a man like him? Daniel fought down the pains that threatened to unman him, and concentrated on what to say next, determined to drag some useful information out of the man who sat watching from behind his desk, like a spider contemplating a fly hesitating on the edge of its web.

"Do you understand the modern world?" he said slowly. "You know an awful lot about the monsters, but what do you know about phones and computers and social media? Does any of that make sense to you? Or do you feel abandoned by a world that's moved on and left you behind? So all you have left is your own private war; a monster fighting monsters..."

"You are venturing into dangerous territory," said Edward. "We're here to talk about your life, not mine."

Deep inside, Daniel smiled slowly. He was getting close to something; he could feel it. He kept his voice carefully casual, as though they were just talking.

"How have you survived all these years?" he said. "A man so completely different from every other man? Walled up in your own private kingdom because you know people would drag you out into the street and beat you to death with their bare hands, if they found out who and what you really are? How have you endured being so alone, for all these years?"

Edward grinned suddenly. "I'm only alone when I choose to be. You'd be surprised how attractive pure evil can make a man, in some women's eyes. But if you're asking what I think you're asking, then no, there has never been a single soul in my life that I was close to, who mattered to me at all. And I like it that way. I don't need anybody."

"There's always the organization you founded," said Daniel. "Jekyll & Hyde Inc. Do you see them as your family?"

"Hydes don't do love, or sentiment," Edward said calmly. "We don't have any need, or any use, for friendship or loyalty. We stand alone, because we can. Once you've taken the Elixir, you'll stop asking questions like these. Because the answers won't matter to you anymore. You won't give a damn for the state of the world, or the people in it. Because Hydes stand outside all of that—predators, in a world of prey."

"You're not exactly selling this new life to me," said Daniel. "Why would I want to become someone like that?"

Edward leaned forward across his desk, his eyes holding Daniel's as he went on the attack.

"I've read your file, policeman. You have no friends or family, because they all deserted you when your life changed. You keep trying to fathom me, but I have no trouble seeing right through you. Everything you care about has been taken from you, leaving you alone in the world. Nothing left to make your life worth living . . . apart from a raging need to make the monsters pay for what they did to you. I can make you strong enough to take the world by the throat and shake some personal justice out of it. And you do want that, don't you?"

"To do the right thing? To make a difference? Yes," said Daniel. It was the only thing he was still sure of.

Edward clasped his huge hands together. "There's a war going on in the secret parts of London, between the organization I created and the organized crime of the monster Clans. And there's a place in that war for you . . . if you want it."

"What use can I be?" Daniel said harshly. "You must know what the Frankensteins did to me."

"Jekyll & Hyde Inc. is finally getting ready to wipe out all the monster Clans," said Edward. "It's taken me a long time to reach this point, and now I need warriors. Not just soldiers who can follow orders, but someone who's prepared to do whatever it takes to win. Because they hate monsters almost as much as I do."

He pulled open a drawer in his desk, brought out a glass vial half full of liquid, and placed it on the desk between them. Daniel couldn't keep from leaning forward, for a better look.

"Dr. Jekyll's infamous Elixir," said Edward. "The same potion that produced me from the depths of a lesser man's mind. Never aging, and growing stronger with every year that passes . . . because I will never again turn back into the small man who first drank this potion."

"You don't trust him to approve of what you're doing?" said Daniel.

"He always was weak," said Edward. "Never daring to pursue any of the things he really wanted. And there's always the chance I might turn back into a man who should have died long ago." He sat back in his chair, and his smile widened. "This is what you've been seeking your whole life, Daniel: a chance to be strong enough to do what needs doing. Drink it . . . and release the real you."

Daniel picked up the vial, and was surprised at how steady his hand was. "What's in it?"

"Think of it as rocket fuel for the imagination," said Edward. "Something that can rebuild your body according to your deepest desires."

"How can a drug do that?"

"What do you care?"

"Will I become . . . like you?"

"It's different for everyone," said Edward. "The Elixir gives shape to all your deepest desires, makes them manifest in new flesh and blood and bone. Your hidden fires will produce a furnace to shape the new you."

"A man with no conscience?" said Daniel.

"What use is a conscience to a man set on revenge? I'm offering you a chance to bring down the monsters who ruined your life. Who destroy the lives of everyone they touch. Why are you even hesitating?"

Daniel frowned. He wasn't sure.

"Why did Paul send me here?"

"I have contacts inside all the Clans. Paul gave me your file. He knows I'm always looking for a few good men with monsters inside them. Now either drink the potion or get the hell out of my office. I have a war to fight."

The Elixir didn't look like anything special. It didn't glow with a sinister light, or heave and roil inside the glass. It was only a thick colorless liquid . . . and just possibly a way out of hell. A chance to have a life again, and strength enough to force the world to make sense. In the end, that was all that mattered. Daniel unscrewed the cap, and then looked at Edward.

"Will it taste bad?"

Edward seemed a little taken aback, presented with the one question he hadn't anticipated.

"It's been so long I honestly don't remember. Does it matter?"

"No," said Daniel.

He gulped the oily stuff down and it exploded inside his head. Every color was suddenly overwhelmingly vivid, every sound full of depth and meaning. The whole world seemed to snap into a sharper focus. The change when it came wasn't painful, it was orgasmic. Daniel cried out with joy as his flesh melted, surging this way and that over rapidly thickening bones. He half fell out of his chair, and then lurched back and forth across the office, growing taller and stronger in sudden bursts. He snatched up his walking stick from beside the chair, and broke it in two with no effort. He threw the pieces away and laughed out loud, and Edward laughed with him. Like two wolves howling in the night, just for the sheer savage pleasure of it.

Daniel looked down at himself. He'd grown large enough to burst open all the buttons on his shirt. His whole body buzzed with new strength. He felt like he could take on every monster in the world, and trample them underfoot. And then a voice called out to him— but it wasn't Edward's. Daniel turned slowly to look at a mirror hanging on the wall. His face filled the glass, grinning back at him.

"Welcome to the new you," said his reflection. "What are you going to do now?"

"I haven't decided yet," said Daniel. He moved over to stand before the mirror. "What are you supposed to be—my conscience?"

"Hardly. I'm the voice in your head that tells you what you really want, instead of what society thinks you should want. I'm all the ideas that come to you in the small, slow hours of the morning. Think of all the appetites we can indulge, and the pleasures we can sink ourselves in. And then, we can punish everyone who ever hurt us. Not just the monsters, but all the bastards who refused to believe us. We can tear them apart with our bare hands and dance on the pieces. What do you say?"

"Not right now," said Daniel. "I have things to do."

"I'll be waiting," said his reflection.

Daniel turned away from the mirror to look at Edward. "Did you hear any of that?"

Edward shrugged. "What goes on inside your head is your business."

Daniel glanced back at the wall, and wasn't entirely surprised to find there was no mirror hanging there. He looked down at himself and smiled slowly.

"Is this change permanent?"

"If you want," said Edward. "Another dose of the potion will turn you back into your old self—but why would you want to be such a small and broken thing, when there is life to be lived and monsters to be slain?"

"When do I get to fight these monsters?" said Daniel.

"When you're ready," said Edward. "You've a way to go yet. You can make a start by choosing your new name."

Daniel thought about it, and then smiled.

"Daniel Hyde. Because, basically, I'm still me."

"Of course you are," said Edward Hyde.

Chapter Four
AS FIRST DATES GO...

✤ ✤ ✤

"IF YOU'VE FINISHED TALKING to yourself," said Edward, "there's work waiting to be done."

Daniel looked at him, and then deliberately sat down in his chair again. "I have questions, before I agree to do anything."

"Really?" said Edward.

He got up and came out from behind his desk again. He sauntered over to Daniel, and kicked the chair out from under him. Daniel fell sprawling to the floor, and then rolled quickly to one side to avoid Edward's boot, as it went sweeping through the air where his head would have been.

Daniel scrambled back onto his feet, fists raised, and Edward smiled and nodded approvingly.

"That's more like it. Hydes don't take shit from anyone. But for now, you take my orders and you don't argue, because I know what's going on and you don't."

"Like what?" said Daniel, not lowering his hands.

"The Frankenstein Clan is holding its annual gathering right here in London, in just a few hours," said Edward. "How would you like to go there, and kill every single one of them?"

"Kill them?" said Daniel.

"Does the thought honestly bother you? After everything you saw?"

Daniel remembered bodies strapped to tables with their guts ripped out. Remembered bloody-gowned surgeons bent over a living victim like vultures. Remembered what happened to his friends, and to him ... But he was strong now. Strong enough to avenge the dead and protect the living. To be the kind of man he'd always wanted to be; the knight in shining armor who slayed dragons. He was ready to take on the Clans, and wade in their blood till every last one of them was dead ... But just because he'd drunk the Elixir, that didn't mean he had to be like Edward. He would be Daniel Hyde, the man who made himself a monster to put an end to monsters. He took a deep breath, and slowly lowered his hands.

"I can't slaughter an entire Clan on my own," he said.

"Oh, I think I can find someone to help you out," said Edward. "Can't let you have all the fun."

"Hold it," said Daniel. "The Frankenstein Clan is meeting in London, this evening ... and I'm told to report here today? I don't believe in coincidences like that."

"I've been fighting my private war for so long ...," said Edward. "I've waded in blood, just to get one inch nearer to my goal. Followed stratagems I knew wouldn't pay off for generations, just to bring me closer to this moment. You are merely the latest part in a scheme to bring down all the monster Clans."

Daniel glared back at him, refusing to be impressed or intimidated.

"What would you have done if I hadn't come to see you? Or if I'd decided not to drink your potion?"

Edward leaned back against his desk. It groaned loudly under his weight.

"In the unlikely event of something not turning out the way I calculated, I do have other irons in the fire. But you seem most likely to approach this task with the proper attitude. I like a man who knows how to hate. So: down to the third floor with you, and make yourself known at door number seven."

"Who am I meeting?" said Daniel. "Someone who owes you a favor?"

"I own this entire building," Edward said airily. "The best thing about an extended life like mine is that long-term investments really do pay off. Every office on every floor of this building is a part of Jekyll & Hyde Inc."

"So this is all just one big front," said Daniel. "Something for you to hide behind."

"If you like," said Edward. "I prefer to think of it as camouflage.

All the monster Clans know about me, but they have no idea how big my organization has grown."

"If you've been a thorn in their side all these years, I'm surprised they haven't tried to do something about you," said Daniel.

"Oh, they have," Edward said happily. "I've lost count of all the assassins the Clans have sent sneaking in here. But I just kill the killers, eat the bodies, and send whatever bits I don't fancy back to their Clan in a nice little box tied up with ribbons. Along with a recipe for stew. Now stop cluttering up my office and get your arse out of here. I don't want to see you again until every member of the Frankenstein Clan has been wiped off the face of this earth."

"I'm still waiting to hear how I'm supposed to do that," said Daniel. "Or what a Frankenstein Clan even consists of. Are some stronger than others? Is there some kind of organization? You can't just send me out there without any information."

"I'm not. Your partner is waiting behind door number seven," said Edward. "Along with a detailed plan. And please: no improvising."

"What if something goes wrong?" said Daniel.

"Then I won't see you again. Unless the Clan decides to send you back here in a box tied up with ribbons."

Daniel had time to think, as the elevator descended. The idea of killing Frankensteins lit a definite fire in his heart, but he thought there was a limit to just how much of a monster he was prepared to be. Killing for revenge didn't bother him at all. Killing to avenge innocent victims—he could get behind that. But slaughtering an entire Clan . . . They couldn't all be monsters.

The elevator doors opened onto the third floor, and Daniel strode off down the corridor. It occurred to him that it had been a long time since he'd been *able* to stride. He leapt into the air for the sheer joy of it, and was startled at how close to the ceiling he came. He jumped again, and punched the ceiling with his fist. Great flakes of plaster rained down, and Daniel grinned broadly as he brushed the flakes off his shoulders and then set off down the corridor again. He'd never felt so gloriously alive. Like he could do anything, anything at all, and never have to care about the consequences.

And it didn't worry him in the least, that the idea didn't worry him at all.

He finally came to a halt before the right door, and knocked cheerfully.

"What do you want?" said a voice from within.

Daniel blinked a few times. "This is Daniel Hyde?"

"About time," said the voice. "Get in here. You're late."

A great many responses crossed Daniel's mind, none of them likely to make a good first impression, so he just opened the door and went in. This office was more modern, with stylish furniture, all the latest equipment, and a large, drooping rubber plant in one corner. From off to one side came a series of low thudding sounds, and Daniel turned to see a woman throwing knives at a dartboard. They chunked heavily into the center of the board, each thin blade quivering with the force of its impact. The woman turned unhurriedly to face Daniel, hefting the last knife in her hand.

"Just getting my eye in," she said.

Daniel nodded, lost for words. At six and half feet tall, the woman was a few inches taller than him, with a physique like a body builder; but she also had the sleek grace of some powerful exotic animal. In her smart business suit and black string tie, she looked seductive and glamorous and extraordinarily dangerous. A great mane of crimson hair cascaded down past her shoulders, her eyes were a fierce green, and her mouth was wide and mocking. And as Daniel stood there, taking it all in, the woman threw her last knife right at his face.

Daniel's hand snapped up faster than he could think and caught the knife, stopping its point an inch short of his eyeball. He looked speechlessly at the woman, and she grinned back at him.

"Just checking you really are one of us. Nothing personal."

"A knife to the eye strikes me as about as *personal* as it gets," Daniel said coldly. "Please don't try that again."

"Of course not," the woman said reasonably. "Not now. I've run out of knives."

Daniel examined the blade. It was light and slender, with an excellent balance. "Is this what we're going to use at the Frankenstein gathering?"

"Not unless the plan goes seriously wrong. I am Valentina Hyde; always Tina, never Val. I'll be your partner in the mass slaughter to come."

Daniel tucked the knife away in an inside pocket. "I'm still not sure how I feel about that..."

Tina threw herself at him, like a jungle cat going for the throat. Her first punch was so powerful it would have taken Daniel's head clean off his shoulders if it had connected, but his reactions started him moving the same moment she did, and her fist sailed harmlessly past his cheek. She lashed out with both hands, again and again, but he avoided most of the blows and blocked the rest. She tried a few karate kicks, and he evaded them easily, as though they were both just moving through the steps of a familiar dance.

Daniel finally decided he'd had enough, ducked inside Tina's reach, and punched her right between the eyes. The blow rocked her back, and while she was off-balance Daniel grabbed her and threw her across the room. She tucked and rolled and was quickly back on her feet again, her eyes full of the light of battle and something else besides. She grinned at Daniel, snatched up a heavy chair and threw it at him. He backhanded it to one side, but while he was busy doing that she picked up the massive oak office desk and brought it slamming down on his head.

The impact alone should have been enough to kill him, but he barely felt it. Daniel punched her in the face again, putting all his weight into the blow. Tina fell back a step, but appeared entirely unhurt. The desk had split in two over Daniel's head, so she tossed it aside. The two of them surged forward and slammed together, trading punches that would have killed a lesser mortal. And neither of them felt any pain or took any damage. Tina grinned, as she saw him realize that.

"Now you're getting it," she said, laughing breathlessly. "This is what it means to be a Hyde."

She grabbed Daniel with both hands, and he grabbed her, and they wrestled fiercely, both of them using all their strength to try and subdue the other. Tina fought to get in close, her teeth snapping at Daniel's face, and it took all his strength to hold her off. They raged back and forth across the office, smashing through the furniture and fittings as though they were made of paper. Daniel laughed loudly. He felt like he could do anything, because there was nothing in the world strong enough to stop him. The Elixir had rewritten all the rules in his favor. By the time the two of them finally broke apart they had wrecked everything they touched, and the rubber plant was in tatters.

They ended up standing head to head, so close Daniel could feel her breath beating against his face, and see the sweat running down hers. But he didn't feel hurt, or even tired. He felt . . . exhilarated. There was a definite sexual charge on the air, an almost overwhelming attraction that was pulling the two of them even closer. Tina laughed at the look on Daniel's face, and ostentatiously relaxed. She lowered her hands and stepped back, and after a moment so did he.

"I just wanted to be sure you were up to the job," said Tina.

Daniel was still fighting a desire to get his hands on her, one way or another. He could tell Tina knew exactly what he was feeling, and that it amused her. He breathed deeply, forcing his raging blood down. Because he couldn't do all the things he needed to do, if he couldn't control himself.

"Just because I'm a Hyde, doesn't mean I'm always going to act like one," he said finally.

"Well," said Tina. "You're no fun."

She turned her back on him quite casually, found a chair that had survived more or less intact, and sat down in the midst of the wreckage. Daniel searched for something to say, couldn't think of anything, and settled for finding another chair and sitting down opposite her.

"Now we've introduced ourselves, I'll brief you on the mission," said Tina.

"That would be helpful," said Daniel.

"We'll be invading the annual gathering of the Frankenstein Clan. And just to put a smile on your face, we are talking about the entire family, so whoever destroyed your old life will definitely be there. What else do you need to know?"

"Edward assured me there was a plan," said Daniel.

Tina shrugged. "The plan is simple: go where they are, kill everyone we see, and not get caught doing it."

A cold rage seethed in Daniel's heart, at the thought of finally getting his hands on the monsters from the cellar. The sheer strength of the emotion disturbed him, and he had to force it down before he could speak calmly and clearly.

"Will it be just the family at this gathering, or can we expect to run into some of those oversized thugs as well?"

"Each faction in the family runs its own collection of creatures," Tina said easily. "Patchwork things, pieced together from graveyard leftovers. They act as bodyguards, to protect the factions from each other, and as general servants and security guards. Fortunately, they're all muscle and no brain."

Daniel frowned. "Exactly how many people, and creatures, are we talking about?"

"Around three hundred," said Tina. "Maybe more, if we're lucky."

"You really think we can wipe out that many of them on our own?" said Daniel.

"Providing we use a big enough bomb," said Tina. She laughed at the look on his face. "What did you think we were going to do—march in there and beat them all to death with our bare hands?"

"That does sound like something I'd enjoy," said Daniel.

"Oh, me too," said Tina. "But it would be far too time-consuming. And some of them might get away."

Daniel leaned back in his chair, and studied her thoughtfully. "So, you're my new partner. You're not what I was expecting."

"I know," said Tina. "You thought I'd be taller."

"I came here to fight monsters," said Daniel. "Not act like a terrorist."

Tina shrugged. "Potato, tomato. Hydes are all about the winning."

"Question?" said Daniel.

"Ask away," Tina said generously.

"Why is Edward trusting a newcomer like me with such an important mission?"

"You have more reason than most to hate Frankensteins," said Tina. "And Edward believes in motivation."

Daniel nodded slowly. "Do they really all have to die? Are none of them worth saving?"

"Long years of doing favors for those in power have made the Frankensteins untouchable," said Tina. "And corrupt from top to bottom. The only justice they'll ever face is what we hand out. Do you have a problem with getting your hands dirty?"

Daniel wasn't ready to answer that, just yet. "Why is Edward only sending the two of us?"

"Because there aren't that many Hydes," said Tina. "Never have been. At present there are nine of us, including you. And everyone else is busy."

"Why so few?" said Daniel.

"Because the Elixir kills most of the people who take it," Tina said calmly. "Blows the heart apart like a firecracker in a rotten apple."

Daniel stared at her. Tina grinned.

"You didn't know that when you drank it, did you? Not everyone has a Hyde in them," she said. "The Elixir needs rage and hatred to fuel the change, and the kind of inner strength you only get from seriously motivated people."

Daniel finally got his voice back. "Why didn't Edward tell me that, before I drank the potion?"

"You think he *cared*?" said Tina. "He's Edward Hyde! He probably thought it was funny. Would it have made any difference if you had known?"

Daniel decided he'd rather talk about something else. "How does Edward know where the Frankenstein Clan holds its annual gathering?"

"He's been trying to get a hold over someone on the inside for ages," said Tina. "Unfortunately you have to be family to be a Frankenstein. But just recently one of them approached Edward: a young researcher who'd had the idea of combining the Hyde Elixir with a Frankenstein creation, to produce something new and more powerful. Edward was convinced the Frankenstein wouldn't be able to resist trying the potion himself, so he only provided a very dilute solution. Just enough to produce a single short-term change. Once the Frankenstein turned back, and wanted more. He was hooked. An addict. He had no choice but to come to Edward—and the price was the gathering's location."

"This man betrayed his own family?" said Daniel.

"Never even hesitated. Being a Hyde is very addictive."

"So," Daniel said heavily. "Just the two of us, a bomb, and no backup. How dangerous is this going to be?"

"What do you care?" said Tina. "Only a few hours ago you were dying by inches."

"How do you know that?"

"I've read your file. Edward passed it around."

Daniel winced. "Has everyone read it?"

"Pretty much," said Tina. "We all enjoy a good laugh. And we like to know who we might be fighting beside. Provided the subject survives the Elixir, of course."

Daniel decided it was time to change the subject.

"Where are the Frankensteins holding their little jamboree? In a hospital, or an abattoir?"

"In a nice hotel," said Tina. "Because they like to think of themselves as businessmen. Now pay attention. The whole point of this little get-together is so they can tell each other how successful they've been, and show off some of the awful new things they've created. The best of them are rewarded with higher status, and the least successful are eliminated. Right there, in front of everyone. It helps keep the rest of family on their toes—and besides, they enjoy it."

"Do we know where to look for them?"

"They've taken the entire penthouse floor for themselves. So, no innocent bystanders to worry about. Not that I ever do."

"And how long have we got, before this gathering begins?" said Daniel.

"Oh, hours," said Tina. "More than enough time to get you ready."

"I *am* ready," said Daniel.

"Not even close," said Tina. "To start with, you're going to need a whole new outfit if we're to look the part and infiltrate the hotel unchallenged."

Daniel nodded reluctantly. "Edward said he owned every part of this building. Does he have his own personal tailors here?"

"Being this big means we always have trouble finding clothes," said Tina. "So it only made sense to bring the rag trade in-house. They have their own little cubbyhole, down on the first floor."

Daniel nodded. "I suppose it'll make a nice change from plainclothes."

"I have no idea what you're talking about," said Tina.

The tailors turned out to be two grim-faced figures in long-tailed morning suits that made Daniel think of undertakers. Their long and gloomy office was packed full of cloth samples, rails of ready-made clothes, and dummies in half-finished suits standing shoulder to shoulder like watchful guardians. Daniel had barely stepped through the door before the tailors swarmed all over him, measuring everything with flying tape measures. Tina left them to it, disappearing into the rear of the office.

The tailors finally fell back and conferred briefly, before reaching into the rails and bringing out a tuxedo. They thrust it into Daniel's arms, and then disappeared silently into the shadows. Daniel looked around. There didn't seem to be any changing room, so he just stripped off his old clothes and dropped them self-consciously on the floor. He took a moment to admire his amazing new body, and then put on the tuxedo and studied himself in a standing mirror.

He couldn't help but smile, as the James Bond theme played in his head. The tuxedo was stark black and white and fitted perfectly, with an almost indecent snugness. A blood-red bow tie added a touch of color. His reflection winked at him. Daniel pretended he hadn't seen that. He was still struggling with the bow tie when Tina reappeared, wearing a long burgundy evening dress with wide slits in the sides, rising all the way to the hip. Daniel couldn't help but stop and stare.

"Very elegant," he said. "But perhaps just a bit drafty?"

"Sleek and stylish and yet and at the same time entirely suitable for mayhem," Tina said briskly. "What are you doing with that tie?"

"It keeps fighting back," said Daniel.

He stood very still as Tina moved in to tie it for him. He half expected her to try and strangle him with it, but her fingers were quick and surprisingly gentle. She finally stood back to look him over and nodded, satisfied.

"You'll do."

Daniel glowered at the shadows the tailors had vanished into. "How much is all of this going to cost us?"

"Edward pays for everything," said Tina. "Though given the structure of Jekyll & Hyde Inc., I'm pretty sure a lot of the time he's paying himself."

"All right," said Daniel. "Where now? To the armory, to pick up the bomb?"

"That's already waiting for us, down in the lobby," said Tina. "All we have to do is smuggle it into the gathering, hit the timer, and retire immediately to a safe distance. What could possibly go wrong?"

"I could make out a list, if you like."

"I *have* done this before," said Tina.

"I won't ask," said Daniel.

"Best not. Come on; once we've picked up the bomb we've time for a few drinks, at this nice little bar I know."

Daniel looked at her. "You want to take a bomb into a bar?"

"Best way to get served," said Tina.

Daniel considered his tuxedo, and her evening gown. "Won't we seem a little overdressed?"

"Trust me," said Tina. "Where we're going, no one will give a damn."

The bomb had been placed in a pleasantly anonymous tote bag, and then left standing not all unobtrusively by the lobby's front door. Tina glanced inside the bag, picked it up, and slung it casually over her shoulder.

"Before you ask: yes, the bomb is quite definitely big enough. Don't ask me what it is, or how it works. In a world of vampires, werewolves, and Hydes, a small but insanely powerful bomb is only a minor miracle."

"But what about the blast radius?" said Daniel. Trying to sound like he knew what he was talking about.

"It's a shaped charge," Tina said patiently. "All we have to do is put it in position underneath the penthouse floor, and the blast will rise up and take out the entire Frankenstein gathering."

"Won't that be a bit hard on the hotel?" said Daniel.

"The owners know who they're in business with," said Tina. "So really, they have it coming."

"I think I'm more concerned with how this bomb was just dumped by the door," said Daniel.

"No one gets into the building unless we want them to," said Tina. "There are cameras everywhere."

Daniel frowned. "I didn't see any."

"That's rather the point," said Tina. "The best security is the kind you never see coming. Now let's go; and try not to bump into me while we're walking down the street."

Daniel opened the door for her. "Could we go back to my original idea, about beating the entire Frankenstein Clan to death with our bare hands? It seems so much safer."

"If you don't stop whining, I will beat you ever the head with this tote bag," Tina said severely. "Stop thinking so small! You're a Hyde now!"

"Lead me to this bar," said Daniel. "I feel in need of a whole bunch of drinks."

"Well," said Tina. "That's more like it."

The Frog and Princess turned out to be a hole-in-the-wall affair, with far too much character for its own good. Underlit and more than a bit rough, the bar was surprisingly full for the time of day. With the kind of drinkers Daniel just knew it wouldn't be wise to turn your back on.

"What is this?" said Daniel. "Happy hour?"

"Not even a little bit," said Tina.

She barged unceremoniously through the crowd to get to the bar, and everyone competed to see how quickly they could get out of her way. Daniel wandered along behind her and noticed that people were giving him plenty of room too. It might have been the tuxedo—or the touch of Hyde in his face. The bartender recognized Tina immediately, and looked like he wanted to hide behind something.

"Don't start whimpering," said Tina. "You know I hate that. It's not like anything's even happened yet."

"It will," said the bartender. "*You're* here."

"Give me a bottle of brandy and two glasses," said Tina. "Then batten down the hatches. It's going to be a stormy afternoon."

The bartender quickly produced the brandy and the glasses, and pushed them toward her.

"And I'd only just got the place looking nice again, after the last time you were here . . . The brandy is on the house, and I am now off to lock myself in a toilet cubicle and sob bitter tears until it's safe for me to come out again."

Tina grabbed the bottle and nodded for Daniel to pick up the glasses. She turned her back on the rapidly departing bartender and headed for an empty table.

"What was he so upset about?" said Daniel, doing his best to keep up.

"Treat them mean, to keep them keen," Tina said cheerfully. "He loves it, really."

She dropped into her chair and dumped the tote bag on the floor, ignoring Daniel's wince. He took his time sitting down opposite her, just to show he was his own man, and set the glasses down between them. Tina filled both glasses to the brim, gulped the brandy down, and immediately refilled her glass. Daniel sipped his drink carefully, and looked away from Tina to study the other people drinking in the bar. It seemed safer.

"Why is everyone watching us?"

"They all love it when a Hyde turns up," said Tina. "Means a good time is guaranteed for all."

"Then why do they all look so angry?"

"They're just playing hard to get."

"I'd feel better if we were preparing for our mission," said Daniel.

"We are," said Tina. "We are getting ourselves in the right mood, and girding our loins for battle. I do so hate an ungirded loin. And I thought we might use the time to get to know each other a little better."

"You've read my file," said Daniel.

"That's who you used to be," said Tina. "You're someone else now."

Daniel shook his head firmly. "I'm still me."

"It's cute that you think that," said Tina. She belched, and scratched her ribs unself-consciously. "Try to keep up, Daniel. All the hidden dreams and desires that you've spent your entire life suppressing have been let out of their cages. Rejoice! You can do anything you want now, and you will. Get some of that brandy inside you; it'll help cushion the shock."

"We're going to be working soon," said Daniel, not hiding his disapproval as Tina poured herself a third glass of brandy.

"Hydes can handle their drinks," said Tina. "We can indulge all our appetites, and never have to pay the price."

Daniel looked at her. There had been something in the way she said that...

"What kind of person were you, before you drank the Elixir?"

Tina's voice was suddenly quiet and reflective. Her gaze was far away, lost in yesterday, as though she was looking at someone else's life.

"I was a party girl," said Tina. "The legendary good time had by all. I came from a nice, respectable family, with all the comforts and everything to live for—so of course I couldn't wait to throw it all away. I ran off to London the first chance I got, and less than a year later I was dying by inches, just like you . . . except I did it to myself. And then Edward happened to be around when I started a fight in a club, and he saw something in me."

"He offered you the Elixir?"

Tina snorted loudly. "I grabbed it out of his hands. Couldn't wait to be somebody else."

"Did you know it could kill you?"

"I didn't ask; but I wouldn't have cared. I was a drunk, a junkie, and riddled with so many STDs I was a danger to be near. Now look at me. I've been fighting Edward's war for ages—not for any cause, or because I'm grateful to him. It's just so much *fun*."

"Does Edward know that?"

"Who knows what goes through that old gargoyle's mind? He probably does. Probably thinks it's funny. And a very suitable attitude for a Hyde."

"Have you killed many people?"

"Not people, Daniel. Monsters."

Daniel must have looked like he doubted her, because she leaned forward and fixed him with a cold stare.

"I have hammered a stake into a vampire's chest, and cut a werewolf's throat with a silver knife. I once beat a Frankenstein surgeon to death with my bare hands, because he wouldn't say he was sorry for what I'd caught him doing to a child with a scalpel. You only think you know what monsters can do. Before this, Edward used me as his private assassin, to take out targeted individuals who might have got in the way of his plans. Now he's finally unleashed me on the Clans—and I couldn't be happier."

Given what they were planning, Daniel supposed he should find that reassuring, but he wasn't sure that he did. He looked round the bar again. All the other customers had given up even pretending to drink or talk to each other and were looking steadily at Daniel and Tina, as though they were waiting for something to happen. Daniel drank some more brandy. It didn't help.

"How much longer, before we can go after the Frankensteins?"

"There's plenty of time," said Tina. "More than enough to let off a little steam."

She took a firm grip on the brandy bottle, leaned back in her chair, and looked challengingly around the bar. A man at the next table grinned at his friends, caught Tina's eye, and raised his voice to make sure she heard him.

"Will you look at that? They'll let any kind of trash in here, these days. I know what you are, sweetheart, and what you need. So why don't you come over here and get down on your knees, where you belong?"

His friends laughed loudly, and then they all leered at Tina, daring her to do something.

Daniel set his glass down and started to get up, but Tina was already on her feet. She sauntered over to the next table and smiled down at the man who'd made the remark. And then she smashed the bottle over his head with such force that his face was slammed down into the table. The bottle broke, blood flew on the air, and the man didn't move again. One of his friends jumped to his feet, shouting obscenities, and Tina rammed the jagged end of the bottle into his face and twisted it. He fell back, screaming, his face a horrid mess.

The other men overturned the table in their eagerness to get to Tina, but she just stood her ground, grinning. She punched one man in the face with such force that all his bones shattered, back-elbowed another in the throat, and then picked up the discarded table and hit the others with it, sending them flying.

Daniel took his time getting to his feet. Tina seemed to have matters comfortably in hand.

More men came charging forward, from all over the bar, and Tina laughed happily as she went to meet them. Facing overwhelming odds, and not giving a damn. Tina struck men down and trampled them underfoot, a vicious Valkyrie in an elegant evening gown, and no one could stand against her. Though that didn't stop an awful lot of men from trying.

More patrons joined in, on both sides, and just like that everyone in the bar was fighting everyone else. Blood flew, people crashed this way and that, furniture was broken up to provide improvised weapons—and Daniel finally understood what everyone had been waiting for.

Tina took on anyone who came within reach, laughing out loud with uncomplicated enjoyment. Daniel finished the brandy in his glass, and made his way unhurriedly through the seething mob to guard Tina's back. Fists came flying at him from all directions, but he didn't even bother to dodge them. They might have been ghosts, for all the effect they had. He was a Hyde now, and nothing in the everyday world could hurt him anymore. At first he only hit people who got in his way, but after a while he developed a taste for it, and hit hard enough to break bones and smash in faces—because they all looked like the kind who deserved it.

The man who once needed a cane to walk now broke chairs and tables over people's heads, and laughed as he did it.

Daniel and Tina Hyde fought back to back, and no one could stop them from doing anything they liked to anyone they didn't like. Daniel threw one particularly annoying man through a plate-glass window and, not to be outdone, Tina threw another through a door that was closed. In the end, the remaining combatants realized they would have to clamber over the bodies of the fallen just to reach the two Hydes, and that seemed to sober them up. They turned away, and rushed for the hole in the wall where the front door used to be. Daniel and Tina were left standing alone, surrounded by the battered and the unconscious.

Tina produced a delicate handkerchief from somewhere about her person, and set about cleaning the blood off her hands. Daniel checked his own hands, and found they weren't even bruised. Tina saw him frowning.

"Don't worry. Edward will pay for the damages and the surgeries. He always does."

"This has happened before?" said Daniel.

"I told you: Hydes come in here all the time. All nine of us."

"Then I'm amazed anyone else does."

"They love it," said Tina. "All the local villains and hard cases turn up regularly, just so they can test themselves against us. Make no mistake, these people we just fought were bad men. They were looking for a fight, and would not have responded to reason." She put away her handkerchief. "Time we were on our way."

Daniel checked his tuxedo, but it seemed to have survived the brawl without any damage or bloodstains.

"You look fine," said Tina.

"You too," Daniel said generously.

"Don't I take you to the best places?" said Tina.

Daniel looked sharply at her, as the penny dropped. "This was an audition, wasn't it? To see how I'd do."

"To make sure you had a taste for it," said Tina. "And of course you do. You're a Hyde."

Daniel started to say something, and then stopped. Because Tina was right. She smiled at him happily.

"Let's go kill a whole bunch of Frankensteins."

"Can we pick up the bomb first?"

"Perfectionist."

Tina summoned a taxi by pulling her dress back to show an awful lot of thigh. A black cab screeched to a halt right in front of them, and they climbed in. The back seat was barely big enough to hold both Daniel and Tina, and they had to lower their heads to keep from banging them on the roof. Tina instructed the taxi driver on where to go, and he took one look at them in his rearview mirror and decided he wasn't in the mood for conversation.

One extremely rapid journey across London later, the taxi slammed to a halt outside a very elegant hotel. Tina was first out of the cab, not even glancing back. Daniel paid the fare, added a grudging tip, and then asked the driver for a receipt.

"What are you doing?" said Tina.

"I want my expenses reimbursed."

"Stop thinking like a policeman," said Tina. "If you want your money back, take it off the bodies of some dead Frankensteins."

The taxi driver threw his cab into gear and accelerated off into the traffic. Daniel didn't blame him. He took his first good look at the hotel, and winced internally. It all seemed very grand.

"How are we going to sneak in?" he said. "Find a side door, or a servants entrance?"

"Hydes don't sneak," said Tina.

"But there's a doorman. In a uniform. And a top hat."

"Then he'd better not get in our way," said Tina. "Or I will knock him down and walk right over him."

In the end, the uniformed doorman bowed politely and opened the door for them. Daniel put it down to the tuxedo and the evening gown. The huge hotel lobby was brightly lit, welcoming in an overpowering sort of way, and packed with rich and important-looking people. The kind who were probably born looking elegant and feeling entitled.

Daniel squared his shoulders and strode forward, and the crowd just naturally parted to let him through. Tina strolled along beside him, taking the various admiring glances as her due. Daniel was surprised to find he got a few looks too, and did his best to act as though that was entirely normal. When they reached the elevators at the rear of the lobby, Daniel hit the call button with a flourish. The doors slid open, and he and Tina stepped inside. An elderly couple dressed to the nines went to join them, but Tina gave them a look and they decided to wait for the next one. She hit the button for the floor under the penthouse level, and the doors closed.

Daniel allowed himself to relax a little, and tugged at his bow tie to loosen it.

"Leave it alone," said Tina, not even looking at him. "It's fine."

"I can't believe we got in so easily," said Daniel.

"It's all about looking the part," said Tina. "Now all we have to do is place the bomb where it needs to be, and it's good night, sweetheart for the entire Frankenstein Clan."

"You really think it's going to be that easy?" said Daniel.

"Edward has been planning this for longer than you and I have been alive," said Tina. "Trust the man."

Daniel looked at her. "Trust Edward Hyde?"

"Trust him to know what he's doing."

Daniel nodded slowly. "I would have liked to watch the Frankensteins die."

"You see?" said Tina. "You were born to be a Hyde."

"No," said Daniel. "I was made one."

The elevator doors chimed politely and Daniel braced himself for enemy action, but when the doors slid open the corridor was empty. He gestured for Tina to stay where she was, and stepped cautiously out of the elevator to look around.

"No guards, no security presence," he said quietly. "Where is everybody?"

"The Frankenstein Clan booked the whole of this level as well as the penthouse, to ensure their privacy," said Tina, with something very like patience. "It's off-limits to everyone else. Is it all right for me to come out now? Because I'm going to."

Daniel scowled up and down the corridor. "There must be some kind of security. Surveillance, armed guards, regular patrols..."

"A hotel like this has all kinds of security," said Tina. "But it's been shut down on both of these floors. Because the Frankensteins don't want the rest of the world to know what they get up to. All the systems have been rerouted to the Clan's own security center on this floor, so they can keep an eye on things. Thanks to our inside man, the one Edward has been paying off with weakened Elixir, we know where the center is. All we have to do is go there, and put it out of action."

"So someone is watching us, right now," said Daniel.

"And probably wondering why we're standing around," said Tina, just a bit pointedly. "Let us go and enlighten them, in a sudden and violently overwhelming way, so we can be about our business."

She started off down the corridor, and Daniel moved quickly to join her.

"How are we supposed to find this center? Do you have a map, or hotel satnav on your phone?"

"Edward showed me a map earlier," said Tina. "I memorized it."

Daniel looked at her. "You can do that? Because you're a Hyde?"

"No, because I'm a woman with enough sense to think ahead. Try to keep up."

She increased her speed, and Daniel had to hurry after her. He was getting a little tired of always having to play catch-up. Not because he wanted to be in charge, necessarily, but because he didn't like feeling he was the only one who didn't know what was going on. He scowled at Tina's unresponsive back. He couldn't help remembering that the last time he'd followed someone's orders blindly, it hadn't worked out too well.

He also remembered Nigel saying, *If you can't see the patsy in the deal, it's you.*

Two corridors and a sudden left turn later, they were standing outside a door with a surveillance camera set above it, regarding them suspiciously with its unblinking red eye. Tina smiled and waved.

"What are you doing?" said Daniel.

"I'm being intriguing," said Tina, still smiling at the camera. "I can't just break the door in because it's probably alarmed, so I have to fascinate the guards into opening the door for us."

"You really think they're going to do that?"

"Of course. They might be Frankensteins, but they're still men."

There was the sound of several locks disengaging, and the door started to open. Tina kicked it hard and the door slammed all the way back, knocking the guard off-balance. Tina surged forward, and knocked the man cold before he could react. Daniel saw another guard reaching for an alarm, but he'd started moving the same moment Tina had, and was in the room and upon the guard before he could get anywhere near the switch. He hit the guard once, and he collapsed. Daniel looked quickly around the control room, but there was no one else on duty.

A long row of monitor screens showed what was happening on both floors. Daniel looked for a way to shut them down.

"Don't," Tina said immediately. "If the systems stop working, that will sound an alarm."

Daniel nodded, and checked the screens carefully.

"I'm not seeing the gathering anywhere."

"No cameras allowed at the big beanfeast," said Tina. "What happens at the Frankenstein gathering stays at the gathering."

"How do you know all these things?" said Daniel.

"I told you, Edward has been planning this for ages. And he's had me rehearsing this raid for months. Apparently, we were waiting for you. Or someone like you."

"All right," said Daniel. "What do we do?"

"Kill the two guards, and leave the system to run itself. It can watch what it likes so long as there's no one here to react to what it sees."

Daniel looked at the unconscious guards. "Kill them?"

"You're the one who wanted to beat the whole Frankenstein Clan to death with your bare hands," said Tina.

"I didn't mean in cold blood."

"Then think of what they did, to you and your friends," said Tina. "And all the other people the Frankensteins have preyed on. See if your blood is still cold."

Daniel remembered the cellar under the bookstore. The blood

and the bodies, and the horror of it all. His hands closed into fists, but he still couldn't move. Tina sighed impatiently, and stamped on the guards' necks. The sound of vertebrae breaking was very loud in the quiet.

"You'd better toughen up, Daniel; because if you don't the monster Clans will eat you alive."

Daniel looked at the two dead guards. He wanted to think that because they were Frankensteins, they must have done something to deserve this. But that was still a step too far. He looked steadily at Tina.

"Is this what it means, to be a Hyde? To kill without caring?"

"No. It means you care enough about the victims to kill the people who need killing."

"Where do we have to go, to set the bomb?" said Daniel.

"The Clan will be whooping it up in the main banquet hall. We have to locate the room directly underneath it."

"And you know where that is?"

"Of course." She lightly tapped her head. "It's on the map."

Tina made her way confidently through the maze of corridors, only to stop abruptly when they rounded a corner and came face-to-face with two large gentlemen in hotel uniforms who moved quickly to block their way.

"Sorry, Sir and Madam," said the larger of the two, though he didn't sound particularly regretful. "This floor has been reserved for a private function. Unless you have invitations . . ."

"Of course we do," said Tina, smiling brightly. "I've got mine right here."

She stepped forward and kicked him in the balls so hard his whole body lifted up off the floor. While the other guard was gaping at that, Tina punched him out. Both men were unconscious by the time they hit the floor, and probably grateful for it.

"Are they Frankensteins?" said Daniel.

"No, just hotel flunkies moonlighting for cash in hand."

"What do we do with them?"

"Leave them," said Tina. "We don't kill innocent bystanders unless we have to. This is a private war."

She set off down the corridor. Daniel looked at the unconscious bodies, and told himself he didn't give a damn. He was a Hyde. But he still stepped carefully around them as he hurried after Tina and moved quickly in beside her.

"I thought we'd be a little more subtle," he said. "Given that we're taking on an entire Clan and its security people."

"Hydes aren't built for subtle," said Tina.

"I noticed that," said Daniel.

A brisk walk and several sharp turns later, Daniel and Tina had to stop again because the way ahead was completely blocked by even more very large men in hotel uniforms. Given the sheer size of them, Daniel had no doubt they were Frankenstein creations. They stood shoulder to shoulder, blocking the corridor from wall to wall. There was something inhuman, unnatural, about the way they held themselves; as though they weren't properly put together. Or perhaps because they no longer remembered how to stand like people. Their faces were blank, and Daniel only had to look at their eyes to know there was nobody home. They were just machines made out of meat, waiting to be told to do something awful.

"Do we kill them?" Daniel said quietly.

"I like the way you're thinking, but no," said Tina. "We don't want to give away our presence this early. All we have to do is tell them to go be somewhere else in a loud and confident voice, and they'll do it. They're conditioned to obey authority figures."

She strode right up to the hulking creatures and snapped out her order—and they immediately turned and stomped off down the corridor. Apart from one, who stood his ground and started to say something. Tina punched him so hard his entire face collapsed, and her fist buried itself so deep in his head it took her two hard jerks to get it out again. The dead man collapsed, while Tina shook blood and gore from her hand.

Daniel stared at the terrible damage she'd done, and didn't know what appalled him the most: that Tina was so easy about it, or that he was already thinking how good it would feel to do something like that to a Frankenstein.

"From now on, anyone we encounter will either be a part of the Clan, or one of their creatures," said Tina. "You can't hesitate, Daniel, or they'll kill you. And you know what they'd do to you after that."

"I remember," said Daniel. "I still have nightmares about what I saw."

Tina looked at him. "You're going to have to let go of that cellar eventually."

"Yes," said Daniel. "But not yet."

When they finally reached the right room, Tina had a key. Daniel didn't ask. There was a limit to how much smugness he was prepared to put up with. She strode straight in, and after a quick look back down the corridor, Daniel went in after her. The room seemed pleasant enough, with lots of comfortable furniture. It didn't look like it deserved what was about to happen to it. Tina reached into her tote bag, and Daniel watched interestedly as she brought out a simple metal box. No control panel, no flashing lights, just a single activating button. Daniel felt obscurely disappointed that it wasn't red.

"Fetch me a chair," said Tina. "I need to attach this to the ceiling."

Daniel brought her a chair. Tina stepped up onto it, and pressed the box hard against the ceiling. It stuck there quite happily when she took her hand away. She pressed the button firmly, and climbed down again.

"The timer was preset for sixty minutes. More than enough time for us to get far, far away, before it blows the lid off the hotel."

And then they both looked round sharply, as the door behind them slammed open and a tall, Aryan superman type burst in. Blond and blue-eyed, he was wearing an Armani suit and a desperate expression. Tina's hands closed into fists and she started forward, but the newcomer was already holding out both hands beseechingly.

"Please, you must listen to me! I'm Peter Frankenstein, Edward Hyde's inside man."

Tina stopped reluctantly and glared at him. "You were given strict instructions not to come anywhere near this hotel! Oh to hell with it; someone as stupid as you doesn't deserve to live."

She started forward again, but Daniel grabbed her arm. "Let's hear what he has to say."

Tina threw off his hand, shrugged reluctantly, and then scowled at the newcomer.

"Well? What do you want?"

Peter lowered his hands, but not before Daniel realized they were shaking. The Frankenstein looked genuinely scared at being so close to two Hydes, but he made himself meet their gaze steadily.

"Something awful is going to happen at the gathering. I need you to put a stop it. The family's gone too far, this time..."

He broke off, unable to continue. Daniel looked at Tina.

"What could do that to a Frankenstein?"

"Have to be something pretty appalling," Tina admitted grudgingly.

"Talk to us, Peter," said Daniel. "What is it that's going to happen at the gathering?"

The Frankenstein had to swallow hard before he could say anything.

"I wanted to use the Hyde Elixir Edward provided to make new creations that were stronger and more capable of following orders. But I wasn't getting anywhere, so I handed the process over to my superior in the family, telling him I'd bought a dose of the diluted potion on the black market. And somehow he made it work. A whole new kind of creation... It's going to be presented at the gathering, as their latest triumph. Please, you have to do something! I've seen it... Not dead or alive, but trapped somewhere in between. Frankensteins are one thing. They are idiotic brutes, but they *are* alive in some manner, like animals. This is not. It's a walking corpse that thinks it's alive, a ghost in the machinery of man. Just aware enough to know that it shouldn't exist..."

"I say we kill this fool, and get the hell out of here," said Tina.

"No," said Daniel. "He risked a lot, coming here." He turned to the Frankenstein and nodded at the door. "Leave this to us. We'll deal with it."

Peter looked at him steadily. "I didn't betray my family for a taste of the Elixir. I never touched it. I had to turn against them because they betrayed everything we were supposed to be. We dedicated our lives to defeating death, not creating a better kind of slave."

He turned abruptly and left the room. Daniel looked at Tina.

"Does he know about the bomb?"

"Of course not," said Tina. "We couldn't risk him warning the Clan."

"We need to check this out."

"Give me one good reason."

"Because this new creation is part Hyde—and it's suffering."

"The bomb will kill it, along with the Frankensteins," said Tina.

"I want to rescue it," said Daniel.

"Why?" said Tina. "Because you couldn't save your friends from what happened in the cellar?"

"Maybe," said Daniel. "I won't know till we get there."

Tina sighed heavily. "All right! We'll take a look. It will be a thrill to race against the bomb's timer. But I'm not promising anything."

"Of course not," said Daniel.

They ran all the way up the stairs to the penthouse level, because the elevator was bound to be guarded, but neither of them was short of breath when they got to the top. Daniel eased the swing door open, and took a good look around the empty corridor. Tina shouldered her way past him.

"You have got to get over this protective nonsense."

Daniel stepped cautiously out into the corridor to join her.

"How much time do we have?"

"Not enough. Let's get moving."

"You know the way?"

"The layout on this floor should be the same as the one below."

"What if it isn't?"

"One more question out of you that I don't like, and I will punch your head through a wall."

Daniel sniffed. "Probably your idea of foreplay."

She smiled briefly. "Don't distract me."

They moved quickly through the empty corridors. There was no sign of life anywhere, and all the doors were firmly closed. The constant silence was starting to grate on Daniel's nerves when Tina stopped suddenly, and gestured at the corner ahead.

"We have to pass the main elevator to get to the banquet hall," she said quietly. "Which means we're going to have to deal with whoever or whatever is guarding it." She gave Daniel a hard look. "No mercy, and no holding back. Do you have a problem with that?"

"No," said Daniel. "Let's just concentrate on the life we're saving."

"Why are you so determined to save this new Frankenstein creature?" said Tina.

"Because I need to believe I'm not just a killer," said Daniel. "That I'm only doing this to save innocent lives."

"Hydes don't do sentiment," said Tina.

"This one does," said Daniel.

"You'll get over it," said Tina.

She went flying round the corner, with Daniel right behind her. Half a dozen hulking creatures in oversized suits stood before the elevator doors, along with a spiky-haired young businesswoman in a smart city suit. One of the creatures turned to look at the new arrivals, and Daniel stumbled to a halt as he realized the Frankenstein creation had Oscar's head set on its shoulders. The eyes stared right at Daniel and didn't know him. Tina reluctantly stopped with Daniel, as the young businesswoman turned to see what was happening. Her eyes widened with shock as she recognized Daniel. He smiled at her coldly.

"Hello again," he said. "Remember me? From the bookstore? You worked behind the counter. You killed my friends."

She shook her head like a child, as though she could make him go away just by wishing it.

"They told me you were dead!" she said finally.

"Should have tried harder," said Daniel.

She turned abruptly to her creatures. "Kill them!"

"You deal with her, Daniel," said Tina. "She's your unfinished business. I'll take the late-night horror shows."

She surged forward, slamming into the midst of the creatures. She lashed out with inhuman strength, and necks broke and skulls shattered. Tina laughed out loud as bodies dropped to the floor. The young businesswoman produced two brightly shining scalpels from her sleeves and launched herself at Daniel, hacking and stabbing viciously. She was fast, but Daniel was so much more than he used to be. He avoided the blows easily, twisting and turning so the scalpels always missed him, and then he punched the businesswoman in the face. She fell back, and Daniel went after her. She saw something in his face, and horror filled her eyes.

"You're a Hyde!"

"I'm what *you* made me," said Daniel.

"Let me go. Please. I'm no one important."

"You're a Frankenstein. And I still have really bad dreams about that cellar."

"It was just business! And it's not like we took anyone who mattered."

"Everyone matters."

"Then let me go."

"Sorry," said Daniel. "But I'm a monster now. Just like you."

He started forward again, and she quickly lowered her scalpels.

"Wait! I know things. There must be something you want to know..."

Daniel stopped. "I did wonder: how were you able to shrug off that Taser?"

"Genetically engineered transplants. Physical upgrades. We all have them."

"You experiment on yourselves?"

"We share the wealth. We're better than everyone else, because we're made that way."

"I saw what you did to Oscar," said Daniel. "And I know what happened to Paul. But what did you do to Nigel?"

He was still speaking when her hand snapped forward, and one of the scalpels flashed toward his throat. Daniel snatched it out of midair, turned it around, and sent it flying back. The thin blade plunged through her left eye, and she dropped to the floor. Daniel looked down at the body for a long moment. This wasn't closure... but it was a good start. He turned to Tina, who was standing grinning over a pile of dead creatures. Daniel didn't look to see which of them had Oscar's face. It didn't make any difference. Tina looked back at the dead businesswoman, and then smiled at Daniel.

"Did it feel as good as you hoped?"

"Maybe. It's complicated."

"Hydes don't do complicated." She looked at her watch. "We really need to get a move on."

"Yes," said Daniel. "Let's get this done."

He strode off down the corridor, leaving her to catch up with him.

Two larger-than-usual creatures in ill-fitting suits stood guard outside the banquet hall. Daniel and Tina charged down the corridor and killed both creatures while they were still reacting. Daniel didn't hesitate, and didn't care. He helped Tina move the bodies away from the door, and glanced quickly up and down the corridor.

"I'm not seeing any sign of backup. I can't believe they thought they could get away with just a couple of guards."

"Typical Frankenstein arrogance," said Tina. "They couldn't believe anyone would dare attack them at their own gathering."

Daniel tried the door. To go with the hotel, the door had an old-fashioned latch on it. It was locked.

"Do we break it in?"

"Too noisy," said Tina. "Fortunately, I never leave the house without these little beauties."

She produced a set of skeleton keys, some of them looking rather high tech, and had the door unlocked in a moment. She eased it open, and slipped quickly through the gap. Daniel followed her in, and quietly closed the door behind them. The huge banquet hall was brightly lit by a series of elegant chandeliers, and packed full of long tables with pristine white tablecloths, all but buried under the very best in food and wine. There were floral displays and ice sculptures, and all the trappings of wealth and power. No expense had been spared—or even considered, from the look of it. Sitting at the tables were hundreds of perfectly ordinary-looking men and women in exquisitely tailored outfits. No surgeons in blood-spattered gowns, no mad doctors with staring eyes, no faces steeped in evil or marked by a lifetime's cruelties. They could have been any business community, come together to attend a formal dinner and celebrate the year they'd had. Except for the rows of oversized creatures standing inhumanly still as they watched over the diners.

At the end of the hall a distinguished-looking man was on his feet, addressing the Frankenstein Clan.

"Once again, it's been a very good year. Rich and powerful people the world over owe their extended lives to the very special organs we provide—and we are careful to never let them forget that. Our researches continue: into rejuvenating the deserving old, enhancing the lives of people who matter, and learning all there is to know about life and death. We lower our hands into human depths, and create marvels. We are the cutting edge of Humanity!"

He stopped, so they could applaud him and one another. The clapping went on and on, as though they couldn't bring themselves to stop. In the end, the speaker had to raise an admonitory hand before the self-congratulation reluctantly died away.

"But . . . we are still struggling to achieve the eternal goal of the Frankensteins," the speaker said sternly. "To bring the dead back to life. Our patchwork creations always seem to lack something. A certain vitality. It's almost enough to make you believe in souls . . ."

The people at the tables laughed politely, and some glanced briefly at the creatures standing behind them. Nothing moved in the empty faces that looked back.

"But not anymore!" said the speaker. "Allow me to present something new; restored from the grave, rejuvenated and remade . . . Dead tissues infused not only with life, but the beginnings of intelligence. A new hybrid creation, worthy to serve the Frankenstein Clan! I give you: the perfect slave!"

He nodded to two men standing by the rear door. They opened it, and wheeled in a metal frame holding a naked, hulking creature, standing upright and secured in place by lengths of heavy steel chain. Surgical scars crisscrossed a body bulging with muscles, but it was the eyes that caught everyone's attention. They were alive and aware—and driven to the edge of madness. The new creation knew what he was, and hated it. A dead man walking, going nowhere. Just alive enough to know he still had both feet in the grave. Tears ran jerkily down his face. But even this horrible awareness was totally different from that of a normal Frankenstein creation. The whole of the Frankenstein Clan rose to their feet, laughing and cheering and madly applauding.

Daniel felt sick to his soul. For all their fine words, the Clan had produced nothing more than a reanimated corpse that knew what it was. He looked at Tina.

"He doesn't want to be rescued," she said flatly. "Let's get out of here. The bomb will kill him, along with the rest of the Clan."

"What if the bomb isn't enough?" said Daniel. "We have no way of knowing how strong the Frankensteins and the Elixir made him."

"We can't rescue him without giving away our presence, and putting the bomb at risk!" said Tina.

"We have to do something!" said Daniel. "Would you want to go on living like that?"

Tina looked at the new creation, and shook her head.

"No. But what can we do?"

Daniel produced the knife he'd taken from Tina earlier, and his arm snapped forward. The long thin blade flashed through the air to bury itself in the creature's right eye, and Daniel thought he saw a fleeting gratitude in the scarred face, before the body slumped lifeless in its frame.

Everyone in the banquet hall turned around in their seats, to take in Daniel and Tina standing by the doors. Daniel smiled at them coldly, while Tina waved cheerfully.

"Don't mind us! Just passing through. Hope your evening goes off with a bang."

"Get them!" The voice of the Clan's spokesman was thick with rage at being so openly defied. None of the Frankensteins sitting at the tables so much as stirred in their chairs, but the rows of creatures standing behind them turned as one and lumbered steadily toward the two Hydes. Dozens of dead things, pieced together from the remains of better men, with murder on what was left of their minds. They moved slowly at first, but soon built up a head of speed as they closed in on their prey.

Daniel stood his ground, his face as set and implacable as theirs. He'd faced this scene so many times before in his nightmares that it had lost much of its power over him. In fact, this was better, because he was looking forward to getting his hands on these creatures. He wasn't helpless anymore. He was a Hyde. Part of him wanted to see the creatures as victims of the Frankensteins, like the hybrid, but in his mind's eye he could still see the death of his friends in that awful cellar, at the hands of things just like these.

"Time we were leaving," said Tina.

"No," said Daniel, his chest so tight he had to force the words out. "Not yet. I have unfinished business to attend to."

His hands clenched into fists, and he could tell from the look on Tina's face that his smile was a very cold thing. He *needed* to face the Frankenstein creatures. Needed to stand his ground and let them come to him, so he could hurt them they way they'd hurt him, and his friends. It was the only way he'd ever be able to leave the cellar behind him. He barely felt Tina grab his arm, until she used all her strength to turn him around and face her. He yanked his arm free, ready to shout at her if that was what it took—and then stopped as he realized that, while her face was angry, her eyes were understanding.

"You can't physically hurt them, Daniel!" she said urgently. "You can't. They don't feel anything, because they're just dead men walking. But they can hurt us. Or at the very least, hold us here until it's too late to get away."

And just like that Daniel remembered the bomb, with its preset timer ticking away. He nodded stiffly, and turned to follow Tina as she headed for the door.

But his moment of indecision had given the creatures just enough time to catch up with them. Daniel was within arm's reach of the door when a heavy hand dropped onto his shoulder, and dead fingers clamped down with sickening force. He cried out at the pain, as the creature hauled him back from the door, and then he threw off the creature's hand with an effort, turned back, and punched it in the face with such force that its head snapped all the way round, the neck broken. The creature staggered backward, head lolling to one side at an unnatural angle, but it quickly recovered its balance and came forward again. Behind it came more of the Frankenstein creations, closing in on the Hydes with cold, relentless purpose.

Daniel lashed out at them with all of his Hyde strength, grunting out loud with the effort he was put into every attack, but his fists only jarred against the cold unyielding flesh. Bones broke and shattered under his blows, but none of it was enough to stop the dead men pressing forward. Tina threw punch after punch with happy abandon, hitting one creature so hard under the sternum that she must have crushed its heart—but no blood flowed from the creature's mouth, and the expression on its face never changed. The Frankensteins made their creations to last. They kept on pressing forward, a crowd of cold merciless hands reaching out to rend and tear.

Daniel forced down his anger, so he could concentrate on what was in front of him. He focused on the creatures' weak spots, breaking their extended arms with swift, calculated blows, shattering leg bones with vicious kicks, and even thrusting two fingers deep into unseeing eyes. The crippled creatures fell sprawling to the floor, but there were always more, stepping uncaringly over the fallen to take their place. Daniel lashed out again and again, hitting them as hard as he could, until his fists were bloodied and aching from the impacts, but it was like fighting death itself. He could hold it off for a while, but he couldn't stop it.

Tina fought tirelessly at his side, kicking the legs out from under the creatures and then stamping on their necks when they were down. She laughed breathlessly as she fought, delighting in the mayhem. She grabbed two handfuls of a creature's clothes, hauled it off its feet and lifted it above her head, and then threw it down the hall. It flew through the air and smashed into the tables, sending good food and wine flying, and scattering the panicked Frankensteins. She managed the same trick several times, because the creatures never learned—no matter how hard they landed, they always got up and came back for more.

Most of the Frankensteins were on their feet now, screaming conflicting orders at the creatures, but none of them made any attempt to get involved themselves. Perhaps because they were businessmen, and such direct action would be beneath them. But some of the younger Frankensteins were so incensed, or saw an opportunity to make an impression, that they left the safety of the tables to advance on the Hydes with scalpels shining brightly in their hands. The Clan spokesman yelled for them to come back, but they pretended they hadn't heard him. The young men and women broke into a run, smiling maliciously, with blood and punishment on their minds. One after another they threw themselves at Daniel and Tina, only to be struck down so hard they never got up again. Daniel took a certain satisfaction in that, remembering the bloody-handed surgeons standing over gutted corpses, but there just wasn't enough time for him to savor it properly.

He was breathing hard now, his heart hammering painfully fast in his chest. It seemed there might be a limit after all to Hyde strength and endurance. He drove the dead men back with a flurry of blows and looked quickly about him, his eyes darting over fallen creatures still struggling to rise, and more dead men coming, and then he smiled suddenly as his gaze fell upon the nearest table. He called out to Tina and pointed, and she got the idea immediately. They charged right at the nearest creatures, sending them stumbling backward with lowered shoulders and great sweeps of their arms. They grabbed hold of the table and heaved it over onto its side, despite its weight, and then used it as a barrier to force the crowd of creatures back. Daniel and Tina kept their heads carefully low, so the hands reaching over the table couldn't find them. Some of the creatures took hold of the table and began to tear it apart.

Daniel suddenly let go and stepped back. Tina looked at him sharply, but he shot her a reassuring smile. He'd just remembered what she said earlier, about how the creatures were conditioned to obey authority figures. He took a deep breath, and raised his voice so it would carry over the screaming Frankensteins. He glared at the creatures, and stabbed a finger at them.

"*Stay!*"

And for a moment, the creatures did. Held where they were by the simple power of a direct command. Tina started to turn away and head for the door, but Daniel wasn't finished yet. He couldn't forget the hybrid in its chains, and the gloating satisfaction in the spokesman's voice. He reached across the table and took a firm hold on the nearest creature's head with both hands. He braced himself, and tore the head right off. As the headless body toppled slowly backward, Daniel pulled back his arm and threw the head with all his strength. It rocketed down the length of the hall, and hit the Clan spokesman in the face with such force that his head all but exploded. Blood flew on the air, and the Frankensteins nearest him shrank back, crying out with shock. Daniel grinned like a wolf.

The Frankenstein Clan fell silent, staring at Daniel with wide, stunned eyes. The creatures still weren't moving. Daniel looked upon his work, and knew it to be good. Tina tapped him politely on the arm.

"If you've quite finished..."

"I think so," said Daniel.

"Did that make you feel any better?"

"Do you know?" said Daniel. "I really think it did."

"Good," said Tina. "Can we go now?"

"Right behind you."

They turned their backs on the shocked Frankensteins and their motionless creatures, and sprinted for the door. The Frankensteins suddenly started screaming orders again, and the dead men tore the table apart and stamped forward through the wreckage. Daniel and Tina barely had time to haul open the door and throw themselves through it before the creatures were almost upon them. The Hydes slammed the door in their cold, empty faces, and then Daniel held it closed with all his strength while Tina locked it quickly with her skeleton key. She broke the key in two, leaving half inside the lock, and then she and Daniel backed quickly away from the door. It was already shaking and shuddering in its frame, as cold fists pounded and hammered on the other side. The two Hydes didn't wait to see the heavy wood crack and splinter; they were already running down the corridor. Daniel heard the door start to fall apart behind him, but kept his gaze fixed firmly on the way ahead.

"How long do we have, before the bomb goes off?"

"I'm not wasting time looking at my watch!" Tina said loudly. "Shut up and run!"

"I *am* running!"

"Then run faster!"

They reached the swing door at the far end of the corridor, hauled it open, and went racing down the stairs. They hadn't got far when the stairway seemed to suddenly rise and fall, as though the whole building had shrugged. The walls cracked and fell apart, and great pieces of stone rained down into the stairwell. Daniel and Tina were thrown off their feet, and sent tumbling headlong down the shaking steps. They finally slammed up against a wall, and Daniel threw himself across Tina, covering her body with his own as large pieces of jagged stone rained down. He gritted his teeth, refusing to move, as they crashed into him again and again. And then the lights went out, and choking smoke and dust filled the air.

Eventually, the stairway stopped shaking. Emergency lights flickered on, diffusing dimly through the smoke-filled air. Daniel and Tina slowly dug their way out from under the rubble. Daniel rose painfully to his feet, absently brushing debris from his dust-covered tuxedo. Tina stood up, shook herself briskly, and then glared at Daniel.

"I can look after myself!"

"You're welcome," said Daniel.

Tina shook her head. "Let's get out of here. I hear flames, to go with the smoke."

Daniel nodded. The air was growing distinctly hotter. He started down the cracked stairs, kicking pieces of rubble aside, and Tina slipped in beside him.

"Burn in Hell, Frankensteins," Daniel said quietly.

"You see?" said Tina. "You *are* a Hyde."

Daniel turned to smile at her, as a thought struck him.

"You know, as first dates go . . ."

"Don't push your luck," said Tina. But she smiled as she said it.

Chapter Five
HYDES AT THEIR PLAY

✜ ✜ ✜

THE HOTEL EVACUATION went pretty smoothly, all things considered. By the time Daniel and Tina emerged from the stairwell and into the lobby, all the alarm bells were ringing their heads off, and the hotel staff was guiding people to the nearest exits with calm, reassuring words and the occasional boot up the backside. Daniel and Tina just slipped in with everyone else, and were immediately anonymous in the midst of the crowd.

Once they'd made it outside, the two Hydes stood on the opposite side of the street, and looked up at the top floor of the hotel. Most of it was wreckage now, consumed by flames and wreathed in clouds of thick black smoke. The sound of sirens drew steadily closer, announcing that fire engines, ambulances, and police cars were on their way. Though what the emergency responders were going to do when they arrived, apart from point and shrug a lot, wasn't clear to Daniel. Tina laughed happily.

"Told you the bomb would do the job. Say good-bye to the Frankenstein Clan."

Daniel just nodded. He was watching the crowd outside the hotel grow even larger, as people continued to spill out onto the street. He couldn't see anyone who appeared to be injured, but many of them were shocked and shaking. They clung to one another like people who'd just survived a train crash or a shipwreck. When the bomb had blown the top off the building, a lot of them had no doubt thought they were going to die. They didn't know they were just collateral damage in someone else's private war.

Daniel had killed the Frankensteins easily enough, in the end, but he had to wonder if killing was *supposed* to be that easy. It seemed that as a Hyde, he could get away with anything, but he was still human enough to care about the price other people might pay for his actions. And he had to wonder if what was left of his conscience would be enough to keep him from doing something even worse, in the future. Could he be a killer of monsters, without becoming a monster?

"You're feeling guilty," said Tina. "Don't. Hydes don't *do* guilt. Concentrate on the things that really matter."

"Such as?" said Daniel.

"I'm *hungry*," Tina said brightly. "I could eat a horse, and the saddle, and whoever happened to be sitting on it at the time. Aren't you hungry?"

Daniel discovered he wasn't just hungry, he was ravenous.

"I could eat," he said.

"I know a really good pizza place, not far from here," said Tina.

"Of course you do," said Daniel.

She bristled a little. "What's that supposed to mean?"

"Just that you always know where everything is," Daniel said smoothly.

"Damn right," said Tina.

The pizza parlor wasn't particularly big or impressive. It had streaky windows and a bunch of brass fittings that clearly hadn't been polished in years, but it was still pretty full, which at least argued that the food was good. Daniel had lived in London long enough to distrust any fast-food establishment that wasn't packed with people at this time of the night. A sign in the window said: BUY ONE, AND GET ANOTHER OF THE SAME SIZE FOR EXACTLY THE SAME PRICE! Tina slammed the door open and strode in like royalty visiting the less fortunate. Daniel followed on behind, feeling just a little self-conscious about his dust-covered tuxedo.

But no one had any eyes for Daniel. The staff took one look at Tina and all their faces fell, as they recognized her. Daniel distinctly heard one waiter mutter to a waitress, "Run. Save yourself," before realizing it was already too late. The staff fell back from the crowded tables, abandoning their customers, and ended up huddled together in the main aisle like sheep in a thunderstorm, wide-eyed and trembling.

Daniel looked at Tina. "They remember you."

"I know!" Tina said happily. "I do like to leave a little reputation behind me, wherever I go."

"You're not going to start a fight here, are you?"

"Not until after we've eaten," said Tina. "Or we'd never get served."

Some of the customers were studying her covertly from behind raised menus, convinced by her incredible looks and presence that she must be some kind of celebrity. Tina ignored them all with magnificent disdain, which just made them even more certain. She caught the eye of the headwaiter and summoned him over with an imperious gesture. He emerged reluctantly from the protection of his fellow staff, a short and sturdy man who looked like he ate a lot of pizza. He approached Tina like a man walking to the scaffold, but he kept his back straight and his head up, and even managed a professional smile.

"Ms. Hyde . . . back again, so soon? We don't deserve such an honor."

"You're right, you don't," Tina said briskly. "We want a private booth, right at the back—but nowhere near the toilets, if you like having your kneecaps where they are."

"Of course, Ms. Hyde. Please follow me."

The headwaiter bowed to Tina, and then glanced briefly at Daniel in a way that suggested he was amazed anyone would choose to be with her, before leading them quickly to the rear. He ushered Daniel and Tina into a private booth, saw them both comfortably seated, and then grabbed two oversized menus from a nearby table. The man and wife who'd been perusing them weren't actually done yet, but one look from Tina was all it took to keep them from protesting. The headwaiter had a sheen of sweat on his face by now, but he still hung on to his composure with both hands. Daniel checked out the prices in the menu, and smiled just a little desperately at Tina.

"How about we go Dutch?"

"No one's going to ask us to pay," said Tina.

Daniel glanced at the headwaiter, but he had nothing to say, so Daniel looked back at Tina.

"Not ever?"

"Of course not. We're Hydes."

Tina glanced quickly through the menu, tossed it aside, and fixed the headwaiter with a stern look.

"I want the biggest pizza you've got, with every kind of topping piled high, and a stuffed crust."

"I'll have what she's having," said Daniel.

The headwaiter nodded quickly and headed straight for the kitchen, so he could hand in the order personally and get the hell away from the Hydes. Daniel sat back in his seat and looked thoughtfully at Tina.

"Well...So much for the Frankenstein Clan."

"Take a deep breath," said Tina. "See? The world smells better without them in it."

"Who's next on the list?"

She shrugged. "That's up to Edward. He's been planning this operation against the Clans for a really long time."

"Why did he choose *now* to start his war?"

Tina fixed Daniel with a hard look. "He said he'd been waiting for someone like you. Which I took as a bit of an insult. I've been his good left hand for ages, striking down the ungodly from ambush and disrupting Clan business from the sidelines."

"So why didn't he trust you to plant the bomb on your own?"

She shrugged in a way that suggested there was a lot she could say, but chose not to for the moment.

"Edward doesn't answer questions."

The headwaiter came back with a huge pizza expertly balanced on each hand. He set them down before Daniel and Tina with a flourish, and then quickly retreated several steps, just in case.

"That was quick," said Daniel.

"They just want us out of here as fast as possible," said Tina. "This is probably someone else's order. Isn't that right, Maurice?"

The headwaiter smiled, wished them "Bon appétit," and then hurried back into the kitchen to hide. Daniel studied the massive pizza before him. He took a deep breath and an amazing smell filled his head. He grabbed hold of the pizza with both hands, and stuffed his mouth with the biggest bite he could manage.

Daniel wolfed all of it down with ferocious appetite, and Tina did the same. They didn't bother with the cutlery provided, just tore the pizzas apart with their bare hands and crammed the pieces into their mouths. The two Hydes devoured their meals at incredible speed, and then sat back in their chairs and grinned at each other. Daniel didn't feel stuffed, or even satiated, just pleasantly full.

"So," Tina said brightly. "Dessert?"

And then the main door slammed open and every conversation in the place broke off as Edward Hyde came swaggering down the main aisle.

He was wearing a really expensive suit, complete with a gold watch chain stretched across his waistcoat, but he still looked like someone had dressed up a demon. His arrogant rolling gait only emphasized his squat and muscular frame, and he lurched down the aisle like he'd come to avenge a deadly insult with extreme malice. He was grinning broadly, as though just by being there he was playing some vicious practical joke on the world. Customers he passed flinched back in their chairs, to put as much distance as possible between them. They didn't just looked scared, they seemed actually sickened by Edward Hyde's sociopathic presence, as though he suffered from some form of moral leprosy and they were afraid it might prove contagious.

The staff looked like they wanted to just drop everything and run, but Edward ignored them, heading straight for Daniel and Tina. But even though he kept his gaze fixed on them, it was obvious he knew the effect he was having on everyone else—and that he was enjoying it.

He dropped down into a chair opposite Daniel and Tina, without waiting to be asked or even greeted. A lot of the customers were leaving, abandoning their unfinished meals so they could make their escape before the trouble started. The staff clustered even more tightly together, looking as though they were wondering which of their many sins they were being punished for. One waiter had put his arm around a waitress, who was sobbing quietly.

Daniel wondered what all the fuss was about. He remembered how badly he'd been affected the first time he saw Edward, but now the man's presence hardly bothered him at all. Maybe he was getting used to being around monsters—or perhaps being a Hyde changed how he saw the world. Edward beamed happily around the private booth, and Tina glared right back at him.

"What the hell are you doing here? Checking up on us?"

"I am celebrating the destruction of the Frankenstein Clan," said Edward.

"But you *never* leave your building! You always said you had too many enemies, out in the world."

He shrugged his massive shoulders. "It's not often I have reason to celebrate."

"Would you like to order some pizza?" said Daniel.

"I've already eaten," said Edward.

Tina smiled sweetly. "Anyone we know?"

"I've talked with our contacts inside the hotel," said Edward. "They confirm that no one survived the destruction of the top floor. They'll be digging bodies out of the wreckage for weeks to come. There are bound to be a few Frankensteins who weren't at the gathering, but I can always have our people hunt them down later. Out in the open and on their own, they'll make easy targets."

Daniel thought about Peter Frankenstein, but didn't say anything. He didn't want to attract Edward's attention to a young man who'd tried to do the right thing. He just hoped Peter got a good head start. He realized Edward was giving him a knowing look.

"How does it feel, now you've had your first taste of revenge?"

"Better," said Daniel.

"You mustn't be disappointed that it wasn't more hands-on and personal," said Edward. "In the end, all that matters is that your enemy is dead."

"Are the other Clans as bad as the Frankensteins?" said Daniel.

"Worse, if anything," Edward said cheerfully. "Come and see me the day after tomorrow, and I'll see you're provided with everything you need to take down the Vampire Clan."

Daniel frowned. "Two gatherings, set so close together?"

"It's that time of the year," said Edward.

"And the vampires will be gathering here in London as well?"

"The monster Clans are great ones for tradition," said Edward. "Fortunately for us."

Daniel started to ask why Edward had waited for him in particular to show up before lighting the blue touch paper on his war, but Edward had already risen to his feet and was heading back to the main door. The few remaining customers watched him pass with horrified fascination. A young waitress emerged unsuspecting from a side door and Edward Hyde crashed right into her. He could have avoided her, but he chose not to. His sheer bulk sent the waitress sprawling to the floor in front of him and he walked right over her, trampling her underfoot. The sound of bones breaking carried clearly on the quiet, before being drowned out by the waitress's screams. No one moved to help her because it was already too late—and because nobody dared. Edward strode out into the night and didn't look back once.

The remaining customers gave him time to get some distance away, and then bolted for the door, fighting each other in their eagerness to be somewhere else and start forgetting everything they'd seen. The staff gathered up the sobbing waitress and carried her off, disappearing through the kitchen door. And just like that, Daniel and Tina were the only ones left in the place.

"You said we're not supposed to hurt innocent bystanders," said Daniel.

"We aren't," said Tina. "But that's Edward Hyde. He doesn't give a damn about rules. Even the ones he makes himself."

"So you're fine with what he just did?"

"He's the boss," Tina said steadily. "I decided not to get involved. And so did you."

"It wouldn't have made any difference," said Daniel.

"Exactly," said Tina. "Of course, if he ever tries to pull that shit on me, I'll kill him. And he knows it."

"But you won't stand against him."

"I owe him. Just like you. He made it possible for us to kill monsters."

"Why is that so important to you?" said Daniel. "You know why I'm doing this. But are you killing monsters to protect the innocent, or just for the thrill of testing yourself against them?"

Tina smiled. "Depends on the mood I'm in."

Daniel sat back in his chair and regarded her thoughtfully. "What will you do when all the monsters are dead?"

"Take the weekend off. And then...make sure Edward gets everything he has coming to him. What will you do? Give up being a Hyde? Drink the potion again, and go back to being a broken man? I don't think so. I know all there is to know about addictive behavior, and being a Hyde is the biggest rush there is."

"So what do we do, when all the monster Clans are gone?" said Daniel. "Fight each other?"

Tina laughed softly. "Not a bad idea. But the Clans aren't responsible for all the evil in the world. There'll always be someone who needs a good kicking." She rose abruptly to her feet. "You know what? I feel like dancing. I have energy to burn and the night is young. How about you?"

Daniel didn't even have to think about it. Destroying the Frankenstein Clan had satisfied his need for revenge, but he still felt a need to be doing something. And since it wasn't time yet to go off and kill vampires . . .

"Dancing sounds fine," he said. "I take it you know a good club?"

"I know all kinds of clubs," said Tina. "Of course, I've been thrown out of most of them. Just for exuberance, and general high spirits. Not that any of them could keep me out if I wanted in. I know—the Constantine Club! I haven't been there since before I was a Hyde."

"Then let us go there, and dance up a storm," said Daniel.

One new intimidated taxi driver and a short drive later, they were standing outside an impressive-looking nightclub with rococo neon stylings, oversized bouncers at the door, and a long queue of bright young things waiting to get in, including a number of minor celebrities (the kind famous for being famous). A few of them were haranguing the stone-faced bouncers, shouting, "Don't you know who I am?," which Daniel had always considered self-defeating. Some offered bribes and some threatened violence, but the bouncers had heard it all before and hadn't been impressed the first time.

The Constantine gave every impression of being the kind of club that would normally never admit someone like Daniel, but the bouncers took one look at Tina and just waved her in, either because they saw the Hyde in her face, or because they knew trying to keep her out would be more trouble than their job was worth. They waved Daniel in with her, not even giving him a second glance. He was with Tina, and that was all they cared about. No one in the queue objected; they knew the way the world worked.

Daniel thought he would have preferred it if one of the bouncers had tried to stop him, so he could beat the crap out of them for past refusals. Another part of him was disturbed that he felt that way. It really wasn't like him. As he strode through the nightclub door, Daniel had to wonder whether the Elixir had changed more than just his body.

The cavernous interior was almost painfully bright and shiny, with flashing lights, revolving patterns on the dance floor, cascading fountains of champagne, and music so loud Daniel couldn't even tell what kind it was. Not that he gave a damn. For dancing, all you really needed was a beat.

The club was packed with people immersed in the music and the dance. Security guards hovered on the fringes, keeping an eye on things. Daniel couldn't help noticing the way they all fixed their attention on Tina the moment she stepped out onto the dance floor. And then he felt a little better when some of them decided he needed watching too. Tina found an open space and started to dance; Daniel did his best to keep up with her.

Tina moved like a dream, all elegant grace and animal power, stamping her feet and snapping her head back and forth, so that her great mane of long red hair danced almost as wildly as she did. Daniel had never considered himself much of a dancer, but since he was sure no one would be watching him when they could be looking at Tina, he felt free to do whatever he wanted and just enjoy himself. The beat from the music got into his blood, and without really trying his movements began to echo Tina's, until it became one dance being performed by two people—a wild and sensuous thing, maddening and exhilarating. Daniel and Tina grinned at each other, lost in the moment and loving it.

They danced for hour after hour without ever pausing, and neither of them ever felt tired. They didn't even raise a sweat. Everyone else gave them plenty of room. Some applauded, some cheered, and some even tried to copy their movements, but no one could match Daniel and Tina's incredible grace and energy. People came and went as the evening progressed, but the Hydes danced on. Until one man burst out of the surrounding crowd to confront Tina, his face full of surprise and shock. He ignored Daniel, raising his voice to make himself heard over the din of the music.

"Val? That is you, isn't it? It's me—Erik!"

Daniel expected Tina to drive the man away with a look or a harsh word, but she just kept on dancing. Erik moved in closer and

Daniel got ready to do something, but the concerned look on the man's face stopped him. It was obvious he knew Tina, from somewhen in the past. She suddenly stopped dancing, and Daniel stopped too. Erik tried to smile at Tina, but it faltered and fell away in the face of her refusal to acknowledge him.

"What happened to you, Val?" said Erik. He started to reach out a hand to her, and then pulled it back, not sure what to do. He swallowed hard, and tried again. "It's been such a long time since any of us saw you here. And look at you! You look amazing! What have you done to yourself?"

"I'm not Val," said Tina. Her voice was flat and empty, but something in it cut through the general din. "I'm someone else."

"Oh come on, I'd know you anywhere, Val! We were all so worried when you just disappeared . . ."

"I'm not Val. Now go away, Erik. I don't want to have to hurt you."

All the color dropped out of his face, as though he'd just been told someone he knew had died. He tried one last smile, but there was nothing in Tina's face to encourage it. So the man from her past had no choice but to turn away and disappear back into the crowd. Tina watched him go, and didn't say anything.

Daniel decided Tina needed a moment to herself. He asked her if she'd like a drink, and she nodded, not looking at him. Daniel made his way through the crush of bodies to the bar. A lot of people smiled at him, complimenting him on his dancing and his choice of partner, but none of them got in his way. They seemed to sense that might be dangerous. He asked the bartender for a bottle of brandy and two glasses, and got served immediately, which was a new experience for Daniel. He didn't offer to pay, and after a glance at security, the bartender didn't ask.

Daniel took his time getting back to Tina, so she could recover herself. He glanced at his watch, and was astonished at how long they'd been in the Constantine. It shouldn't be possible for anyone to dance for hours on end without a break. He wasn't the least bit tired; he felt like he could dance forever. Perhaps Hydes weren't just about the violence, after all. But when he finally caught up with Tina again, another man was talking to her. Or rather, talking at her.

This was no leftover from her past, just an overweight man in fashionable clothes that didn't suit him, trying to get Tina to go somewhere private with him. She wouldn't even look at him, but he was too rich and entitled to take no for an answer. He stopped talking and started shouting, until finally she looked him in the eye and said something that made him flush bright red.

"You can't speak to me like that!" the man yelled. "This is my party, and everyone here has to do what I say!"

He stabbed a finger in Tina's face. She took hold of his arm, and broke it with one quick flex of her hand. He screamed so loudly that even people who carefully hadn't been watching turned to see what was happening. Tina saw the bottle of brandy Daniel was holding, and put out a hand. Daniel reflected that this might lead to the *least* amount of violence from Tina. He gave her the bottle, and she hit the screaming man over the head with it. The bottle exploded and the man was driven unconscious to the dance floor. Daniel decided they wouldn't be needing the glasses after all, and tossed them aside.

The music cut off abruptly, as security men came rushing forward from all directions. The loud guy must have been someone really important. The other dancers scattered, and Daniel and Tina moved quickly to stand back to back. The security men didn't seem at all intimidated by Tina, despite what had just happened. They had a job to do, and they were going to do it. And if that involved beating the crap out of two uppity newcomers who didn't know their place . . . well, every job has its perks.

Daniel almost had it in him to feel sorry for them. Almost.

He waited calmly for the first security guards to come within reach, and then he punched out the first one, back-elbowed a second, and headbutted a third in the face. Bodies crashed to the floor, and took no further interest in the proceedings. The biggest guard of all loomed up before Daniel, and lashed out with a fist that would have put an end to anyone else's evening. Daniel avoided the blow easily, and then pivoted on one foot and kicked the man in the chest with such force that he went flying backward and took out three more security men along the way. Daniel laughed out loud, and looked hopefully around for some more trouble to get into.

Half a dozen large muscular types fell on him, hoping for safety in numbers. Daniel just had time to wonder why the Constantine Club felt the need to employ so many security guards, and then he was knocking them down and throwing them to one side. His speeded-up reactions allowed him to see what the guards were going to do before they did it, and then take them down with a series of swift and vicious blows. He felt the impacts as they traveled up his arms, but his hands took no damage and he didn't feel any pain. He was a Hyde, and the world and everything in it was just there for his amusement.

But even as he was punching men out and stamping on them while they were down, it occurred to Daniel how calm he was feeling. Faced with a small army of thugs and bullies, he never even came close to losing his temper. Probably because he was too busy enjoying himself. It wasn't like a real fight; it felt more like dancing.

He finally ran out of people to hit, and took a moment to stretch slowly. He wasn't even out of breath. People who had previously admired his dancing were now standing well back and staring at him in horror. As though a wild animal had somehow found its way into their civilized world. Bodies lay all around Daniel, broken and bloodied and extremely unconscious. He looked to see how Tina was doing, and found her standing calmly to one side with her arms folded. It occurred to Daniel that he hadn't actually seen her doing any of the fighting. He raised an eyebrow.

"You didn't look like you needed any help," said Tina. "And I was interested to see if you could handle all of them on your own. Did you have a good time?"

Daniel smiled. "Yes, I did."

"I've had enough dancing," said Tina.

She took him by the hand and led him out of the nightclub. And everyone scattered to get out of their way.

Outside the nightclub, there was no sign of the queue, and all the bouncers had run away. Tina walked out into the road in front of an oncoming taxicab, and it screeched to a halt right in front of her. She turned to look at Daniel.

"Come back to my place."

Daniel raised an eyebrow. "You could make it sound more like an invitation, and not an order."

"You want to—don't you?"

"From the first moment I saw you," said Daniel.

"Then that's all that matters."

They leaned close together in the back of the taxi, smiling broadly, lost in each other's eyes. Anticipation filled the air, as though there was someone else in the back seat with them. Their faces were so close that Daniel could feel Tina's breath on his face, and the raw animal musk of her scent filled his head.

It had been a long time since he'd had anyone in his life.

He glimpsed the taxi driver watching them in his rearview mirror. He looked scared out of his wits. Apparently there was something about Hydes smiling that disturbed the hell out of anyone who wasn't a Hyde. The thought just made Daniel smile even more.

Some time later, to Daniel's surprise, Tina suddenly leaned forward and rapped imperiously on the partition between them and the driver. When he reluctantly glanced back at her, Tina brusquely ordered him to stop the cab. The driver was so eager to be rid of his passengers he slammed on the brakes and brought the cab to a very abrupt halt. Tina threw the door open while the taxi was still rocking back and forth and got out, not even glancing back to see if Daniel was following. He clambered out of the cab, taking his time to make a point, and saw that they'd stopped next to a tree-lined path overlooking the River Thames. Tina glared at the taxi driver.

"You. Stay here, while we go for a little walk. When we come back, you can take us the rest of the way."

"You have got to be kidding," said the driver. "I'm not hanging around here while you make up your mind what you want. I've got other fares waiting."

He was doing his best to sound calm and determined and not at all troubled by the two Hydes, but he wasn't fooling anyone. Tina leaned in close to the driver's window and fixed him with a hard look.

"You. Stay here, while we go for a little walk. Or there will be trouble."

"Hell with this," said the driver.

He slammed the taxi into gear, but Tina had already pulled the door open. She reached in and ripped out the driver's seat belt, tossed it carelessly to one side, and then grabbed hold of the driver and hauled him bodily out of the cab. His loud protests gave way to screams as she dragged him across the leafy path to a set of iron railings, and then lifted him up and threw him into the Thames. Daniel hurried over to stand beside her and look down at the river, feeling just a little relieved when he saw the driver swimming strongly for the bank.

It had all happened too quickly for Daniel to intervene, but he wasn't entirely sure he would have if he could. The driver had been very rude, when all his instincts should have told him that was a really bad idea. Daniel turned to Tina to make some kind of comment, and found she was already striding off down the path. As though nothing out of the ordinary had just happened. And perhaps for her, it hadn't. Daniel sighed, shook his head, and went after her. If only to see what she'd do next. Tina didn't even glance at the Thames, just stared straight ahead. Daniel quickly caught up and moved in beside her, and then strode along in companionable silence as he wondered what to say.

"Why did you want to stop here?" he said finally.

"I needed somewhere quiet," she said, still not looking at him. "Somewhere I could think."

Daniel nodded. He was sure he was picking up some kind of vulnerability behind the brisk words. Something very much at odds with her usual determined exuberance. He decided not to press the point, just for the moment, and walked along beside Tina, giving her time to decide whatever it was she needed to say. She did slow her pace a little, which made it feel a little less like she was trying to put something behind her.

The early hours of the morning lay sprawled across London like a comforting blanket, tucking the city in so it could sleep peacefully. The whole setting seemed very quiet and very peaceful, with hardly any traffic passing by, and not another pedestrian to be seen anywhere. As though Daniel and Tina had the river walk and the night all to themselves. A light breeze came gusting down the path, playfully tousling their hair. The trees suddenly fell away behind them, and streetlamps dispensed pools of gentle golden light interrupted by periods of darkness, so that Daniel and Tina were constantly walking out of the light and into the dark, and then back again. Their footsteps sounded slow and deliberate, as though they knew what they were doing. It all seemed peaceful enough, but Daniel didn't think Tina had stopped the cab just so she could take the air and enjoy the atmosphere. She didn't seem to be paying any attention to the sights and sounds of the night. Instead, her head was bowed and her gaze was turned determinedly inward.

More time passed, and she still hasn't said anything, so Daniel decided he'd better make the first move, and get the ball rolling.

"Are you having second thoughts?" he said carefully. "About us?"

Tina shot him a quick look, accompanied by a smile that came and went before he could decide what kind of smile it was.

"This isn't about us. And it's definitely not about *you*, so stop worrying. It's about the Frankenstein Clan."

"You're having second thoughts about what we did there?" said Daniel.

"I don't know," said Tina. "I spent a year training, getting myself ready to kill every single one of them, but now it's over I'm not sure how I feel about it. I didn't act out of moral outrage over what the Frankensteins have been doing, like you. Edward trained me to see all the monster Clans as my enemy, because as long as any of them survived, they would never stop trying to kill me. All the monsters hate the Hydes, so it's always been a case of get them, before they get us."

"Why do the monsters hate Hydes so much?" said Daniel.

"Because Edward wouldn't stoop from being a monster, to be just a criminal," said Tina. "Simply by being what he is, he reminds them of what they used to be."

"What about you?" said Daniel. "Why did you join Edward's war?"

She shrugged. "I didn't do it for revenge, like you. I never lost anyone I cared about to the Frankensteins." She paused. "There's never been anyone in my life that I cared about. Before you."

She still wouldn't look at Daniel.

"What about Erik?" he asked.

"I was a junkie. I hardly noticed him back then."

He moved in a little closer, and didn't say anything. They strolled along beside the Thames, listening to the distant lap of the waters and staring straight ahead. Tina's hand reached out, and took hold of Daniel's. There was none of the Hyde strength in her grip, just a quiet companionable pressing of flesh against flesh. Daniel squeezed Tina's hand reassuringly in return, but she didn't respond. She was frowning hard now, appearing more puzzled than anything, as though she was struggling to find just the right words to help her explain what she was feeling to Daniel.

"At first," she said slowly, "Edward just sent me out to spy on the Clans. So I could see what they did, and learn to hate them. When he finally turned me loose on individual targets, I didn't even hesitate. And it felt good, so good, testing my strength and skills against things that would kill me in a moment, if they could. I was a predator who preyed on predators, and I never felt so alive as when I was wading in blood and death. But still . . . I always felt there should be more to it than that. It wasn't until I saw what the Frankensteins had done to that hybrid that it became personal for me. Because even for Hydes, there are some lines you just can't cross without giving up what it means to be human. The Frankensteins had to die . . . Not because the monster Clans are at war with Edward Hyde, but because putting them down was something that needed doing. When I saw what they'd done to that man, and what they intended to do to so many others . . . suddenly I saw all of the Clan's victims. And I felt what you did—your rage, and your need to do something. It wasn't about self-defense, or being part of Edward's plan, it was just the right thing to do. Something I'm not used to feeling."

She broke off abruptly, as though she'd run out of words. Daniel gave her a moment and then nodded encouragingly, to show he was doing his best to understand.

"Edward trained you—personally? To be a killer of monsters?"

"It was always Edward," said Tina. "Never the organization. Ever since he made me a Hyde, and saved me from my old life. I owe him so much . . ."

"Did he ever . . ."

"You have got to be kidding!" Tina looked at Daniel for the first time, grinning broadly at the very thought. "I'm *really* not his type. Too much woman, for him . . . And do you really think I'd have *let* him? I would have kicked him out a high window if he'd ever tried anything, and he knew it. If anything, he is a kind of father figure, I suppose. And I don't do daddy issues. No, it was all about learning how to fight, how to kill, and how to stay alive during it. Molding me into his own personal assassin. I worked some missions for him, earning my spurs by taking out some of the minor players on the sidelines, but it was only ever people who *served* the Clans, never the monsters themselves. For that, I had to wait until you showed up. I'm still not sure why."

She looked sharply at Daniel, but all he could do was shrug. Tina sniffed loudly.

"I spent ages familiarizing myself with all kinds of weapons, and taking out my frustrations on the small fry. Plotting tactics, and coming up with plans . . . I don't know why I was so patient. I could have walked away. There was nothing to stop me. I could have left Jekyll & Hyde Inc. anytime, and made a new life for myself. And to hell with the monsters."

"But you thought you owed him . . ."

"Hydes don't do duty or obligation," Tina said flatly. "Edward never once put any pressure on me, just promised me that the time would come when I would get to kill monsters. And I wanted that. I needed to test my strength and my skills against something worthy of them. People like the hard men in that bar earlier weren't any challenge, just a warm-up. Something to stir the blood, and put us in the right mood."

"So how did it feel, when you finally got to take on the Frankensteins and their creatures?" said Daniel. "Was it everything you'd thought it would be?"

"I'd been trained to kill them, and I did," said Tina. There wasn't a scrap of emotion in her voice. "When I saw what they'd done to that hybrid, it wasn't about a contest of equals anymore. It was about stopping something awful, and removing it from the world."

She glanced at Daniel, and managed another brief smile. "Maybe we should have gone along with your plan, and beaten every single Frankenstein to death with our bare hands. That might have felt more satisfying. But somehow . . . I don't think it would. In the end, it was more like putting down poison for rats. A necessary thing. I don't know . . . Maybe I'll enjoy killing the vampires more. Because they don't pretend to be human."

They walked some more, just strolling now, in no hurry to get anywhere. They had the night and the path all to themselves, and as much time as they needed to get things in order. Tina was still holding Daniel's hand. He wasn't sure if she realized that, and didn't want to say anything that might make her feel self-conscious about it. But it did seem to him that he should take this opportunity, to try to encourage her to open up more. That it might help her, if she could talk more about her life. Daniel certainly wanted to hear more about it.

"Why did Edward train you personally? Does he often have... favorites?"

"Not as far as I know," said Tina. "He doesn't normally take a personal interest in anyone. We're all just there to fight his private war for him."

"He told me he had enough soldiers," said Daniel. "That he needed warriors now, to finally bring down the Clans."

"I suppose I should be grateful that he chose me," said Tina. "But I'm really not. There's something about Edward Hyde..."

"I'm a Hyde, too," said Daniel. "Is there something about *me*?"

She turned to look at him, and this time her smile deepened. "No. You're nothing like Edward."

"Well," said Daniel. "That's a relief."

She laughed suddenly, gave his hand a squeeze, and then let go of it. She turned around and went striding back the way they'd come, moving so quickly Daniel had to break into a run to catch up. There was a definite bounce in Tina's step, and her frown was gone.

"I've been trying to decide how I feel," she said cheerfully. "Now all the Frankensteins are dead. And you know what? I feel alive! They're dead because they deserved to be; and we're alive because we chose to be. Nothing else matters."

And that was all she had to say, until they got back to the waiting taxicab. Daniel took a quick look around, but there was no sign of the driver anywhere. Which was probably just as well. Tina pulled open the driver's door, and then stopped abruptly. She turned to smile at Daniel.

"Would you like to come back to my place?"

Daniel grinned. "Since you're asking so nicely, I'd love to."

Tina grinned back at him, her eyes dancing, and then she turned quickly away and settled herself comfortably behind the steering wheel. Daniel went round to the other side, and sat down beside her.

"Are we stealing this cab?"

"Of course!" said Tina. "Because it's here!"

She revved the engine, slammed it into gear, and sent the cab racing off down the street. Daniel laughed happily, and beat out a tattoo on the dashboard with both hands.

It was early in the morning, and the city sprawled before them like an open invitation. Tina put the hammer down, and everything else on the road hurried to get out of their way.

Some time and several near misses later, Tina brought the taxi to a halt and they both got out. The apartment building in front of Daniel was old-school impressive, with a lot of history behind it, right in the middle of a really select area. Rows of trees lined the quiet street, along with old-fashioned black-iron streetlamps that shed a pleasant glow over the scene. The kind of place where everyone knows your face, usually from the financial or the society pages. Not at all the kind of setting Daniel had expected for Tina Hyde.

She took hold of his hand again, and led him toward the front door. Daniel could feel the power in her grip, that could crush a brick to powder or rip out a monster's throat. And the strength in his own hand, if he chose to use it. Something was building between them that felt dangerously explosive. Daniel didn't feel nervous, or uncertain. It was going to happen, and they both knew it. But somehow Daniel also knew that it wasn't going to be like anything he'd ever experienced before. Because Hydes did things differently.

The door opened to a combination keypad, and the uniformed security man nodded respectfully to Tina from his little office. She ignored him, so Daniel did, too. They took the elevator all the way up to the top floor, shooting glances at each other and exchanging smiles. Neither of them said anything; they didn't have to. The penthouse corridor was coolly elegant, with thick carpeting and expensive-looking prints on the walls, and the quiet charm that shrieks of serious money. Tina's apartment turned out to be comfortable, but entirely lacking in character. No photos or personal touches, and only the most anonymous fixtures and fittings. Nothing to indicate that Tina had ever tried to stamp her personality on her surroundings.

"What did you expect?" she said. "Rows of fluffy toys, and lace doilies everywhere?"

"No," said Daniel. "I didn't expect that."

"This is just where I am, when I don't have to be somewhere else."

"I know the feeling," said Daniel.

"Thought you would," said Tina.

She grabbed hold of him and slammed him back against the wall. He hit it hard enough to knock all the breath out of an ordinary man, but Daniel just grinned, grabbed two handfuls of her big red hair and hauled her face in close for a kiss. She turned her head at the last moment, and sank her teeth into his neck. He gasped, and then bit her bare shoulder, growling loudly as he worried at her flesh. The blood in his mouth was sharp and exciting. Their heads came up, and they kissed each other fiercely. Blood ran down their chins.

They rioted back and forth across the living room, wrestling and rolling on the floor. Not for control, but just for the fun of it. They crashed through the furniture, leaving it in pieces behind them. When they'd had enough of that, they knocked the bedroom door clean off its hinges in their eagerness to get into the room, and then they stopped abruptly, facing each other. They were both breathing hard, but it had nothing to do with their exertions. Without having to say anything, they both took the time to strip off their clothes, so as not to damage them.

When they were done they slammed together again, two naked bodies pressing hard against each other, as though they couldn't stand the thought of anything separating them. They kissed until they were panting for breath, and when they finally hit the bed Daniel enjoyed the most animalistic, frightening, and intense sex he'd ever experienced. Because Hydes don't hold anything back.

They finally ended up lying together in the wreckage of the bed, nursing their wounds and grinning at each other.

They huddled in close, sweat slowly drying on their bodies, as their breathing returned to normal. The sun was starting to show its face, and a faded gray light sneaked in past the drawn curtains, outlining various dim shapes in the bedroom. Most of which appeared to be broken, or at least walking wounded. Daniel lay stretched out on his back, one arm around Tina's shoulders, while she rested a hand over his heart. He felt wonderfully comfortable, as though this was where he was supposed to be. He started to say something, and Tina slapped him lightly on the chest.

"I'm not much of a one for pillow talk. So unless it's something important, like where the bathroom is..."

"There's something you're not telling me," said Daniel. "If we're going to stay this close, and I want that more than anything, there can't be any secrets between us. You know what happened to me; but I need to know what happened to you."

Tina slowly raised her arms, holding them up before her and turning them back and forth.

"You can't see the scars," she said slowly. "But I can. They'll always be there for me, even though they disappeared after I drank the Elixir."

She lowered her arms again, staring out across her wrecked apartment, so she wouldn't have to look at Daniel. When she finally began to speak again, her voice was entirely calm, almost casual. As though she was talking about somebody else. Daniel lay very still, so as not to distract her.

"I had to dig the razor blade in deep," said Tina. "To make sure I was doing a good job. I knew it wouldn't be enough to just slice across the wrists; I had to hack open all the veins, right up to the elbow. Otherwise some well-meaning idiot might find me and save me. It hurt like hell, and I cried a bit, but I was determined to get it done. Don't judge me, Daniel. You don't know what my life was like, back then. I would have done anything to get away from it."

Daniel took his time answering, to make sure his voice was calm. He didn't want to do anything that might discourage her from finally opening up to him.

"How did you survive something like that?"

"I didn't. Edward saved me. He followed me from the nightclub, after he saw me start a fight and then win it. He told me later he smelled the blood through the closed door, smashed it in, and found me bleeding out in the bathtub. He force-fed me the dose of Elixir he'd brought with him, and it closed my wounds and saved my life. He could have given me the choice to drink it, and I would have. I would try anything back then, the worse for me the better. And the Elixir made me the woman I am today."

She waited, still staring out at the gloom, to see what he would say. Daniel slowly raised a hand and put it over hers, on his chest.

"So Edward caught both of us at the lowest point in our lives," he said quietly. "I wonder if we might have chosen differently, under other circumstances."

"We were both dying by inches," said Tina. "Edward let our old selves die, so we could be Hydes. We have so much to thank him for."

"Do we?" said Daniel. "I haven't been a Hyde long, and already I'm worried I might become as much of a monster as the things I'm supposed to fight. I never killed anyone before I wiped out the whole Frankenstein family. Never wanted to, no matter how bad things got when I was in uniform. But then I lost my friends, my old life, and everything that mattered to me. I sometimes wonder if the best part of me died in that cellar. When Edward offered me the Elixir, I was ready to become a monster, just for a chance to get my life back. And for revenge, of course."

"You are not a monster," Tina said firmly. "Trust me, I'd know."

"I believe you," said Daniel.

They laughed softly, and snuggled together. Tina wedged a leg in between Daniel's, and caressed his foot with hers. Daniel kissed her shoulder.

"So, Edward is sending us after the Vampire Clan next," she said.

"The werewolves, the vampires, or the mummies?"

"What makes you think I know?"

"Because he spent so much time working with you. He must have discussed his plans."

"Of course he did," said Tina. "I couldn't get him to shut up about them. The Vampire Clan should be next on the list."

"Have you ever seen a vampire?"

"No."

"I have."

Tina looked at him sharply. "Up close?"

"Up close and personal," said Daniel. "I thought my old friend Paul died in that cellar, but the vampires dragged him out and turned him, just so they could make him answer their questions. He came to my flat, after I thought he was dead, just so he could tell me I needed to see Edward Hyde."

"What did he look like?" said Tina.

Daniel thought for a moment, considering his answer carefully. "He looked . . . different. As though he'd lost some important part of himself that made him the man I used to know. Or, more likely, it was taken from him."

"Hardly surprising," said Tina. "Vampires are just corpses disguised by a glamour. Leeches on two legs."

Daniel stirred uncomfortably beside her. "He was still my friend. He sent me to the one man who could help me."

"And you think he did that out of the goodness of his heart?"

"He didn't have to do it," said Daniel. "You know, I wasn't scared of him, not really. I think...because I still felt bad, that there was nothing I could do to save him, back in the cellar."

"You can still avenge him," said Tina. "Wipe out the whole Vampire Clan, and make sure no one else will ever have to suffer the way your friend did."

Daniel pushed his head back into the pillow and stared up at the ceiling, looking for answers he didn't have.

"But what will I be like, after I've killed all the monsters? What will all that blood and death do to me? Would I even recognize the man I'm going to become?"

"You ask the oddest questions," said Tina.

"Somebody has to," said Daniel.

He turned his head to smile at her. He could see her face clearly with his Hyde eyes, and he wanted her to see his.

"Have you never compared the person you are now with who you used to be?"

Tina lifted her arms briefly, and then let them fall back again.

"That person is dead, and she was happy to die. I'm someone else now. Don't you like her?"

"You know I do."

"Good. Because you really wouldn't have liked the old me. I didn't."

"Who was the man in the nightclub?" said Daniel. "The one who remembered you, from before?"

"Erik..."

"Were you close?"

"We might have been," said Tina. "But he asked too many personal questions."

She smiled at Daniel, to show that was meant to be a joke, but Daniel wasn't so sure. He looked steadily at Tina, to show he wanted a proper answer to his question, and she stirred uneasily.

"Back then, all I cared about was having a good time, all the time.

And Erik had the money, and the connections, to make that possible."

"But if you were having such a good time..."

"Why was I so determined to kill myself? Because too much fun wears you out. The more you do, the less you enjoy it. Until finally I got so tired all I wanted was to go to sleep and never have to wake up again."

Daniel could still hear an echo of that tiredness in her voice. He wanted to take her in his arms, and hold her so tightly it would drive all the bad memories away... But somehow he knew that if he tried, and it was the wrong moment, Tina would get up off the bed and walk away.

"Why do you suppose Edward decided to save you?" he said finally.

"Because he saw something in me that he could use," said Tina. "The same reason he made you a part of Jekyll & Hyde Inc.: because he has a war to fight, and he needs people like us."

"He said he wanted warriors," Daniel said slowly. "But I think he meant patsies. People he could use and then discard."

"Only if we let that happen," said Tina. "We both have good reasons to want the monsters dead, but once they're all gone... Edward won't need us anymore."

Daniel looked at her thoughtfully. "You think he might try to kill us?"

"Of course! He's Edward Hyde!"

"Sometimes I forget what that name means," said Daniel. "You remember how he walked right over that poor waitress?"

"I've seen him do worse," said Tina. "In the end, it might come down to us having to get him, before he can get us."

Daniel turned onto his side, so he could look at her directly. "You've given this a lot of thought, haven't you?"

Tina smiled. "I had a lot of time to think, waiting for you to show up so I could get this war started." She stretched slowly, as unself-conscious as a cat. "But who knows... maybe we won't have to kill him. Maybe, once we're not needed anymore, he'll just let us walk away and make new lives for ourselves."

"Maybe," said Daniel.

"You don't sound too convinced."

"Give me time. I'll work on it."

They lay tucked in close together, riding each other's breathing, staring out across the bedroom as the morning light slowly brought it to life. Daniel smiled suddenly.

"Conversations you never thought you'd be having ... My life has gone through so many changes—from policeman, to cripple, to Hyde ..."

"I know what you mean," said Tina. "Do you love me, Daniel?"

"Yes," he said. "Somewhat to my surprise. It sort of sneaked up on me, and hit me over the head when I wasn't looking. Do you ...?"

"No," said Tina. "But give me time. And I'll work on it."

"Well," said Daniel. "That's something."

They laughed quietly together, and then drifted off to sleep.

But later, Daniel woke to find Tina crying quietly beside him. She wouldn't or couldn't tell him why, so he just held her in his arms until morning light filled the room, and she could sleep.

They spent most of the next day and a half in bed, getting to know each other. Laying open their lives, sharing their pains and their triumphs, and all the things they'd never thought they'd be able to tell someone else. At least partly because they were just two Hydes, going up against the strength and power of the monster Clans, and they knew the odds were not in their favor.

When you believe you're going to die, you can say anything.

Love, or something very like it, had caught them by surprise, and neither of them was very sure how much they trusted it. But they were having fun finding out.

It was midafternoon before they finally returned to the Jekyll & Hyde Inc. building. They walked hand in hand across the empty lobby and all the way up in the elevator, but they made a point of separating before they entered Edward's outer office. Not because they were ashamed, but because they didn't want to give Edward anything he could use as ammunition against them. Edward's secretary greeted them graciously enough, but Daniel was convinced she was looking down her nose at the state of his tuxedo. He'd done his best to beat all the dust off, but there was a limit to what even

Hyde strength could achieve. Tina's evening dress was in rather better condition, apart from a few small bloodspots here and there. Daniel and Tina headed for Edward's inner office, but the secretary immediately raised her voice.

"I'm afraid Mister Hyde isn't in, just at the moment. But he did leave a message for you..."

And then she made a point of searching through the papers on her desk, even though Daniel had no doubt she knew exactly where it was.

"He said to tell you that he's in his playroom, on the seventh floor," she said. "And that you're to join him the moment you arrive."

"I know where that is," said Tina.

Daniel looked at her. "Why are you scowling?"

Tina's scowl only deepened once they'd left the secretary's office and set off back down the corridor to the elevators. Daniel kept a watchful eye on her. She'd been in a really good mood all the way across London, and he was concerned at how easily Edward Hyde had wiped the smile off her face. He wondered if changing the subject might help.

"Is that secretary a Hyde?"

"Of course not," said Tina, not looking at him. "Edward has always been very particular about who he shares his potion with. Everyone else just works here."

"She knew about us," said Daniel.

"Wouldn't surprise me," said Tina.

"You think Edward knows?"

"You think he cares?"

"What is worrying you so much, about the playroom?" said Daniel, having exhausted all his small talk.

"Depends what he's got in there," said Tina. "He's always having new things brought in, to play with."

"Why is that worth so much scowling?"

Tina finally turned to meet his gaze, and for the first time Daniel realized that Tina was seriously troubled.

"I don't know anyone who's ever been invited to join Edward in his playroom. He's changing his ways—and that's never a good thing."

They traveled to the seventh floor in silence. It worried Daniel that Tina was so worried. He had to wonder what someone like Edward would have in his secret playroom; whether it involved a brothel, a fight club, or a drug den. Or some seriously unnatural combination of all three. The man was capable of anything.

They finally ended up before the playroom door and Tina knocked loudly, not allowing herself to hesitate. A cheerful voice summoned them in. Daniel tried to go first, but Tina shouldered him out of the way. Once they were inside they both stopped dead in their tracks—because the middle of the room was occupied by a huge steel cage with a full-grown tiger in it.

The animal raged back and forth, snarling at Edward as he taunted and tormented it with a long stick. The tiger slammed its great shoulder against the side of the cage, and its weight alone was enough to shift the cage a few inches across the bare wooden floor. The great cat lashed out through the bars with vicious claws, but though its movements were blindingly fast Edward was always faster, and the tiger never even came close. Edward laughed mockingly, and thrust the sharp stick between the tiger's ribs, deep enough to draw blood. The tiger roared but it didn't flinch, just kept on fighting the bars of its cage in its eagerness to get to Edward.

As Daniel stood there, waiting to be acknowledged, he tried to figure out how Edward had got the tiger and its cage all the way up to the seventh floor. The cage must have been brought up in pieces, he decided, and then assembled inside the playroom. The tiger could have been drugged and carried up, and then allowed to awaken inside the cage. But what was it doing here? Was Edward planning to feed him and Tina to the tiger? Daniel smiled coldly, and stood a little straighter. Let him try . . .

Edward finally looked round, and beckoned them forward. Daniel and Tina kept a watchful eye on the tiger as they approached, but it ignored them. All of the animal's attention was fixed on Edward, as though his very existence offended it. The tiger lashed out suddenly, stretching as far as it could through the bars, straining to reach its hated enemy, but the claws slammed to a halt a few inches short. Edward didn't flinch.

"What is going on here?" said Daniel. He didn't even try to be polite, because he knew it would be wasted on Edward.

"I have contacts at London Zoo," Edward said easily. "People who see to it that I always get the most dangerous animals to play with. They do it partly for the money and partly in the hope that, one day, one of the beasts they supply will kill me."

Daniel looked at Tina, but she was keeping all expression out of her face and saying nothing. He turned reluctantly back to Edward.

"How do you mean, 'play'?"

Edward just grinned at him, taking Daniel's obvious disapproval as a compliment. He walked right up to the cage, and the tiger stood very still. It could sense what was coming. Edward unlocked the cage door, holding the tiger's gaze with his own.

"Stay close, my children, and enjoy the show," he said, smiling easily. "But whatever happens, don't interfere. This is all mine."

He threw the door open and the tiger erupted out of its cage, just a blur of muscles and stripes, as it went for Edward's throat. But Edward wasn't there anymore. He'd moved even as the tiger started its leap, and the tiger only flew through the space where he had been. It spun round quickly to face Edward, and he bared his teeth at it. On anyone else such a thing would have looked ridiculous—but this was Edward Hyde. The tiger actually paused for a moment, acknowledging the very real threat in Edward's snarl.

Daniel moved to put his body between Tina and the tiger, but she immediately pushed him aside so she could get a clear view. Daniel checked how far it was to the main door, just in case he had to drag her out. She could be mad at him afterward, when they were both safe. Even though a part of him did wonder whether Tina could take the tiger.

The huge beast circled Edward slowly, its tail thrashing, head held low, lips pulled back to reveal heavy predator's teeth. It was growling constantly now, like a low roll of thunder. Edward turned slowly, steadily, so that he was always facing the tiger ... grinning so broadly his face reminded Daniel of gargoyles on cathedral roofs. And then Edward threw aside his stick and beckoned to the tiger; and it went for his throat again.

Despite all the strength and power in the tiger's leap, Edward didn't give an inch. He braced himself and lashed out with one massive fist, punching the tiger right between the eyes. The sheer force of the blow stopped the great cat in midair, and it slumped to the ground, only half conscious. The impact alone should have broken every bone in Edward's fist, but he hit the tiger again and again, driving it into the floor. Daniel winced as he heard bones crack and break in the tiger's skull.

The massive beast tried to gather its hind legs under it for another leap, but Edward moved in close, raining blow after blow on the tiger's head. Blood spurted from the tiger's mouth and nose, and then from its eyes and ears. It collapsed on the floor, unable to defend itself. It knew its death was close. It made a low helpless sound—and Edward laughed at it. Daniel stirred, but Tina grabbed his arm before he could do anything, piling on the pressure to hold him where he was.

Edward didn't pause in his attack, hitting the tiger again and again and grunting happily with the effort that went into every blow. Until the tiger let out one last sigh, and stopped breathing. But even after it was dead Edward kept on hitting it, laughing out loud as the body jumped bonelessly from the repeated impacts.

And then, quite suddenly, Edward stopped. He bent over the body, breathing hard, as though inhaling the kill and savoring it; and then he slowly straightened up, took a large handkerchief from his pocket, and set about methodically wiping the blood from his hands. He looked across at Daniel, and dropped him a roguish wink.

"King of the jungle!"

Tina let go of Daniel's arm. She was breathing almost as heavily as Edward, her face flushed from the excitement of the kill. Daniel couldn't help wondering what it would feel like, to go head to head with a living engine of destruction and defeat it with nothing but his bare hands. But even as he thought that, another part of him wanted to kill Edward for what he'd just done. Because it hadn't been a fair fight. The tiger never stood a chance.

Edward must have seen something in Daniel's face, because he stopped what he was doing and summoned Daniel forward with one blood-spattered hand. Daniel didn't hesitate, because Edward would have seen that as weakness. He walked steadily forward, until they were standing face-to-face. He didn't even glance down at the dead tiger. Edward reached out and carefully smeared some of the tiger's blood across Daniel's face.

"There," Edward said cheerfully. "Now you're blooded. One of us."

"Fresh blood?" said a new voice behind them. "You shouldn't have."

Paul Mayer was standing by the door, smiling his saturnine smile while being careful not to reveal his vampire teeth. None of the Hydes had heard him enter; he was just suddenly there, wrapped in his long and filthy coat. Daniel realized he was seeing Paul clearly for the first time, in the sharp, shadowless light of Edward's playroom. The vampire looked even worse than Daniel remembered.

Paul's skin was horribly pale, like a dead thing that had spent too much time underground. He stood straight and still, with nothing human in his posture or composure. Just his presence was enough to raise the hackles on Daniel's neck. Paul was dangerous, a threat to all of them; far more than the tiger had been. The animal just wanted to kill them, but Paul would do much worse, given the chance.

He'd make them like him.

Daniel felt Tina stir at his side, and this time his hand clamped down on her arm, holding her where she was. Memories of old friendship might hold Paul back, but Daniel wasn't sure of that. The thing standing before him only looked like his old friend. Tina threw off Daniel's hand and snarled at Paul, like an animal challenged on its own territory. Paul looked her over insolently, and then let his smile widen so Tina could get a good look at his jagged teeth. Tina fell back a step. She knew when she'd been out-snarled.

"How did you get in here?" she said.

"Because he's one of mine," said Edward. He spoke quite calmly, as though the presence of the undead didn't disturb him at all. "This is my inside man for the Vampire Clan. Though he's supposed to know better than to come here during the day. Or enter my building without checking with me first."

Paul shrugged. He seemed entirely unimpressed by Edward, as though he'd seen worse. And Daniel thought he probably had.

"How were you able to get here, in broad daylight?" he said steadily.

"There are all kinds of hidden ways to get around this city," said Paul. "There is a London under London. When I told you all the monsters went underground, Danny, I meant that literally. They make their homes right under your feet. And that's just the monsters you've heard of. You'd be surprised what else there is, down in the depths. Things even monsters are afraid of. The world is older and stranger than you can imagine, Danny boy. Now let's get on with this. I need my beauty sleep."

"In your coffin?" said Daniel.

"That's for the elders," said Paul. "I just get my own patch of dirt."

"Why do you allow a vampire access to this building, Edward?" said Tina. Her voice was loud, and very cold.

"I summoned him here," said Edward. "So he can help us destroy the annual gathering of the Vampire Clan. Paul is going to tell us exactly where they're going to be."

"Why would he betray his own kind?" said Tina.

"Because I'm not like them," said Paul. "I never wanted to be a vampire. They took away my humanity, made me into a thing of blood and horror, dragged me kicking and screaming out of the light and into the dark. You're going to be my revenge."

Daniel turned his gaze away, to look at Edward.

"How do we destroy the Clan? Another bomb?"

"Yes, and no," said Edward. "A bomb on its own wouldn't be enough. You can't kill what's already dead."

"Undead," said Paul.

"Correct me again and I'll rip out your canines," said Edward. "The point is, the vampires need to be lured into a properly prepared trap. And that's where you come in, my children. You will go to the annual gathering and walk among them. Paul will provide you with the proper passwords. You will then insult and provoke the vampires into chasing you to where you have planted the bomb, so you can trigger the trap."

"How are we supposed to survive that?" said Tina.

"I have faith in you," said Edward.

"Where do we find this gathering?" said Daniel.

"Vampires live in the Underground railway system," said Paul. "Because it's always dark down there. They sleep in abandoned stations, and move back and forth through forgotten tunnels. Like worms in the earth. Sometimes they appear on the usual platforms, when hardly anyone's about, so they can fall on some unfortunate soul and drag them off into the shadows. Vampires ride the trains to every part of London, and then use the hidden ways to get to where they have to be, and do what they have to do. The Tube is such a convenient system, you have to wonder if it was originally designed with vampires in mind. A hiding place and a feeding ground, all in one—"

"Hold it," said Daniel. "Vampires ride the trains, along with the living—and no one notices?"

"No one ever looks at anyone else on the underground," said Paul. "You know that, Danny."

Daniel nodded slowly. "You told me the Vampire Clan specializes in crimes of seduction..."

"No one ever sees what a vampire really looks like," said Paul. "A glamour hides our true nature, so people only see what we want them to. The Clan owns all manner of private clubs where the rich and powerful can go to satisfy the needs and hungers they could never admit to anywhere else. And I'm not just talking about blood drinking, but rather all the strange desires and weird cravings that only a vampire's glamour can make possible. Because we can be anyone you ever dreamed of..."

Tina turned to Edward. "We're going to have to do something about these clubs, after we've destroyed the vampires."

"Of course," said Edward. "My people will take them over. Jekyll & Hyde Inc. can always use a new source of revenue."

Tina looked like she wanted to say something, but she didn't, so Daniel didn't either.

"Tell them where they need to go, Paul," said Edward.

"The annual gathering of the Vampire Clan will be held at the stroke of midnight, in the abandoned Albion Square station," said Paul. "Dress informally, and don't be late."

"Why here in London?" said Daniel. "Why not...Transylvania?"

"Because the monsters have been based here for so long, it feels like home to them," said Paul. "The vampire elders remember when this was a very different city, but they still feel like they own it. That all the people in London are nothing more than livestock, to feed on when they choose."

"That's enough," said Edward, cutting him off. "You've said your piece. Now get the hell out of my building."

Paul just nodded, entirely unimpressed by the disdain in Edward's voice. The tip of a gray tongue emerged, to lick at his colorless lips.

"I wonder what your blood would taste like, Edward? Perhaps you've aged well, like an old wine."

"Too rich for you, boy," said Edward.

He smiled at Paul—and something in that smile made the vampire turn his head away. Perhaps because Edward had been a predator for so much longer—or because only one of them wanted to be a monster.

"Walk with me, Danny boy," said Paul. "We need to talk privately."

The two of them moved off a way. Tina stared curiously after them. Edward didn't seem to care.

"Wipe the blood off your face, Danny," Paul said quietly. "It's distracting."

Daniel took out a handkerchief and cleaned his face as best he could. Paul nodded, appreciating the attempt.

"You look good as a Hyde, Danny. Is your new life everything you thought it would be?"

He glanced back at Tina. Daniel didn't.

"The Frankenstein Clan is gone," he said.

"I know," said Paul. "All the other Clans can't stop talking about it."

"I thought the Clans were too proud to talk to each other?" said Daniel.

"There are bars, and clubs," Paul said vaguely. "Private places, where the lower ranks can meet and drink and talk together, even though they know they're not supposed to. Perhaps especially because they know they're not supposed to. But who else could they gossip with, who would understand?" He looked thoughtfully at Daniel. "Did it feel good, when the Frankensteins died?"

"Yes," said Daniel. "Like a weight off my soul."

"I'm glad," said Paul. "I couldn't get to them. The vampire elders keep me on too short a leash. But I knew you could do it, with a little push in the right direction."

Daniel looked at him. He didn't like the idea that Paul had sent him to Edward just so he could make use of him.

"Did you reach out to Edward, originally?" he said. "Or did he go after you, to be his inside man?"

"Did he buy me, or am I using him?" said Paul. "You're sharper than you used to be, Danny boy. Let's just say there are games within games inside this very private war, and there are more sides than anybody knows. But that isn't the question you should be asking."

"Then what is?"

"Did Edward Hyde provide Commissioner Gill with the original misleading information that sent us to the Frankenstein chop shop?"

Daniel stared at Peter. "Why would he do that?"

Paul shrugged. It looked subtly wrong, like something the vampire remembered doing from when he was alive, but couldn't quite remember why.

"Perhaps because he hoped it would produce someone motivated enough to kill monsters. Someone prepared to do absolutely anything, in their need for revenge."

"Are you sure about this?" said Daniel.

"No. But I listen, and I hear things. Enough to be sure that this whole situation is so hideously complicated that not even Edward Hyde understands everything that's going on. The only thing I am sure of is that I don't want to do this anymore. So when it's all over . . . if I survive, stake me."

"I can't do that," said Daniel. "You're my friend."

"If you *are* still my friend, put an end to me," said Paul. "Because I can't. Trust me, you'd do it without a moment's hesitation if you knew some of the things I've done. Because the elders ordered me to, or just because I wanted to. I'm hanging on to what's left of my humanity by my fingertips—and I'm losing my grip. Promise me that whatever happens, you'll finish me."

Daniel nodded slowly. "I promise."

Paul abruptly turned away, and headed for the main door. His feet made no sound at all on the bare wooden floor. As Paul approached the door it opened on its own, and then closed behind him after he was gone.

"Okay . . ." said Tina. "That's handy."

Daniel walked back to join her. Edward thrust a large folder into Tina's hands.

"This file contains your mission details—everything you need to know, to destroy the Vampire Clan. Follow the plan carefully, and you should come back alive. Now off you go, my children, and put an end to every single one of them."

He looked meaningfully at Daniel. He knew Edward was talking about Paul, but he didn't say anything. He headed for the door, and for once Tina hurried after him.

Chapter Six
THE GLAMOUR OF IT ALL

✣ ✣ ✣

"**WE NEED TO VISIT THE ARMORY,**" said Tina, as they walked quickly down the corridor, putting some distance between them and Edward's playroom.

"For the bomb?" said Daniel.

"Well, obviously," said Tina. "But we're also going to need some pretty specialized weapons, if we want to survive long enough to lure the entire Vampire Clan to their death and destruction."

"Yes," said Daniel. "About that . . ."

"Edward has been working on his plan for years," said Tina, hefting the heavy mission file he'd given her. "I'm sure he's thought of everything."

Daniel gave her a look. "You're being very trusting, all of a sudden."

"I trust the plan," said Tina. "No one knows more about monsters than Edward Hyde. Surviving the plan . . . is up to us." She grinned at Daniel. "Come on—we're going to walk right into the vampires' annual gathering, call them a bunch of names to their faces, and then lead them by the nose to our very own killing ground. What's not to like?"

"This can only go well," said Daniel.

"Exactly!" said Tina.

The Jekyll & Hyde Inc. armory turned out to be a massive warehouse that took up half of the first floor. There were no guards on duty, and no obvious surveillance cameras; nothing that Daniel could see to stop anyone just wandering in when they felt like it. The only sign on the unlocked door said simply: PLEASE DON'T DROP ANYTHING. Given the armory's casual attitude to delivering its bombs, by just dumping them at the front door, Daniel supposed he shouldn't be surprised. He pushed the door open cautiously, and when nothing immediately bad happened, he allowed to Tina to go in first—so he could use her as a human shield if necessary. She strode confidently through a maze of open shelving and display cases, packed with all kinds of weird weapons and intriguing devices, some of them old enough to qualify as steampunk. And while there was a definite sense of a place for everything and everything in its place, nothing on the shelves was labeled or identified, so that most of the time Daniel was reduced to guessing wildly as to what he was looking at. He stuck close behind Tina as she marched down one narrow passageway after another, under lights that seemed designed to hide things in shadows. They finally found the person in charge sitting comfortably in something that was not so much an office, more like a converted cupboard.

"This is Miss Montague," Tina said cheerfully. "She knows everything there is to know, when it comes to ruining a monster's day."

"Oh hush, child," said Miss Montague. "I just have a gift for death and destruction."

Miss Montague was a gray-haired little old lady, in a nice cardigan with puppies on it. She had a pleasant face and an easy manner, and the kind of bright eyes you just knew didn't miss a thing. Daniel had to keep fighting down an urge to tell her that the dog had eaten his homework. He was pretty sure Hydes didn't do that. Miss Montague sat behind a desk—on which all the paperwork had been ruthlessly sorted into In and Out trays—knitting something long and shapeless. The needles clacked loudly, never pausing, all the time she talked to Daniel and Tina.

"Back again so soon, dear?" she said cheerfully to Tina. "You can't have used up everything I gave you last time, or most of London wouldn't still be here."

"We are finally ready to take down the Vampire Clan," said Tina, just as cheerfully. "What strange and appalling weapons would you recommend for us?"

"I recommend that you stick to the basics, dear," Miss Montague said firmly. "I always say, you can't go wrong if you stick to the basics. And always carry extra ammunition."

"Can I have this?" said Daniel. "I really like the look of this."

The compressed-air machine pistol that fired miniature wooden stakes had all but jumped off the shelf into his hand. It looked like something he could do some serious damage with, and he really liked the idea of being able to stake vampires from a safe distance.

"Oh, you don't want that, dear," said Miss Montague. "The gears are always jamming, and it has an unfortunate tendency to blow back and perforate the user."

Daniel reluctantly put the machine pistol back where he found it. Tina picked up a flashlight with a really large battery pack.

"What does this do?"

"Theoretically, it generates special wavelengths of light designed to undo the effects of a full moon, and force a werewolf back into its human form," said Miss Montague.

"And does it?" said Daniel.

"Not noticeably," said Miss Montague. "It just makes bits of their fur fall out. The only reason our last tester wasn't killed was because the wolf pack couldn't chase him for laughing."

Tina put the lamp back, while Daniel picked up a pair of scissors that smelled strongly of spices.

"And these?"

"Specially treated to cut the bandages off a living mummy," Miss Montague said patiently. "Providing you can get close enough."

Daniel put the scissors down again, and gave Miss Montague his very best hard look.

"Does anything here work?"

"Of course, dear! It wouldn't be much of an armory if we couldn't supply you with something absolutely guaranteed to rain on a monster's picnic. But it's not like there's a manual when it comes to developing new ways of disposing of vampires, werewolves, and mummies. We are constantly trying out new methods and tactics, but in the end it all comes down to trial and error." She shook her gray-haired head sadly. "We get through more field agents that way… which is why I always say, stick to the basics. You always know where you are, with the basics."

"At least tell me you have another bomb for us," said Daniel. "Preferably something even more powerful than the one we just used to destroy the Frankensteins."

Miss Montague smiled modestly. "It did do the job nicely, didn't it? Took the top right off that hotel. I saw it on the news. Apparently all kinds of terrorist organizations have come forward to claim responsibility, which is always helpful in our line of work. And it served the hotel right; you wouldn't believe what they charged me for using the minibar, the last time I stayed there. And the porn channel was a great disappointment. But that bomb was merely a standard whizzbang. I have something much more emphatic for you, this time." And then she broke off from her knitting, to look sharply at Tina. "Please put that down, dear. We don't want a nasty incident, do we?"

"But what is it?" said Tina.

"A black hole in a jam jar."

Tina put the jar back on the shelf, very carefully. "Really?"

"It's a very special kind of jam jar," said Miss Montague. She sighed quietly, put aside her knitting, and got to her feet. "I can see I'm going to have to sort out what you need personally, if we're to avoid sudden bangs and unpleasant stains on the carpet. Not that there are any carpets, despite all the forms I've filled in. Come along with me, dears—and from now on don't touch anything if you like having fingers."

When she came out from behind her desk, to stand blinking mildly in the gloomy passageway, Miss Montague turned out to be barely five feet tall. But her back was straight and her gaze was still sharp as she bustled between the towering shelves, making sudden turns without warning or hesitation. This was her territory, and she knew every inch of it. While Daniel wasn't even sure which way he'd come in. Miss Montague did pause briefly to coo affectionately at a cat dozing on a low shelf. Tina put out a hand to pet it, and her hand went straight through.

"Ghost cat," said Miss Montague. "See where curiosity gets you?"

But Tina had already stopped listening to her, having become far more interested in something else. She strode over to a large wooden case, half hidden in the shadows, and studied it curiously.

"What is this?"

Daniel moved over to join her. The long, rectangular box was blunt and basic, with no detailing, apart from a really big padlock to hold the heavy lid securely in place.

"It looks like a coffin," he said slowly. "Only twice the normal size. It has to be at least ten feet long, maybe more. Miss Montague, why do you have a giant coffin in your armory?"

"It's not a coffin, as such," said Miss Montague. "It's a container. Built to provide long-term storage, for a very important specimen."

"You mean there's someone alive in there?" said Tina, studying the long box with even more interest.

"Not someone," said Miss Montague. "Some*thing*. Now please come along, dears. That really isn't anything you want to mess with."

"Oh, I really think I do," said Tina. "Edward never mentioned anything to me before about a coffin in the armory, and if it's that secret I want to know all about it."

She stood before the coffin with her arms folded firmly, in a way that suggested she was perfectly prepared to stand there until hell froze over and congealed, if that was what it took to get an answer. Miss Montague pinched the bridge of her nose and sighed heavily, recognising someone just as stubborn as herself.

"Well if you must know..."

"Oh, I must," said Tina. "I really must. Or I won't sleep at night."

"It all goes back to when Dr. Jekyll was creating his Elixir," said Miss Montague. "You don't just test a new drug on yourself and see what happens. You try it out first on a test animal."

"And the original test animal is what's inside this coffin?" said Daniel.

"Yes, dear. But it's really not a coffin. As such."

"But why is there a really big padlock on this coffin, Miss Montague?" Tina said sweetly. She leaned over to study it, and then straightened up abruptly to stare suspiciously at Miss Montague. "Is the lock there to keep something from getting out? Is the test animal still alive?"

"An interesting question," said Miss Montague, "given that the box has been securely sealed for longer than I care to think. I suppose it's like Schrödinger's famous cat: there's no way of knowing whether the subject is alive or dead until you open the lid. But I really wouldn't recommend it. The creature could be very angry, after being locked in there for so long. Not to mention extremely hungry."

Daniel decided he was quite ready to accept that and let it go—but it only took one look at Tina's face to tell him that she wasn't.

"Why is the test specimen still in there?" she said stubbornly. "And why does Edward keep it locked up in his armory?"

"Well, you know how he is, dear," said Miss Montague. "He thought he might have a use for it. Edward never throws away anything he thinks might come in handy one day."

Daniel frowned at the oversized coffin. "I'm not sure I'm following this. The whole point of Dr. Jekyll's Elixir was to release all the evil vitality in a man. But can animals be good, or evil?"

"What's inside that box was quite definitely evil," Miss Montague said firmly. "I've read the history. Apparently it wrecked half of the good doctor's laboratory before he was able to bring it under control with an extremely powerful soporific. He had to build that box specially to contain it securely. Now do please come along, we have a great deal to do."

Tina folded her arms again, and Miss Montague shook her head slowly.

"Oh, very well . . . if you must. But I'll have to ask Edward if he'll authorize a little peek for you. The lock has a combination, and I don't know the numbers."

"I'll bet I could crack it," said Tina.

She took hold of the heavy padlock with one hand, and it jumped open in her grasp. She snatched her hand away, and the lock fell to the floor with a loud thud. There was a pause, and then the coffin lid rose an inch before slowly falling back again. Something stirred inside the coffin.

Miss Montague grabbed Daniel and Tina by the arms, and hauled them backward. They went along with her, never once taking their eyes off the long box. Something growled loudly, like the biggest dog in the world. The whole coffin shuddered, and the lid rattled loudly. Miss Montague quickly slipped behind Daniel and Tina, putting them between her and the danger, and they were so surprised they let her do it.

"I had no idea that padlock was so sensitive!" said Miss Montague, peering between them. "All these years I've left that box strictly alone, just as I was told. I never even dusted it. And all this time, the lock was ready to just fall off... Someone should have said something! I should have been told!"

The lid flew open and fell away, and a giant rat burst out of the coffin to crouch on the floor before them. It was impossibly big, twice the size of a man, bulging with muscles and covered in thick dark fur. It had mad red eyes, clawed hands like a man, and a long tail that lashed angrily behind it. The Hyde of rats... It opened its great jaws to reveal teeth like a shark, and made a sound like an angry foghorn. Tina glanced down at Miss Montague.

"What do we do?"

"You keep it occupied and I'll run for help, dear."

Daniel looked at Miss Montague. "Really?"

"Well, I don't know! That box was never supposed to be opened!"

"But this is an armory!" said Daniel, not taking his eyes off the enormous rat for one single moment. "There must be some weapon in here we can use against it!"

"Oh, I don't think Edward would want us to kill it," said Miss Montague. "Not after he's preserved it for all these years."

"In the current circumstances, let's assume he would," said Tina. "Find something!"

"Let me think..." said Miss Montague, and then she suddenly disappeared into a side passageway.

The rat stared unblinkingly at Daniel and Tina, hunching its powerful shoulders. Thick ropes of saliva fell from its mouth as the jaws worked thoughtfully. And then the rat charged right at them, squealing like a fire siren.

Tina didn't hesitate. She ran straight at the rat and jumped right over it. The rat's head came up, jaws opening wide, but Tina had already landed gracefully behind it. She spun around and grabbed hold of the rat's tail with both hands. She grimaced at the feel of the naked pink flesh, but dug her heels in deep and hauled hard, dragging the rat backward. It squealed deafeningly in protest, while its claws dug deep furrows in the floorboards. It tried to turn its head around to see what was happening, but there wasn't enough room. And while it was distracted, Daniel grabbed hold of the heavy wooden box with both hands, heaved it into the air, and then brought it slamming down on top of the giant rat. The huge creature collapsed and lay there stunned, pinned down by the weight of the coffin. Tina quickly let go of the tail, and rubbed her hands hard on her hips.

"Nice use of lateral thinking," she said cheerfully. "Now help me get the bloody thing back inside the coffin."

They pushed the box off the rat, and then manhandled the great weight of the thing back into its coffin. Daniel retrieved the lid and slammed it back into place, and then they both sat on it, using their weight to hold it down as the rat began to stir again. They clung on to the sides of the coffin, but the rat wasn't strong enough to throw both of them off—or at least, not yet. Daniel glared around at the various passageways in search of Miss Montague.

"Whatever you're looking for, it had better not be an exit!" he said loudly. "Get back here with something useful, even if it's only a really big piece of cheese."

Miss Montague came hurrying back—with a really big grenade in her hand. She gestured for Daniel and Tina to get off the lid. They looked at her dubiously, but she was already pulling the pin, so they jumped down and backed quickly away. The lid started to rise, and Miss Montague popped the grenade through the opening, then forced the lid shut again and slipped the padlock back into place. There was a muffled explosion from inside the coffin, and then it all went very quiet.

"What was that?" said Tina.

"Rat poison," said Miss Montague. "Well . . . mammoth poison, actually. But it'll do the job."

"You have a mammoth problem?" said Daniel.

"Not anymore," said Miss Montague.

They all studied the coffin carefully, but there were no more sounds or signs of movement.

"At least now we know whether it's alive or dead," said Tina.

"Let's hope so, dear," said Miss Montague. She studied Daniel and Tina for a long moment, and then smiled suddenly. "You worked very well together, dears. Reminded me of when Edward and I were a team, back in the day."

Tina looked at her sharply. "You worked missions together? Out in the field?"

"He wasn't always such a recluse," said Miss Montague. "Now come along, dears, and let's get you kitted out for the fray."

She bustled off down a new passageway, not even glancing back at the coffin. Daniel and Tina looked at the unmoving box and then at each other, shrugged pretty much in unison, and went after her. A few sharp turns later, Miss Montague started grabbing things off shelves and thrusting them into Daniel's and Tina's arms: wooden stakes, holy water ampules, garlic gas grenades . . . and a really big silver crucifix on a chain for each of them.

"I'm not religious," said Daniel.

"Vampires are," said Miss Montague, in the kind of tone that made Daniel wonder where his gym bag was.

She also presented them with two large bulbs of fresh garlic and made Daniel and Tina crush them in their hands, and then rub the juices all over their exposed necks and wrists.

"Just what you need to keep you from being bitten," she said briskly. "No, don't throw them away, dears! Put them in your pockets. If all else fails, you can eat the garlic and breathe in the vampires' faces."

"Does that repel vampires?" said Tina.

"More like melts their faces off, dear," said Miss Montague.

"Why does garlic work?" said Daniel.

"Beats the hell out of me, dear," said Miss Montague. "Presumably the vampires know, but they're not telling."

The new bomb turned out to be another flat metal box with just the one button. Only this time it came with a remote control, which Miss Montague handed to Daniel.

"Hit the button on the bomb to activate it, and then hit the remote to set it off. We can't depend on a timer with this mission. If you're going to lead the vampires into a trap, only you can decide on the right moment to trigger the explosion."

"You know about the plan?" said Tina.

Miss Montague smiled sweetly, and fixed Tina with her worryingly bright eyes. "I helped Edward work out most of the details."

"I didn't know you and he worked so closely together," said Tina.

"Oh, we used to be very close, a long time ago." Miss Montague laughed softly at the look on their faces. "You young people, you think you invented sex."

Daniel decided he was going to concentrate on the remote control. Just another box with a single button, presumably because you really didn't want complications when the shit was clogging up the fan. He wanted to ask Miss Montague if she had one with a red button, but he didn't feel like pushing his luck.

Miss Montague finished up by handing Tina a powerful flashlight, to help them find their way through the dark Underground tunnels, and presented Daniel with a small mirror, so he could quietly check who was and wasn't human. And then she gave them both backpacks to carry everything in. She stepped back and looked them over critically.

"Allow me to wish you both the very best of luck," she said. "Because you're going to need it."

"So," said Daniel, after they'd left the armory. "Where now? Back to the tailors, for new outfits?"

"Hell with that," said Tina, slinging her pack carelessly over one shoulder. "I'm keeping my nice evening dress. It's lucky."

Daniel thought about everything they'd been through. "Really?"

"We're alive, and the Frankensteins aren't."

"Do Hydes do superstition?" said Daniel.

"This one does."

"Then I'm hanging on to my tux," said Daniel. "If only because it makes me look like James Bond."

"I am very definitely not a Bond girl," said Tina. "Modesty Blaise, maybe."

"I thought she wore a catsuit?"

"Only because she was drawn by a man. I have better fashion sense."

"All right," said Daniel. "Where are we going now?"

"According to Edward's file, to see a vicar about a river."

They traveled across London on a series of Underground trains. Tina quietly briefed Daniel from the file, while he kept a careful lookout for any vampires who might be traveling with them. Paul's words had made an impression. The few other people in the carriage all seemed entirely ordinary, but he checked them out with his concealed mirror anyway, just in case. None of them paid any attention to what Tina was saying, because everyone minds their own business on the Tube.

"Can't I just read the file for myself?" said Daniel.

"No," said Tina. "This is my file. Edward gave it to me. Now pay attention . . . There are lost rivers that run underneath London. Once they coursed through the heart of the city, part of its everyday trade and commerce, but now they're built over and largely forgotten. One of them is the River Fleet. We are going to visit the source of that river, where a vicar is waiting to bless it for us so that all the waters of the Fleet will be holy."

"Hold everything and blindfold the horses," said Daniel. "Edward Hyde has a vicar working for him?"

Tina looked at him pityingly. "He has all sorts of people on his books, from all walks of life. Because he never knows when they'll come in handy. Some are bought and paid for, and some he blackmails or intimidates into doing their bit."

"That sounds like Edward," said Daniel. "How many of these people have you actually met?"

"Just the ones Edward wanted me to work with," said Tina. "He only ever tells people what he thinks they need to know. Most of what I've learned about Jekyll & Hyde Inc. comes from gossiping with the support staff. I've been told there are some people who work for Edward because they believe it's the right thing to do. Making a deal with the devil for a chance to finally get rid of the monsters. They think they're fighting on the side of the angels."

"Aren't they?" said Daniel. "Isn't killing monsters a good thing?"

"Of course," said Tina. "I'm simply not sure that's why Edward is doing it. Does he really strike you as someone who does the right thing for the right reasons?"

"He must have *some* reason," said Daniel.

"Maybe it's professional jealousy," said Tina, "because he can't stand the idea of anyone being a bigger monster than he is. Or perhaps he just finds the whole idea of monsters fighting monsters amusing."

"Wouldn't surprise me," said Daniel.

Tina consulted her file again. "The official source for the River Fleet is supposed to be two streams on Hampstead Heath, but according to this, Edward has been able to track down the real source."

"Amazing, the information that man has," said Daniel.

"Not really," said Tina. "People tell him things. He has a very compelling personality, as you've seen."

"Whether they want to or not?" said Daniel.

"Wouldn't surprise me at all," said Tina.

They left the train at Paddington Station, and set off through a variety of unofficial passageways until they were deep in the unfinished workings of the long-delayed Jubilee Line Extension. Daniel and Tina descended through increasingly dark and deserted tunnels, in a bobbing pool of light provided by her flashlight. Daniel assumed Tina was following a map in her head, but wouldn't give her the satisfaction of asking. But even as they moved through one tunnel after another, he couldn't shake off a slow creeping feeling that they weren't alone; that something was down there in the dark with them. He stuck close to Tina, straining his eyes against the gloom and his ears against the quiet.

Finally an uncertain flickering glow appeared up ahead, and Daniel and Tina hurried toward it. The low-ceilinged tunnel suddenly widened out into a great open cavern, lit by dozens of candles set everywhere there was a reasonably flat surface. A trickle of water ran across the muddy cavern floor, rising up from some underground spring. The source of the River Fleet. A man in a dark suit and a white dog collar was sitting on a folding stool, drinking hot tea from a thermos. He put it down carefully when Daniel and Tina stumbled out of the dark and into the candlelight, and rose to his feet to meet them.

Tall and more than usually thin, he had a gaunt face and haunted eyes. It was hard to tell whether or not he was pleased to see the Hydes; it seemed like there was simply too much sadness in him to allow for anything else.

"You can call me Mr. Martin," he said, in a voice so low they had to strain to hear it. "Here to do what's necessary. You both drank the potion, didn't you? You have the look. No, don't bother to introduce yourselves. I don't care."

He reached down and picked up a large leather-bound bible from the cavern floor. It looked like it had seen a lot of use. He patted the cover absently, like a man with a faithful dog.

"I find comfort in the Old Testament. Especially when it speaks about the end of the world."

"Because it offers you hope?" Daniel said politely.

"Because I'm looking forward to it."

"You are exactly the kind of vicar Edward Hyde would have working for him," said Tina.

Mr. Martin showed them a brief smile. "Needs must, when the devil has a lease on your soul."

He opened his bible to where it was marked, and pronounced his blessing on the source of the River Fleet. His voice became louder and more forceful as he spoke the ancient words. When he was done, the trickle of water didn't appear at all different. He closed his bible, and dropped it carelessly onto the folding stool. He seemed very tired.

"Why are you doing this?" said Daniel.

Mr. Martin looked at him with distant eyes. "They made my wife into a vampire. No warning and no reason; no sign anywhere of God's will or his great plan . . . or at least nothing I could come to terms with. I had to hammer a stake into my wife's heart, while she screamed and fought me, just to give her rest."

"I'm sorry," said Daniel.

"How could you be? You didn't know her." Mr. Martin gestured at the stream he'd blessed. "Drink. You'll need its protection, where you're going."

Daniel and Tina looked dubiously at the muddy water, but Mr. Martin's gaze was implacable. So they both got down on one knee, cupped some of the blessed water in their hands, pulled pretty much the same face at the smell, and then drank the filthy stuff down as fast as they could manage. When they were finished Daniel felt like doing some serious spitting, but he didn't want to seem disrespectful. The Hydes got to their feet again, and Mr. Martin nodded slowly.

"That's it," he said. "We're done. Now go and do God's will . . . or Edward Hyde's. And finish off as many of the bloodsucking bastards as you can."

"What will you do now?" said Daniel.

"Wait here, and listen for the sound of the explosion," said Mr. Martin. "And then, perhaps, I'll get some rest at last."

They left him standing there in the unsteady candlelight, with his bible and his thermos and what was left of his faith.

Daniel and Tina trudged steadily on through dark tunnels and deserted workings. The air was cold and getting colder, as they descended farther into the earth. The only sounds were the ones they brought with them: the scuffing of feet and the rustling of clothing. And the occasional muttered curse as they tripped over something, or kicked out at a scuttling rat.

Daniel was still convinced something else was down there with them, following at a safe distance so it could stay out of the light. He didn't say anything to Tina. He didn't want her thinking he was jumpy.

They passed through a number of deserted stations that no one used anymore, stepping carefully over rusting rails that hadn't known a train since the nineteenth century. The advertising posters on the walls offered faded reminders of products no one remembered anymore, like the ghosts of business past. After a while, painted arrows started to appear on the walls, in a variety of colors.

"Could be the vampires," said Daniel. "Saying: *This way to the party.*"

"Not necessarily," said Tina. "They're not the only things that live down here."

"Okay . . ." said Daniel. "What are we talking about, exactly—mole people, survivors of previous civilizations, or dark Wombles?"

"Old things," said Tina. "From before there was a London. Sleeping away the millennia, waiting for Humanity to disappear. I did some reading on the subject for a previous mission. And learned just enough to make me just a little insecure about being here."

"I didn't think Hydes did nervous."

"They do in places like this. So keep your voice down. We don't want to wake anything."

They kept going, until once again a tunnel opened out into a great open space. Tina's flashlight beam leapt around, illuminating two empty platforms with long-unused rails passing between them. The sign on the wall said FLEET HARBOUR.

"This is where we're supposed to be," said Tina. "The abandoned station next to Albion Square, where the Vampire Clan will already be whooping it up."

Daniel checked his watch. It was well past midnight. He hadn't realized how long they'd spent down in the darkness. He looked quickly around him.

"I'm surprised they haven't set guards here."

"Why should they?" said Tina. "No one is supposed to know where the gathering is, unless you've got an invitation."

"Written in blood?"

"Almost certainly. Vampires are such drama queens."

"Do I get to hear the rest of the plan now?" said Daniel.

"It's really very simple. We attach our bomb to the ceiling. This station was called Fleet Harbour because the River Fleet runs directly above. When the bomb goes off the ceiling will come down, and the blessed waters of the River will fall through. Gallons and gallons of holy water . . . more than enough to destroy all the vampires we're going to lure here."

"Simple enough, I suppose, if not particularly straightforward," said Daniel. "How exactly are we going to persuade the entire Vampire Clan to follow us all the way here from the other station?"

"We'll just have to do something seriously annoying," said Tina. "Shouldn't be too difficult. We are Hydes, after all." She flashed her light up and down the deserted station. "Once they're here, there's nowhere they can go to escape the waters. The River Fleet will fill both of the approach tunnels."

"How are we supposed to survive?" said Daniel.

"You can hold your breath, can't you? Come on, help me stick the bomb to the ceiling."

Daniel craned his neck back, to stare up at the high arching stonework, and then looked at Tina.

"I haven't seen any ladders anywhere."

Tina smiled brightly at him. "I've been thinking about that. I have an idea."

Daniel sighed. "I'm really not going to like this, am I?"

"That's how you know it's a good idea."

Tina clambered up onto Daniel's shoulders, balanced herself carefully, and then stood up straight; but she still couldn't reach the ceiling, so Daniel had to brace himself while Tina jumped into the air. She slapped the bomb against the curved stone ceiling, and it held. She just had time to hit the activating button before she fell back, and Daniel caught her in his arms. She scowled at him until he quickly put her down.

"Tell me you have the remote control."

"In my pocket, ready to go," said Daniel. And then quietly slipped a hand into his pocket, just to check.

"All right! Let's go find the vampires," said Tina. "I've had some really good ideas on how to annoy them into chasing us."

"Of course you have," said Daniel.

It didn't take them long to make their way from Fleet Harbour to Albion Square station. As they drew nearer they heard a rising clamor of voices. Not the usual sounds of people gathered together, but shouts and screams and a particularly vicious kind of laughter. Like a party in Hell, where someone was always going to be the butt of the joke. Lights spilled into the tunnel mouth, in bursts of clashing hues, as though the gathering couldn't decide which color scheme to go with, so went with all of them at once. Tina turned off her flashlight and put it away, and they both stopped just inside the tunnel mouth for a cautious look at what they were getting into.

The vampires were partying on one of the abandoned platforms. Hundreds of figures packed tightly together, dancing and gossiping and milling back and forth, with all the vitality of maggots writhing in a corpse. Screams and laughter rose up from the babble of conversation, like bubbles in poisoned champagne. Down here, in the depths, the vampires didn't have to pretend to be human, and yet still they hid their true nature behind their glamours. Perhaps because they couldn't stand to see what they really were.

"Okay," Daniel said quietly. "How do we do this?"

"I was hoping you'd come up with something," said Tina.

Daniel looked at her. "You're the one with hands-on experience of monsters. I never even knew vampires were real, until Paul showed up the other day."

"Outsiders don't normally get this close to the undead," said Tina, studying the gathering and trying hard not to grimace. "Not and live to tell of it."

"What did Edward's file have to say? He's the man with the plan."

"He was a bit short on details."

"Not to worry," said Daniel. "We have good reasons to be confident."

Tina looked at him. "We do?"

"We have special weapons, and we drank the holy water," said

Daniel. "And on top of that, we have one advantage that the vampires don't."

"I'd love to hear what," said Tina.

Daniel smiled briefly. "They're so powerful, they think they don't have to be smart. All we have to do is outthink them..."

"Okay..." said Tina. "We're doomed."

"Follow me and bluff like crazy," said Daniel. "Come on, we can do this."

"Of course. We're Hydes. And I have every confidence in you."

"That's the nicest thing you've ever said to me."

"Just shows how tense I am."

They left the tunnel mouth and headed for the party on the platform. Immediately, two figures appeared out of the shadows to block their way. Muscular young men in black leather bondage outfits, proudly showing off the bite marks on their necks. Their faces were very pale, but Daniel was pretty sure that was just makeup. He surreptitiously checked the mirror concealed in the palm of his hand, and the reflection showed they were definitely still human. The guards stretched their mouths in humorless smiles, to show off teeth filed to points. Daniel didn't wait for whatever challenges or threats they had in mind; he went straight to the password Paul had provided.

"We're here to see the Beautiful People."

"Of course you are," said one of the guards. He lisped a little, around his sharp teeth. "You're late."

"We're extra security," said Tina. "Checking out the perimeter, after what happened to the Frankenstein Clan."

The two guards stirred uneasily at the name, and then stepped back out of their way.

"Be welcome to the gathering," said the speaking guard. "Indulge yourselves in whatever gives you pleasure, but always remember: be respectful to the masters. This is their party, not ours."

Daniel and Tina strode straight past them, heads held high. Someone had put some wooden steps in place, leading up to the platform, and they were already splashed with blood. Apparently someone had got impatient. A forest of candles set in a tall candelabra shed a diffused glow across the gathering, augmented by colored paper lanterns. It seemed the vampires preferred their illumination old school.

The large crowd milled back and forth, chattering loudly, packed close together as much for mutual support as company. It was easy enough to tell the vampires from their victims: The undead were glamorous creatures, strutting among their conquests like aristocrats of the Pit, their every glance and gesture infused with the arrogance of unchallenged power. But there was still something of the animal about them; of a predator ready to strike out, for any reason or none.

Their clothes came from many times and places, sometimes even different centuries, and the styles clashed like raised voices. Daniel assumed vampires clung to what they remembered from when they were alive and still part of the society they moved through. He wondered how vampires saw the world, now Time no longer had any hold over them. Did fads and fashions just go flashing past, glimpsed in the rearview mirrors of their lives? Things that came and went . . . like their victims.

Daniel studied the undead carefully as they glided back and forth. Impossibly sleek and stylish, they strutted and preened like supermodels on a catwalk in Hell. He couldn't see any common feeling among them, no sense of family like the Frankensteins. He tried to make out the elders, the ancient nosferatu who ran the Clan, but all the vampires looked the same behind their glamours.

Impossibly beautiful, like works of art that had gone off.

Daniel stayed put at the end of the platform, not ready to join the gathering until he had some idea of what passed for normal behavior. The victims were easy enough to identify; there was nothing glamorous about them. Some had made an effort to dress up for the occasion, but shirt collars had been left open to allow easy access to necks, and the women mostly had bare shoulders. Many of them had fresh wounds, and blood soaked into their clothes from recent feedings.

Men and women of all ages and from all backgrounds, they partied fiercely together, determined to convince themselves they were having a good time. And that being at the vampire gathering was their decision. They drank and ate with eager appetites and babbled loudly to one another, to fill what would otherwise have been an awful silence. There wasn't any music.

And whenever one of their undead masters passed by, the victims would immediately fall silent and stare at them with pleading eyes, like a junkie hoping their pusher would be kind.

"What's the point of this gathering?" Daniel said quietly to Tina. "I can't see anyone here wanting to make speeches or announcements about how well the Clan is doing."

"It's all about tradition," said Tina. "The one thing the vampires have in common with the Frankensteins is a need to show off. To establish status and authority by demonstrating how many slaves they have, or how much power they hold over important people in the world above. It's all about rank and station, and keeping score. No one knows how to hold a grudge or maintain a feud like vampires who've walked the night for centuries."

Daniel was still studying the victims. Some were half naked, revealing bodies covered with bite marks and scars, as though they needed to show off what had been done to them; proud of what they had endured, and survived. They'd been used and abused by masters who would never give a damn about them, and yet here they were, back for more.

Because only the one who hurts you can make the pain go away.

And all the while the vampires paraded back and forth, inhumanly alluring and impossibly bewitching, strutting and posing like deadly peacocks. And though they made a point of ignoring the imploring looks from their victims, it was obvious they enjoyed being worshipped. Perhaps because they knew they weren't worthy of it. Daniel strained his eyes against the false faces, trying to see past the glamours; but even though he was a Hyde, he was still human and they so very obviously weren't.

The Frankenstein Clan was born of the Age of Science. The Vampire Clan had its roots in older, darker times.

And then he made a low, shocked sound and plunged forward, leaving Tina to hurry after him. Daniel shouldered his way through the milling crowd, paying no attention to raised voices or injured looks. Tina glared them into silence in his wake, without even slowing. Daniel finally came to a halt, staring at what was left of Commissioner Alicia Gill.

She was down on all fours, like an animal, with a collar around her throat. Being pulled along by a length of steel chain. Daniel looked at the man holding the other end, and he quickly dropped it and backed away. Daniel checked the mirror in his hand, but the reflection showed that Gill was still human. Naked and filthy, covered in cuts and bruises and bites, her face was almost blank, showing nothing but dumb suffering. Because all the personality had been beaten out of her.

Some of the victims had been pointing and spitting at Gill, laughing and kicking her in the hope of attracting a master's approval—but they all found other things to do rather than face the anger in Daniel's eyes.

He remembered Paul saying he made Gill disappear. And that after what Gill had done to them, she deserved everything that happened to her. Daniel had assumed Paul killed her, but apparently that hadn't been enough. The proud and ambitious Commissioner Gill had been dragged down into the darkness and tormented by both the vampires and their victims, just for the fun of it. No wonder the police couldn't find her; she wasn't a part of their world anymore.

Daniel said Gill's name, but she didn't react. Tina watched his back, scowling at anyone who even looked like they were getting too close. No one made any objection. Submission to authority had been bitten into them. Daniel knelt down before Gill, putting his face close to hers. She wouldn't look at him.

"Is that who I think it is?" said Tina. "What would the vampires want with a police commissioner?"

"Someone wanted her silenced, so she couldn't talk about what happened to me and my friends," said Daniel. "The vampires were supposed to kill her, but apparently they thought this would be more amusing." He said Gill's name again, right into her face . . . and very quietly, she said his name.

"Tell me what I need to know, and I'll get you out of here," said Daniel.

"That's not what we're here for . . ." said Tina.

Daniel spun on her. "I need to know!"

Tina nodded stiffly, and Daniel turned back to Gill. "Why did you send us to the Frankenstein chop shop, Commissioner?"

"Told to," she said, in a voice so harsh he had to concentrate on every word. As though she'd damaged her throat from screaming too much. "Orders. From high up. Don't know who. They only way, they said, to get past the glass ceiling. Wanted a promotion. Like you."

"You sacrificed us," said Daniel.

"Yes. Sorry. So sorry..."

Daniel thought he'd have so much to say when he finally saw the commissioner again, but faced with everything that had been done to her, he really didn't.

"You keep wanting to rescue people," said Tina. "But we're not here to save anyone."

"I can't leave her like this."

"Daniel..." said Gill.

"Yes?"

"Please. Kill me."

He didn't argue. Just placed one hand on the back of her neck, and broke it quickly. Her body seemed such a small thing, as it crumpled to the ground. No one around them gave a damn.

There was a time when Daniel would have rejoiced to know that the woman who'd betrayed him and his friends was dead; but now he had a new target for his anger. He rose to his feet and glared at the gathering, and the nearest victims flinched away. They knew a real threat when they saw one. Tina moved in close beside Daniel, and put her mouth next to his ear.

"Don't even think about saving anyone else. All of these victims are addicts, and I know all there is to know about the power of addiction. They don't want to be saved, and they'd fight you if you tried. The best we can do is trigger the bomb and release the holy waters, and wash all the suffering away."

Daniel nodded slowly. "I need to see the vampires die."

"Technically, you've left it a bit late," said Tina.

They managed a small smile.

A striking female vampire appeared suddenly from out of the crowd, to stand before Daniel and Tina. Dressed to the height of 1920s fashion, she wore the long black dress of the silent screen vamp, complete with hanging beads. Her face had no color at all, and even though her night-black hair was bobbed, it was nowhere near as dark as her eyes. She smiled slowly at Daniel with her pale lips, and he felt his hackles rise. It was like having a shadow turn around and fix you with a dark and hungry look. She swayed a little closer, never once taking her eyes off Daniel.

"You're not one of us."

Her voice was deep and sultry, but in a practiced sort of way, as though she'd forgotten what a woman was supposed to sound like. Up close, she smelled of blood and grave dirt.

"We're security," said Tina.

The vampire ignored her, holding Daniel's gaze despite everything he could do to look away.

"I don't know you," she said. "But I want you. Come with me, and I will teach you all the pleasures of the night. For as long as you last."

Daniel tried to say no, but his voice wouldn't work. A slow cold horror ran through him as he started moving toward her, and found he couldn't stop. Until Tina grabbed him by the arm and hauled him back, glowering fiercely at the vampire.

"You can't have him," she said. "He belongs to me."

The vampire lashed out at her. Long black fingernails sliced through the air with vicious speed, but Tina had seen that coming and was already somewhere else. The vampire seemed to see her clearly for the first time. Her eyes widened, and her mouth became a vicious snarl.

"*Hyde!*"

Tina punched her in the mouth with all her strength—and the vampire just stood there and took it. She grinned at Tina, her smile spreading impossibly wide to show off jagged teeth. And while she was busy doing that, Daniel kicked the legs out from under her. The vampire fell to the platform in an ungainly heap, and Tina booted her off the edge.

And just like that, all the noise stopped. Daniel and Tina turned to find all the vampires and their victims standing very still, staring at them with cold and hungry eyes. As though a whole shoal of sharks had just scented blood in the water. The name *Hyde* moved through the crowd in a whisper, as though the word was an obscenity.

"Okay . . ." said Tina. "Now what?"

"Don't say that like this is my fault," said Daniel.

"You're the one who flirted with the old bat."

"She took advantage of me," said Daniel. "Or at least, I'm pretty sure she would have."

"Tell me you have a plan," said Tina.

"Make them hurt," said Daniel.

Daniel and Tina grabbed the garlic gas grenades out of their backpacks, pulled the pins, and lobbed the grenades into the gathering. Pungent-smelling clouds billowed across the platform and the vampires quickly retreated, choking and howling and covering their faces as best they could. Glimpses came and went of the reality behind the glamours as the vampires' concentration was disrupted, revealing decaying corpses wrapped in the rotting remains of their grave clothes. They were really nothing more than things that had died and been buried, and then burst out of their coffins to dig their way out of the ground, so they could walk the world again and feast on the blood of the living. Old-time, old-school monsters, with nothing of Humanity left in them. Some of their victims cried out in horror as they finally saw what it was they'd been worshipping.

But the gas clouds were already beginning to disperse, and Daniel realized the station must have hidden extractor fans working, to keep the air fresh for the victims. Most of them had already moved to surround their masters, forming human shields. Some of them produced knives while others had straight razors, but they all looked ready to use whatever they had.

Daniel glanced at Tina. "Why would they bring knives to a party?"

"To get the party started," said Tina. "It's always all about the blood, here."

Daniel tried to feel some sympathy for the victims, but they made it difficult, by being so obviously ready to kill him and Tina, if they could. They had given themselves, body and soul, to their masters; and they loved it. They bared filed-down teeth, and tried to look scary, as though they were the threat instead of their masters. Daniel met the vicious stares and wildly waving blades with a growing anger. The victims were standing between him and his prey, and he would kill them all if he had to. Because it was necessary, and because the choices they'd made disgusted him.

The vampires searched the underground station with their bloodshot eyes, until they were sure there were only two Hydes, and then screamed at their victims to attack. Without a moment's hesitation, the victims surged across the platform like a pack of maddened animals. They showed no fear of what the Hydes might do to them, perhaps because it was nothing compared to what their masters did to them every night. They crossed the intervening distance in no time at all, and swarmed all over Daniel and Tina.

None of the victims were particularly strong or fast, but there were so many of them they were able to hit the Hydes from every side at once. Punching and kicking, slashing and stabbing with their various blades, desperate to bring the Hydes down. But for all their hate and frenzy, there was no real force to anything they did. Their masters had used them up.

Daniel and Tina struck the victims down with almost casual violence, and bones broke and blood spurted as they fell dead and dying to the platform. The masters had taken so much from them, there wasn't enough left to hold them together. But even as bodies piled up around the Hydes, the remaining victims kept pressing forward. Because they would rather die than fail the ones who'd made them what they were.

In the end Daniel and Tina killed every single victim, because nothing less would stop them. Even after they'd been struck down, they often crawled forward across the blood-slicked platform, to do what they could. Gripping at the Hydes' ankles with clawed hands and trying to trip them, to bring them down to their level. Until the Hydes stamped on their heads or broke their necks, in what little mercy they could show.

Finally Daniel and Tina stood together at the end of the platform, not even breathing hard, with blood dripping thickly from their aching fists and dead bodies scattered around them. For all the insane viciousness of the people he'd just killed, Daniel still had it in him to wish there could have been some other way. This wasn't what he'd come here for. He glared down the platform at the vampires, and they glared back at him, eyes burning like evil stars in their dead faces. The slaughter of their victims hadn't affected them in the least. Because they could always get more livestock, and because it had been a long time since death had meant anything to them. The last of the garlic gas finally dissipated, and the vampires showed their jagged teeth in slow vicious smiles as they realized nothing stood between them and the Hydes. Long-fingered hands flexed slowly, showing off fingernails grown long and sharp in the grave, and hunger radiated from the undead like a heat haze, hanging heavily on the air.

"Nasty-looking things," Tina said flatly.

"Parasites usually are," said Daniel.

Tina took a deep breath, and raised her bruised and bloodied fists. "Let's finish this, and get the hell out of here."

"Sounds like a plan to me," said Daniel. He made an obscene gesture at the watching vampires, and addressed them in a voice thick with contempt. "Come on, then, you bloodsucking little turds, what are you waiting for?"

The vampires surged forward in a solid wave. Their feet made no sound at all, like ghosts in a cemetery. Their mouths were all stretched in the same rictus of rage and malice; not because of what had been done to their victims, but simply because they had been defied. Daniel and Tina waited until the very last moment, and then threw holy water ampules into the nearest vampires' faces. The creatures screamed horribly and fell writhing to the platform as their features melted and ran away. They put both hands to their faces, as though they could hold them together, but holy water and melting flesh oozed between the fingers. The rest of the vampires just kicked them out of the way, concentrating on their tormentors.

The Hydes had already reached inside their backpacks and brought out the ash-wood stakes they'd been given. They held the stakes out before them, and the vampires slowed their advance, but didn't stop. Up close, they didn't look elegant or glamorous anymore. They looked like what they were: animated corpses with burning eyes and mouths packed full of animal teeth. Dead things that stank of the grave and other people's blood.

The gathering fell on Daniel and Tina like a swarm of rabid bats. There was nothing of grace or style in them, only teeth and claws, inhuman vitality, and the hunger for blood that would never end. Daniel thrust his stake into the first vampire to reach him, slamming it in under the breastbone with all his strength. The moment the wood pierced the vampire's withered heart, its unnatural body just disappeared, leaving nothing behind but a few ashes floating on the air. Tina staked her first vampire with an elegant upward thrust, and then yanked the stake out again as the vampire collapsed into dust, so she could move on to her next victim. She laughed in the vampires' faces, and went to her work with a vengeance.

The vampires swarmed all over the Hydes, hitting them from

every direction at once, and Daniel and Tina had to draw on all their resources to match the vampires' strength and speed. Daniel lashed out with his free arm, trying to open up more space to use his stake, but it was like slamming into a stone wall. The vampires took no damage and felt no pain, for they had left all such things behind them, in their graves. There was nothing left of them that could be hurt, except in supernatural ways. Daniel lashed out at the vampires again and again, grunting out loud with the effort he put into driving every blow home, until his hands ached and bled. It didn't stop the vampires, and the fresh blood just maddened them even more. They forced their way closer, past everything Daniel and Tina could do to defend themselves. Death on two legs, up close and personal.

Daniel forced down a rising sense of panic, as vicious fingernails ripped through his clothes and scored the skin beneath. He could feel the blood trickling down his skin. Vicious teeth snapped together, coming closer and closer to his face and throat. It helped that there were so many of them that they got in one another's way, and Daniel found he could use that to distract them. He used one vampire to shield him from another, until they turned on each other in flurries of teeth and claws. He plunged his stake into one vampire chest after another, their inhuman forms offering no more resistance than smoke, but he was slowing down as he tired, and the vampires weren't.

He couldn't even look around to see how Tina was doing, because he didn't dare turn his gaze away from the hideous forms that seethed around him. He'd only lasted this long because the vampires were afraid enough of his stake to keep them at arm's length; but that was all he had, and there were just so many of them.

Finally one vampire darted in under Daniel's extended arm, avoiding the stake, and went for Daniel's wrist. The sharp teeth were within an inch of piercing the skin, when the vampire suddenly jerked its head back, hissing and screeching as it smelled the garlic Daniel had smeared there earlier. The vampire broke off and fell back, just as another vampire discovered Tina was protected in the same manner; and just like that the whole gathering was retreating back down the platform. Daniel and Tina slowly lowered their stakes and leaned tiredly on each other, breathing harshly. Their clothes were torn and ragged, and sharp nails had gouged deep wounds into their flesh. Blood spattered down onto the platform, slowing as the Hydes' wounds healed themselves. The vampires studied them carefully, milling and stirring as the scent of fresh blood called out to them; but still they stayed where they were.

"So," said Tina, drawing in a great breath of air and then coughing harshly as she inhaled some floating dust. "Are you having a good time, Daniel?"

"I'm keeping busy," said Daniel, wiping the sweat from his forehead with a ragged sleeve. His arm was so tired it ached just to raise it. "They really don't like the garlic, do they?"

"We have to hold their attention," Tina said quietly. "We can't let them run and scatter. We might never have a chance like this again."

"We came here to annoy them," said Daniel. "And I think we've made a good start. All we have to do now is infuriate them so much that they'll chase us wherever we lead them."

"How are we going to do that?" said Tina? "Call them bad names and insult their dress sense?"

"Leave it to me," said Daniel. "You head for the tunnel mouth. No, don't argue. I need you to go first and clear the way. Trust me, I will be right behind you as soon as I'm done."

Tina looked at him steadily. "You're not about to do something heroic, are you?"

Daniel smiled. "I have something more practical in mind."

Tina grinned back at him. "Don't keep me waiting."

She jumped lightly down from the platform and onto the rails, and sprinted for the tunnel mouth. Daniel quickly took a step forward, to hold the angry stares of the vampires. He smiled insolently at the gathering, radiating confidence, and they snarled back, confused and wary in the face of a challenge they didn't understand. They weren't used to such casual defiance. They could tell Daniel was planning something, but they couldn't understand what.

Daniel reached inside his shirt, and brought out the silver crucifix on its chain. The vampires flinched, and some turned their faces away. But the cross only had an impact when Daniel thrust it at a particular vampire; the moment he moved on, the cross seemed to lose its power. Or perhaps it just didn't mean enough to Daniel. He'd always suspected the power lay in the faith behind the cross, rather than the symbol itself. Though Daniel had to admit that standing face-to-face with so much evil was starting to make a believer out of him. He put the crucifix away.

"You're all just a bunch of cowards," he said loudly, piling on the contempt. "Tina and I crashed your party, killed all your victims, staked a whole bunch of you... and then drove you off with our garlic cologne! Once we get out of here, we're going to tell everyone that there's nothing special about you. That you're all nothing but leeches with delusions of grandeur."

He turned around, dropped his trousers, and showed his arse to the Vampire Clan. He didn't look back to check their response, just hauled up his trousers, jumped down from the platform, and ran like hell for the tunnel. He passed two dead guards along the way, lying crumpled on the rails with their necks broken. Tina had been busy. Daniel joined her in the tunnel mouth, and the two of them disappeared into the darkness, following the jumping glare of her flashlight.

And behind came the vampires. The whole Clan, desperate to avenge an unforgivable insult. Their dead feet made no sound at all, and Daniel had to glance back to make sure they'd taken the bait. He didn't look again. It was like being chased by a tidal wave with teeth. The two Hydes raced through the deserted Underground tunnel, pushing themselves as hard as they could, knowing the vampires were already closing the gap between them. Because the undead never grew tired or ran out of breath; and because they could not stand to be defied by their livestock. It struck at the very heart of what they believed they were.

Daniel and Tina reached Fleet Harbour station only a few moments ahead of the Vampire Clan. Their muscles ached horribly, and their lungs strained to drag in fresh air. They couldn't hear the vampires behind them, but they knew they were there. They could feel their presence, like a coming storm. Daniel and Tina hauled themselves up onto the platform, clung onto each other for a moment to get their breath, and only then looked back.

The vampires had stopped at the tunnel mouth. They could sense danger. Daniel laughed breathlessly at them, and shot them the finger. Maddened by such continuing defiance, the vampires raced forward. Daniel threw Tina down onto the platform, grabbed hold of a heavy vending machine, and pulled it over on top of them.

"What are you doing?" said Tina, as the weight of the machine pinned them down.

"We don't want the waters of the Fleet to wash us away," said Daniel.

She nodded quickly. "Hit the remote control."

"Got it right here," said Daniel.

He hit the button just as the first wave of vampires came sweeping over the edge of the platform. The sound of the bomb exploding was painfully loud in the closed space. Jagged cracks shot across the stone ceiling, and then a whole section collapsed as the blessed waters of the River Fleet came crashing in. They thundered down like a mighty falls, a whole river diverted from its usual course and forced to find a new way. Churning waters filled the station from end to end, and rose back up to the ceiling, creating an underwater grotto of dark and muddy waters.

The vampires barely had time to scream before the holy water hit them like the hammer of God. Bodies melted and faces fell apart as a great many walking corpses finally gave up the ghost. A few made it back to the tunnel mouth, but they didn't get far before the blessed waters overtook them and dissolved them from the legs up. The entire Vampire Clan was reduced to ashes and less than ashes, as the River Fleet swept on.

Daniel had time to see some of that before a great wave of freezing cold water leapt up over the platform. He took the deepest breath he could, and then the Fleet slammed down. After that Daniel couldn't see or hear anything, and the waters were so cold that soon he couldn't even feel Tina beneath him. All he could do was lie there, in the dark and the freezing waters, buried alive under a River.

Fortunately, it turned out that Hydes could hold their breath for a very long time.

Eventually the River Fleet drained away through the two tunnels as it found a new course, and the waters receded. The platform reemerged, and Daniel and Tina could breathe again. They were both shivering violently, and it took a moment before Daniel was able to gather enough strength to throw off the vending machine. He rolled away from Tina and lay on his back, breathing in the blessed air and staring up at the great hole in the stone ceiling. Water was still dripping from the jagged edges. In fact, wherever Daniel looked water was dripping from something. He checked his wounds, but they had already healed. His clothes were still a mess. Tina rolled onto her side and glared at him.

"You protected me again! I told you, I don't need protecting!"

"I'm sorry," said Daniel. "I was a bit pushed for time. I promise, next time you can protect me."

"Well," said Tina. "That's more like it."

She kissed him, and they held each other tightly, driving out the cold.

"How very romantic," said Paul.

Daniel and Tina broke apart and were quickly up on their feet again. The vampire was standing some distance down the platform, half hidden in the shadows. He was still wearing his long coat, which gave every appearance of being dry as a bone.

"Why are you hiding in the dark, Paul?" said Daniel.

"It's not as dark as my heart," said the vampire. "You look like a drowned rat, Danny boy."

Tina scowled at him. "How did you survive the flooding?"

"I got here early," said Paul. "Stole one of the elders' coffins and tucked it away somewhere safe. Then all I had to do was stay inside until it was all right to come out. Though the coffin did turn out to be not entirely watertight."

He moved forward into the light and Daniel could see terrible burns on his face and hands, from where they'd been splashed by the blessed waters.

"Why are you here?" said Tina.

"Unfinished business," said Paul.

"I know," said Daniel. "I hadn't forgotten."

He produced his wooden stake, but Paul smiled slowly and shook his head.

"I've changed my mind."

Daniel looked into the deep dark eyes of what had been his old friend, and a chill closed around his heart.

"You made me promise . . ."

"The Clan made me a monster," said Paul. "But they're not around anymore. So I'm free to do whatever I want now."

"You sound . . . hungry," said Daniel.

"I'm my own man again," said Paul. "That's all that matters."

"But *are* you a man?"

Paul shook his head slowly. "Low blow, Danny. I'm what I have to be."

"But you don't have to be a vampire," said Daniel. "I can set you free."

"I already am," said Paul. "Freer than I ever was, when I was alive. I only popped in to say good-bye, old friend. Give Edward my regards. Tell him . . . I'll be seeing him."

"No," said Daniel. "I can't let you go, Paul."

"You never could let go of the past." The vampire looked at him thoughtfully. "I'm sparing you for old times' sake, Danny—but don't push your luck. You're still only human . . . while I am so much more. And without the vampire elders to hold me back . . . who knows what I'll become?"

"I can't let that happen," said Daniel. "It's not what my old friend would have wanted."

"Your friend was murdered. He isn't around anymore."

The vampire dropped his glamour, to show what he really was: a rotting corpse, in a coat covered with grave mold and dried bloodstains. Decaying flesh fell away from yellowed cheekbones, and his eyes were like patches of night. His teeth were too large for his mouth, his hands had claws like an animal, and he stank of the grave and all the people he'd killed.

Daniel went forward anyway, stake in hand. Because he'd made a promise, and because he couldn't leave his job unfinished. Tina was quickly there beside him, a stake in her hand too. Paul just stood where he was, smiling his awful smile, waiting for them to come to him. And then he lashed out with inhuman speed, one hand slamming into Daniel's chest like a wrecking ball. It smashed all the air out of his lungs, and sent him flying the whole length of the platform. Daniel hit hard, but still scrambled back up on his feet again. Just in time to see Paul slap the stake out of Tina's hand, take hold of her firmly, and then lower his mouth to her throat.

Daniel raced down the platform. "No! Don't!"

Paul pressed his teeth against Tina's throat, but didn't bite. Daniel crashed to a halt. He knew he'd never reach them in time. Tina stood very still, keeping her gaze fixed on Daniel. The vampire's teeth were pressing just hard enough to dent the skin over Tina's jugular, without breaking it. And then Paul pulled his mouth back a little, so he could smile at Daniel.

"I smell traces of garlic, but it would seem the waters have washed most of it away. And while her clothes may be soaked in the blessed River Fleet, my coat will protect me long enough to do what's necessary. I've spent a long time wondering what Hyde blood would taste like."

Tina back-elbowed Paul in the groin with all her Hyde strength, but he didn't even flinch.

"I'm afraid that's just another of the things they took from me. I have to find my pleasures in different ways now."

"You want Hyde blood?" Daniel said steadily. "Then take mine, instead of hers."

He threw away his stake and walked slowly forward, holding his right wrist out before him.

"Come on, Paul," said Daniel. "Make me a vampire too—and then you'll never have to be alone again."

The vampire stared at him. "You'd give up your life—for her?"

"For you, old friend."

"I could take you both."

"You don't want her, you want me. You said I could never understand what's been done to you—so help me understand."

Paul threw Tina to one side, hard enough to leave her stunned and helpless. The vampire surged forward inhumanly quickly, and his mouth clamped down on Daniel's outstretched wrist. Daniel gasped once as the sharp teeth pierced his skin, not so much from the pain but because it felt like a violation. He could feel the blood rushing out of him, see a soft red flush filling Paul's face, giving it the appearance of life. And then Paul jerked his mouth away from Daniel's wrist and he fell backward, screaming shrilly as all the strength went out of him. His legs collapsed under him and he went sprawling, his face full of a terrible understanding . . . and in just a few moments there was nothing left on the platform but the remains of a body that had died months ago.

"I drank the holy water, Paul," Daniel said steadily. "And now even my Hyde blood is blessed."

He wanted to feel sad for his friend. But Paul died long ago. This was just a walking corpse that thought it was Paul. He looked down at the vicious wound in his wrist and winced, but the damage was already repairing itself. Tina came over to stand beside him, and slipped a supportive arm around his waist.

"Did you know that would happen, when you offered yourself to save me?"

"Of course," said Daniel.

"Liar," said Tina.

"Let's just say... I hoped. Come on, it's a long walk back to civilization."

Tina smiled. "Then let's take the scenic route this time."

Chapter Seven
VOICES FROM THE DUST
✢ ✢ ✢

DANIEL AND TINA spent the next few days at Tina's place, celebrating not dying after all, and only returned to the Jekyll & Hyde building because they didn't want Edward sending someone to bang on their door. As always, there was no one in the lobby. Daniel was beginning to wonder about that. Given that the whole building only existed to house Jekyll & Hyde Inc., why did he never bump into anyone else going about Edward Hyde's business?

When they entered Edward's outer office, the rather more glamorous than she should be secretary gave them her best professional smile.

"Go right on in. Edward has something he wants to share with you."

Daniel looked at Tina. "Is that good?"

"As long as it's not another tiger."

"Beware Hydes bearing gifts," said Daniel.

He barged into Edward's office without knocking, just to make it clear what kind of a visit it was going to be, and then stopped short as the smell of roast meat hit him in the face. Marvelous and mouth-watering, it was like nothing he'd ever encountered before. Tina made a loud appreciative noise. Set on an antique silver platter, the steaming meat was so rare that blood was still seeping out of it. Edward smiled at Daniel and Tina from behind his desk, tore a piece off the large joint, and stuffed it into his mouth. He chewed with uncomplicated enjoyment, already reaching for another piece. Daniel couldn't help remembering how he'd attacked his pizza the night before, as though nothing mattered but satisfying his appetite. Daniel took a deep breath, and the amazing smell filled his head till he couldn't think of anything else. Edward smiled knowingly, and waved them forward.

"This is a haunch off the tiger I killed yesterday. Waste not, want not. Go ahead, help yourselves."

Daniel felt he should object, on behalf of the tiger. What had been done to it was cruel as well as wrong. But he just had to know whether the meat would taste as good as it smelled. Tina had already pushed past him, to rip a piece off the joint and jam it into her mouth. She made ecstatic noises, her eyes closing to slits as blood and juices ran unheeded down her chin. Daniel took a smaller piece for himself, and did his best to eat it in a more civilized manner. The taste was incredible, and before he realized what he was doing he'd emptied his mouth and was reaching out for more.

He stopped himself, with an effort. He remembered Tina saying that Hydes could indulge themselves however they wanted, but he had to believe there was more to him than just his appetites.

He turned away from the meat on the table, looking for something to take his mind off temptation, and his eye was caught by a mirror on the opposite wall. His reflection smiled and nodded to him, and Daniel remembered that there was no mirror in Edward's office. He moved over to stand before his reflection. It was chewing on a really large piece of meat, while blood dripped thickly from its chin. The reflection winked cheerfully at Daniel, and spoke without bothering to empty its mouth first.

"Told you you'd like being a Hyde." It looked past Daniel at Tina, and he glanced back to see her unself-consciously licking blood and juices from her fingers. The reflection sniggered loudly. "She is something, isn't she? No conscience, and no restraint. Ready and willing to do absolutely anything, and never give a damn about the consequences. The only trouble is, eventually you have to get out of bed. How long will it be, do you think, before you're just like her . . . and loving it?"

Daniel started to turn away, and the reflection raised its voice.

"You have to listen to me!"

"No I don't," said Daniel, facing his reflection steadily. "You're nothing but a voice in my head."

The reflection thrust an arm out of the mirror, grabbed Daniel by the shoulder, and pulled him in close.

"How long before I'm the Hyde... and you're just a voice that no one listens to?"

Daniel punched his reflection in the face, but all he hit was the office wall, hard enough to leave a large dent and a lot of cracks. The impact should have broken every bone in his hand, but he barely felt it. Action, without consequences... just what he was most afraid of. He turned away to find Edward and Tina staring at him.

"Just putting down a minor rebellion in my head," said Daniel.

Tina nodded briefly, as though that kind of thing happened every day. Edward started to reach for more meat, and Daniel cleared his throat loudly.

"Maybe I should come back when you're done."

Edward sat back in his chair, smiling easily. "I do so admire a practical man. By all means, let us get down to business."

Tina looked wistfully at what was left of the steaming joint, but Edward pushed the silver platter firmly to one side. Tina dropped sullenly into a chair facing him, and Daniel sat down beside her.

"You need to know why I found it necessary to leave the building yesterday," said Edward, clasping his hands before him in a businesslike way. "I had to meet with my inside man for the Clan of Mummies. So he could tell me where they're going to be holding their gathering this year."

Tina frowned. "What's so important about this particular inside man that you were ready to go to him instead of summoning him here?"

"He would only agree to meet me on his home ground, where he felt safe," said Edward. "He was afraid that if the mummies discovered he'd been talking out of turn..."

"They'd kill him?" said Daniel.

"Eventually," said Edward. "The ancient Egyptians had very strong feelings about betrayal, and they raised torture to an art form. Luckily for us, my man was more angry at them than afraid."

"Would I be right in assuming that this gathering will be taking place somewhere in London?" said Daniel.

"Where else?" said Edward. "And on this very night."

"Of course," said Daniel. "It would have to be."

"The mummies feel at home in London because it contains so many museums," said Edward. "All of them positively stuffed with the spoils of Empire and the treasures of conquest. There's more evidence of the mummies' ancient past here than in the whole of Egypt. But like all the monster Clans, really it comes down to tradition. All the Clan gatherings take place at the same time every year, because tradition is all the Clans have to give themselves a sense of history."

"I'm amazed the mummies haven't postponed it, after what we did to the Frankensteins and the vampires," said Tina.

"That is what the mummies' security people have been saying," said Edward. "But the mummies won't hear of it. Because it might make them looked scared—or worse still, weak. They have added quite unprecedented levels of protection, but nowhere near enough to prevent such talented field agents as yourselves from paying them a little visit later on tonight, and shutting the Clan down once and for all."

"No," said Daniel.

Edward glared at him. "What do you mean, no?"

"Tina and I have destroyed two monster Clans just days apart," said Daniel. "And came very close to being killed on each occasion. Going for a third attack so quickly would be really pushing our luck. Why can't some of your other field agents help us out?"

He looked at Tina, expecting her to back him up. She'd agreed with him one hundred percent when he raised the idea in her apartment. But now she just sat where she was and said nothing.

"We need backup," said Daniel.

"All my other agents are busy."

Daniel had to raise an eyebrow at that. "Doing what?"

"Taking care of the advance planning, to make what you do possible," said Edward. "And then cleaning up afterward, so no one suspects you were ever there."

Daniel frowned. "I thought that was what the support staff were for?"

"There are some things only a Hyde can do," said Edward. "That only a Hyde would have the stomach for."

Daniel looked at Tina, but she was deliberately avoiding his gaze. Reluctantly, Daniel turned back to Edward.

"All right . . . Where are we supposed to look for this gathering of sarcophagus-dodgers?"

"And how big a gathering are we talking about?" said Tina, suddenly taking an interest in the conversation. "Something on the same scale as the Frankensteins and the vampires?"

"Are we going to need another bomb?" Daniel said bluntly.

Edward pretended to be shocked. "Given that the gathering is being held inside the British Museum, I should hope not. Blow up a national treasure? The very idea . . . Fortunately, the Clan itself is surprisingly small. Just nine mummies, kept alive long after their time by drugs no one but them understands.

"The mummies like to boast that the ancient Egyptians invented chemistry, or alchemy if you prefer. That's how they're able to dominate their market—because they create and supply drugs that no one else can match. If you want what they've got, you have to go to them. Of course, once you put control of your life into their bandaged hands, you shouldn't be surprised if they abuse that trust. Just one of the reasons why the Clan of Mummies is the most successful crime organization in the world."

"Then why have I never heard of them?" said Daniel. "I used to be a cop. I thought I knew all about the London drugs scene."

"You didn't know because you didn't move in the right circles," said Edward. "The mummies supply special drugs for special people, because only the elite can afford what it takes to make them feel like gods. But once you start taking the mummies' drugs you have to go on taking them, because if you don't . . . you'll die."

Daniel nodded grimly. "And of course once you're addicted, the price just goes up and up."

Edward smiled happily at Daniel. "I do so love to see the moral outrage in your eyes, Daniel. The way it motivates you to get the job done, no matter what the risk. Dear Tina is an excellent field agent, but she lacks your drive."

Daniel looked at him thoughtfully. "Why do the mummies need money?"

"To fund their researches. They're still searching for the drug that will give them true immortality so they can walk the world freely, instead of being trapped inside withered little bodies wrapped in miles of specially treated bandages. Now . . . this mission will be a little different. You don't have to kill everyone in the organization; in fact, I would very much prefer it if you didn't. All you have to do is kill the nine mummies. Cut off the organization's head, so my people can step in and take over. I've always had an interest in chemicals."

"Hold everything and stamp on the brakes," said Daniel. "You want to continue what the Clan of Mummies has been doing?"

"Unfortunately, the drugs they've created will die with them," said Edward. "Because only the mummies know the formulas. My people will steer the organization into more standard pharmaceuticals. Don't look so shocked, Daniel. You're not a police officer anymore, you're a Hyde. And addicts will always be with us—isn't that right, Tina?"

"The weak will always be weak," said Tina. "And the strong will always dominate them. It's the way of the world."

"Exactly! And spoken like a true Hyde," said Edward. He leaned forward across his desk. "This evening, the mummies will be holding court in one of the Egyptian Rooms. You won't have to worry about innocent bystanders, because the rest of the Museum will be closed all night, officially for essential cleaning and repair work. Fortunately, my inside man found a way for you to enter the Museum unnoticed by any of the guards."

"Okay . . . now it's my turn to say hold it and shoot the horses," said Tina. "What guards?"

"Are we talking armed guards?" said Daniel.

Edward smiled. "The mummies have surrounded themselves with a small army of heavily-armed mercenary soldiers, inside the Museum and out. Is that going to be a problem?"

"You expect the two of us to take on a whole army?" said Daniel. "Are you kidding?"

Tina glared at him. "We can do this; we're Hydes."

"Do this right, and the army won't even know you're there," Edward said calmly. "Your mission file includes a floor map of the Egyptian Rooms, along with the exact locations for every man standing guard. All you have to do is sneak up on them, and enjoy yourselves."

Daniel sat back in his chair, and thought hard. Was this really any more dangerous than taking on a whole Clan of Frankensteins and their creations, or a gathering of vampires and their victims? At least this time they wouldn't have a bomb hanging over their heads...

"Why the Egyptian Rooms?" he said. "Because the artifacts remind the mummies of home?"

"Presumably," said Edward. "After all, there's nothing left of the world they were born into. A whole civilization, gone back into the sand."

"What do they even have to live for?" said Daniel. "What keeps them going, in a world that probably makes no sense at all to their antique minds?"

"They go on because they're afraid of dying," said Edward. "That's what led to them becoming mummies."

"They *wanted* to be mummies?" said Tina.

"Hardly," said Edward. "Remember, they were scientists of a sort, uninterested in anything but the creation of drugs that would let them live forever. However, the priests of ancient Egypt saw what they were doing as blasphemy, and had the nine men mummified alive and entombed. But, of course, they couldn't die, after the drugs they'd already taken. And so they waited out the passing of centuries, locked away in the dark, until their tombs were rediscovered and broken into."

"It's a wonder they didn't go mad," said Tina.

"Who's to say they didn't?" said Edward. He leaned back in his chair, smiling easily. "Think of all those brave scholars and adventurers, trekking into the depths of Egypt, searching out forgotten tombs with nothing to guide them but scraps of maps and hints of history. Now, imagine them breaking down the door of some newly rediscovered tomb, intent on treasure and the thrill of discovery—only to find something in there waiting for them. The bandage-wrapped hand that shoots out of the darkness, to crush a throat or crack a skull. And then... the first faltering steps out of the dark and into the light, as something from the distant past emerges into the modern world..."

"You've clearly put a lot of thought into this," said Daniel.

"Know thy enemy," said Edward.

"What do these mummies look like?" said Daniel. "Are we talking about the bandage jobs from the old horror films? Stumbling along with one outstretched hand, in pursuit of tana leaves or some reincarnated long-lost love?"

"I always thought those movies were very romantic," said Tina, just a bit unexpectedly.

"No one knows what the mummies look like," said Edward. "They keep themselves strictly to themselves. Hardly surprising . . . who else is there, that they could have anything in common with? The world they knew has been dust and less than dust for millennia. The annual gathering is the only time they emerge from behind their usual layers of protection, to meet in person."

"Why would they risk that?" said Tina.

"Nostalgia?" said Edward. "A chance to say *I can remember when it was all sand around here* . . . or simply because all the other monster Clans hold gatherings, and the mummies didn't want to feel left out. Or perhaps it's just vanity, proclaiming *Here we are! Still alive, after all these years. Look on our achievements and despair!*"

"Who's your inside man?" said Tina.

"I had great difficulty finding one," said Edward. "That's one of the reasons it's taken me so long to arrange the complete destruction of the monster Clans. I couldn't risk making a move until I was sure I could bring them all down. Because if even one survived, it would take control of all the territories . . . And of course I couldn't buy the loyalty of anyone in the mummies' inner circle, because they already had more money than they knew what to do with."

"I'm guessing you have other methods for suborning people," said Daniel. "Blackmail, or intimidation?"

"How well you know me," said Edward. "But, much as it pains me to admit it, everyone turned out to be far more scared of the mummies than they were of me. Which gives you some idea of how vicious those monsters can be. Of all the Clans, the mummies have always made the most use of the werewolves, to dispose of outside threats, and the ghouls, to dispose of all the bodies that accumulate in their wake."

"Hold it," said Daniel. "You told us that the werewolves act as muscle for all the Clans . . . but Tina and I haven't spotted anything hairy and dangerous so far."

"I've been wondering about that," said Edward. "In the past the wolves provided security for all the gatherings, but this year the entire werewolf clan has been conspicuous by its absence. It's as though they've disappeared into the deepest part of the underworld."

"Why would they do that?" said Tina.

Edward shrugged. "The last reports I saw mentioned something about an internal power struggle in their clan. It's a dog-eat-dog world in the werewolf clan. I've got people out watching for them, should they decide to reappear. For now, be grateful that the werewolves aren't part of the problem. Silver bullets are expensive."

"Can we get back to your inside man?" said Daniel.

"Of course. Professor Albert Pinder was a part of the British Museum academic staff, specializing in the more obscure areas of ancient Egyptology. Perfectly happy to potter around in his little ivory tower and do the odd job of authentification for the mummies—until he discovered exactly what it is the mummies do for a living. Spitting mad at the thought of his precious Museum being under the control of a criminal organization, he reached out to me."

"How would an academic like Professor Pinder even know someone like you existed?" said Daniel.

"He didn't," said Edward. "But I have people everywhere. When they heard he was looking for someone brave enough to stand up to the Clan of Mummies, the professor was carefully pointed in my direction. I'm told my existence came as something of a shock. Apparently living mummies from the dawn of civilization was one thing, but a 'fictional character' come to life was quite another. Perhaps that's why he insisted on meeting me in person. I like to think I wasn't a disappointment . . . I promised him the complete destruction of the mummies, in return for their exact location and a means of entering the Museum unobserved. Luckily for us, the professor knew a lot about the history of the British Museum, and was able to provide an entirely unexpected means of entry."

"You keep talking about him in the past tense," said Tina. "He's dead, isn't he? Did the mummies get to him?"

"Something like that," said Edward.

Daniel sat up straight, as the penny dropped. "You killed him! That's why you had to go and meet him in person!"

"He lost his nerve," Edward said calmly. "He was ready to betray us to the mummies. I couldn't allow that. They would have set an ambush and killed both of you. So I did what I had to. He died very quickly, if that matters."

"Tell us about the secret way in," said Tina.

"The Museum will be surrounded by mercenary soldiers, so all the usual entrances are closed to us," said Edward. "Even Miss Montague couldn't provide you with enough weapons to get past that level of security."

"She said she knew you, when she was younger," said Tina.

"So she did," said Edward. "Luckily, she's not one to bear a grudge."

"Hold everything and pull the ripcord," said David. "A private army of mercenary soldiers, operating openly in the middle of London? There's no way the police would stand for that."

Edward smiled unpleasantly. "Trust me, all the necessary people have been very well paid to look the other way."

He produced a map from his desk drawer, and spread it out on the desk. Daniel and Tina leaned forward.

"What are we looking at?" said Daniel.

"The sewer systems underneath the British Museum," said Edward.

Daniel stared at him. "Oh, you have got to be kidding..."

"What's the problem?" said Edward. "Too grand to go wading through a little sewage?"

"Well...yes!" said Daniel.

"Hydes don't do sewers," Tina said flatly.

"They do if I tell them to," said Edward. He met Tina's gaze until she looked away, and then continued. "Professor Pinder assured me this is the only way in that no one else knows about. So get used to the idea."

They studied the map carefully. Edward traced one particular tunnel with a blunt fingertip.

"This route leads to an old access point, from the days when certain individuals wanted to move items in and out of the Museum without being seen. Smugglers, forgers, religious fanatics... So, you will enter the sewers unobserved by the exterior guards, follow the tunnels until you reach the access point, and then enter the Museum and take down all the guards standing between you and the mummies."

"How are we supposed to do that?" said Daniel.

"Quietly," said Edward.

"How are we supposed to kill the mummies?" said Tina. "If they're still alive, or at the very least extraordinarily well preserved, I'm guessing it'll take a lot more than a whiff of garlic and a wooden stake to make them lie down and give up the ghost."

Edward smiled. "I think you'll find that fire will do the job quite thoroughly. With so many chemicals in their bodies, they should go up like fireworks. You'll be provided with flare pistols, but please... try not to burn down the whole room in the process. That might attract unwanted attention."

He presented Tina with the mission file, a map of the sewers, and a floor plan for the Egyptian Rooms. Daniel felt a little left out on not being given anything, but couldn't see how to complain without sounding petty.

"Down to the first floor with you, o my children," said Edward. "Where my personal tailors are waiting to outfit you with clothes more suitable for burgling a British institution."

Tina shook her head stubbornly. "I am not giving up my evening dress. It's lucky."

"It won't be, after you've spent some time slogging through London's finest sewage," said Edward. "The smell would travel ahead of you and tap the guards on their shoulders, to let them know you were on your way."

Daniel looked apologetically at Tina. "He has a point."

Tina scowled. "I hate it when people get reasonable. Hydes don't do reasonable. That's half the point of being a Hyde."

"What's the other half?" said Daniel.

"Sensual indulgence and indiscriminate violence."

"That's my girl," said Edward. "Now, off you go and get changed. You'll like your new outfits."

"What if we don't?" said Tina.

"Feel free to complain," said Edward. "See how far that gets you."

Back in the elevator, on their way down to the first floor, Daniel looked steadily at Tina, who was staring straight ahead and hugging the mission file tightly to her.

"Why didn't you back me up, when I said we needed backup in the field?"

"Because it's not easy for me to say no to Edward," said Tina, fixing her gaze on the changing floor numbers so she wouldn't have to look at him. "He made me what I am."

"Doesn't mean he owns you," said Daniel. "I thought not taking any shit from anyone was what being a Hyde was all about."

"You agreed to take on this mission fast enough!"

"Because the mummies need taking down," said Daniel. "But once this is over, I think we're going to have to do something about Edward Hyde."

Tina looked at him for the first time. "What did you have in mind?"

"Something permanent."

"And violent?"

"Almost certainly," said Daniel. "But I can't do it alone. I'm going to need your help."

Tina grinned. "Count me in. Hydes don't do daddy issues."

The grim tailors, looking more than ever like unfrocked undertakers, fell on Daniel and Tina the moment they walked through the door, and thrust into their arms the new outfits Edward had ordered. These turned out to be night-dark one-piece catsuits, complete with built-in boots, all designed to keep out the cold, the waters in the sewer tunnels, and anything else that needed keeping out. Daniel was a little embarrassed when he discovered he'd have to get naked to climb into the catsuit, because they fitted so tightly there wasn't room for any underwear. But Tina shed her clothes so quickly and unself-consciously he didn't see how he could object.

"Just think of the tailors as doctors," said Tina, dropping her underwear to the floor and kicking her shoes to one side. "They've seen it all before, and weren't impressed the first time."

"Really not helping," said Daniel.

He removed his clothes with as much dignity as he could manage, and the tailors immediately grabbed his tuxedo and Tina's evening dress and hurried off with them. Daniel was even more taken aback when he discovered the only way to get into the catsuit was to climb in through the neck hole. He wriggled his way in, struggling to pull the stretchy material over him without giving up what remained of his dignity. The tailors returned in time to watch him do it, which didn't help.

"We should have asked for some talcum powder," said Tina.

"Or a shoehorn," said Daniel.

When they'd finally finished squeezing into the catsuits, Daniel and Tina stood side by side before a tall standing mirror, and studied the result.

"I know a fetish club in Soho where these outfits would win every prize going, and get you worshipped by most of the regulars," said Tina.

"Of course you'd know about a club like that," said Daniel.

"Don't be a snob," said Tina.

"These outfits are really unforgiving," said Daniel, tugging unhappily at the material here and there. "They're so tight they show off every extra pound. Including a few I didn't know I had."

"I wouldn't know," Tina said airily. "I don't have that problem. Anyway, no one's going to see us down in the sewers, and if we do this right, no one we meet in the Museum will live to tell of it."

"Won't there be surveillance cameras?"

"According to the mission file, the whole system will be shut down for the night," said Tina. "The mummies are very private persons."

"It's all right for you," said Daniel. "You look good in everything."

"I do, don't I?" said Tina. And then she surprised him with a kiss, before moving off to try out some extreme stretching, to test the limits of her catsuit. Daniel's reflection looked him over, and shook his head sadly.

"Oh, shut up," said Daniel.

Next, the tailors provided them both with simple gas masks.

"What do we need these for?" said Daniel.

"In case of gas build-ups in the sewers," said Tina.

Daniel started to ask what kind of gas, and then decided he really didn't want to know.

After the masks came the flare pistols, and half a dozen flares each. Tina showed Daniel how to load them, and he paid close attention. It seemed simple enough, but it wasn't something you wanted to get wrong in an emergency.

"There you go," said Tina. "Easy-peasy, lemon squeezy. But remember: we're going to be in a room full of historical treasures, so make sure you hit what you're aiming at. You incinerate it, you bought it."

Finally, the tailors presented Daniel and Tina with two sets of casual clothes, to change into once they'd entered the Museum. Gray slacks and pullovers, and cheap knockoff trainers. Tina turned up her nose.

"I can't be seen wearing something like this! I mean, it's gray! I have my reputation to think of."

"I refer you to your previous comment, about nobody seeing us," said Daniel.

"Don't push your luck," said Tina. "I am just in the mood to hit someone."

"Never knew you when you weren't," said Daniel.

They crammed everything into two backpacks provided by the tailors. Who then handed the Hydes a personal handwritten note from Miss Montague, saying: *Try not to lose everything this time.*

"I don't think that's fair," said Daniel. "It got very busy, down in the Underground. I don't even remember what happened to my old backpack."

"I'm pretty sure I hit a vampire with mine," said Tina. "By the end, I was hitting them with anything that came to hand that wasn't actually nailed down. And I think I lost my flashlight when I stuck it up a vampire's . . . Too much information?"

"Did the light come out his eyes?" said Daniel.

Tina stretched unself-consciously in her catsuit, and Daniel felt like applauding. She gave him a look that said *Down boy*, and then scowled at the mirror again.

"I miss my evening dress. It was lucky."

"Hydes make their own luck," said Daniel.

"Don't you start," said Tina.

Later that evening, they traveled across London in a taxi driven by one of Edward's people, who was either overawed by their presence or had been ordered not to talk to them. Daniel and Tina sat wedged together in the cramped back seat with their backpacks on their laps, and studied the mission file. The taxi finally dropped them off as close as possible to the British Museum, so they could observe the guards from a distance. There did seem to be an awful lot of them.

The mercenaries were all wearing battle armor, and carried their automatic weapons in a way that suggested they were only waiting for an excuse to use them. The few people out and about on the streets gave the soldiers plenty of room, and were careful to avoid eye contact. Daniel and Tina got as close to the Museum as they could, and then slipped down a particular side alley mentioned in the mission file. Streetlamps at either end of the alley provided just enough light for them to find the manhole that would give them access to the sewers. Daniel studied the cover carefully. It looked very solid, and very heavy.

"We should have brought a crowbar."

Tina looked at him pityingly, ripped the metal cover out of the ground with one hand, and threw it away. It rolled an impressively far distance down the alley.

"Sorry," said Daniel. "I keep forgetting."

They leaned over the opening, and a blast of foul air hit them in the face. Daniel and Tina competed to see which of them could appear most stoic. Tina produced a flashlight, and shone it down into the darkness.

"I thought you lost that up a vampire?" said Daniel.

"This one was in the backpack, along with a whole bunch of other useful items," said Tina. "Didn't you look?"

"I would have got around to it," said Daniel.

They descended into the sewers on a series of steel hoops hammered into the brickwork. Tina went first, because she had the flashlight and because she was Tina. The smell grew steadily more appalling, and by the time they reached the foot of the ladder they were both grabbing for their gas masks in self-defense. Once they had them fitted tightly, Tina flashed her light around, and the fierce beam showed them an old brick tunnel with a ceiling so low they were going to have to keep their heads right down to avoid banging them. The partially flooded tunnel was ankle-deep in dark and murky waters that swirled sluggishly around them. Daniel made a sudden surprised sound.

"What?" said Tina.

"Something just bumped into me," said Daniel, with as much dignity as he could manage. "There are things floating in the water."

"What did you expect, in a sewer?" Tina flashed her light up and down the tunnel. "This way."

"You memorized the map again, didn't you?"

"Someone has to."

They followed Tina's light through the tunnel for some time. Strange sounds came and went, in front and behind and off in the adjoining tunnels. Worryingly loud groans and creaks, strange splashing noises, and what might have been some kind of animal moving about. Daniel wasn't sure which he found most disturbing. Tina kept her flashlight moving, but they never saw anything. The murky waters rose slowly up their legs and made a bow wave ahead of them as they progressed. Some of the sounds seemed to be getting closer. Daniel tried to take the lead, but Tina was having none of it.

"Why are you so jumpy?" she said.

"I'm keeping an eye out for alligators," said Daniel. "You know the stories, about how people used to keep the babies as pets, until they grew so big they weren't cute anymore, and then they got flushed down the toilets and ended up roaming the sewers."

"That's just an urban myth," said Tina. "Think about it: what would alligators find to eat down here?"

"Rats, cats, the occasional repairman..."

"Alligators have far too big an appetite to be satisfied with that."

"Really not helping, Tina."

"However..."

"What?" Daniel said quickly.

"I have heard stories about this incredible purple moss that can only be found in the sewers, grown wild and feral on all the various drugs and chemicals that get dumped down here from clubs and parties and private labs. Some say if you smoke the moss, it cranks your inner eye open all the way up to eleven..."

"Can we please concentrate on getting to the access point?" said Daniel.

They pressed on, through a series of increasingly narrow tunnels. Tina kept a careful watch on the walls, just in case.

They'd almost reached the access point when they heard something moving in the waters up ahead. They both stopped, and listened hard. Tina velcroed the flashlight to her belt, so she could have both hands free, and light jumped around the brickwork every time she moved. Daniel leaned in close, so he could murmur in her ear.

"If Professor Pinder told the mummies about the access point before Edward got to him, they could have sent some of their mercenaries down into the sewers to wait for us."

"Good," said Tina, and Daniel could hear the grin behind her gas mask. "I could use a little exercise, to warm me up for the main event."

"I really don't like what I'm hearing," said Daniel. "It sounds... big."

"Could be guard dogs," said Tina.

"I am not killing any dogs," Daniel said firmly. "I like dogs."

"We are talking expertly trained military attack dogs," said Tina. "You try saying *Nice doggie* and patting one of them on the head, and they'll have your throat out before you can figure out why you're making that strange whistling noise when you breathe."

"It can't be dogs," said Daniel, straining his eyes against the gloom ahead. "There's no way they'd be able to stand the smell. I've got a gas mask on and *I'm* having trouble coping."

"What else could it be?"

"I have a feeling we're about to find out."

"Good," said Tina.

They moved slowly forward, the murky waters lapping up around their thighs. They rounded the next corner and then stopped again as they found their way blocked by half a dozen living nightmares.

"Alligators!" said Daniel. "Look at the size of them!"

"Those are crocodiles," said Tina.

Daniel looked at her. "How can you be so sure?"

"The mummies are big on tradition," said Tina. "And the old-time pharaohs really got off on throwing their enemies to the crocodiles."

Daniel studied the huge creatures carefully. At least ten feet long, they had dull gray scales, mouths packed full of teeth, and cold, unblinking eyes. Packed tightly together, they filled the tunnel from wall to wall like a living barrier. They hadn't just arrived, after a wander through the sewers—they'd been carefully placed in position to insure no one got past them. While Daniel was still trying to work out how anyone could have arranged that, one of the crocodiles turned its head to look at Daniel—and then lurched forward, heading straight for him. All the other crocodiles surged after him, their short, stubby legs churning through the dark waters. Daniel thrust a hand into his backpack for the flare pistol.

"No!" Tina said sharply. "Any flames could ignite a pocket of gas and blow up the tunnel."

"Then what are we supposed to do?" said Daniel, reluctantly taking his hand out of the backpack. "Those things are really picking up speed."

Tina's laughter filled the tunnel. "Let them come. I always wanted to fight a dinosaur."

"You're weird," said Daniel.

There wasn't much room to maneuver in the tunnel, so Daniel and Tina just stood their ground and waited for the crocodiles to come to them. The moment the first of them came within reach, Daniel slammed his fist down hard on top of the crocodile's head. The skull broke under the impact, and the crocodile's head was forced down into the water. All Daniel had to do then was hold it there until the beast drowned.

Tina grabbed the next crocodile to arrive, and hauled it up out of the waters. The great jaws snapped at her viciously, but she easily evaded them and slammed the creature against the wall. Brickwork shattered, and the crocodile went limp in her hands. She turned the semiconscious creature around, took a firm hold on its tail, and then used her crocodile as a flail to bludgeon the others to death. Tina whooped loudly, as she brought the dying crocodile hammering down again and again. Blood spattered across the walls and stained the waters. Some of the crocodiles tried to back away, but Tina brought her crocodile slamming down with vicious force until nothing was moving.

One crocodile did manage to get past her and lunged at Daniel, its jaws stretched wide. Daniel grabbed them with both hands, and held the beast back as it strained toward him. Finally he forced the jaws apart until the muscles tore, and then broke the crocodile's neck.

Daniel and Tina dropped their dead crocodiles and listened carefully, but everything was still and silent. Daniel let out a breath he hadn't realized he'd been holding, and allowed himself to relax. The mummies must have thought six oversized reptiles would be enough. And if the intruders had been anyone else, they would have been right. A thought struck Daniel, and he turned to Tina.

"Didn't the ancient Egyptians worship crocodiles?"

Tina shrugged. "They worshipped pretty much everything at one time or another, often in strange combinations."

"So we just killed the mummies' gods?"

"Start as you mean to go on," Tina said briskly.

It took them a while to clamber over the dead crocodiles and continue on their way, but the access point to the British Museum turned out to be just around the next corner. An ancient trapdoor in the ceiling, it opened easily to Hyde strength and persuasion, and Daniel and Tina quickly pulled themselves up and into the Egyptian Rooms. Which turned out to be unusually dark and gloomy because all the electricity had been turned off. Instead, dozens of candles and oil lamps had been set up all over the place, giving the setting a warm yellow glow like the patina of age. There didn't seem to be anyone else around.

"I'm guessing this isn't a power cut," Daniel said quietly. "Just the mummies making themselves at home."

"Like this place isn't creepy enough at night," said Tina. She glared around at the various Egyptian artifacts, as though daring them to start something.

Daniel took off his gas mask, and the smell from his catsuit hit him like a punch in the face. He all but ripped the suit apart getting out of it, and Tina did the same. They changed into their casual clothes, stuffed the soiled catsuits into their backpacks, and then dropped them through the trapdoor into the sewer—remembering at the very last moment to take out the flare pistols and the flares first, and distribute them in convenient pockets.

They closed the trapdoor quietly, and then Tina consulted the map in her head and pointed the way. They set off through the Egyptian Rooms, moving so quietly they didn't even disturb the flames on the candles. Ancient artifacts loomed up out of the gloom, dead reminders of a dead world. Stylized faces stared out of the shadows with eyes that never closed, and tall figures of forsaken gods watched sternly from their pedestals as the Hydes padded softly past them.

And then Daniel gestured urgently for Tina to stop, as he spotted the first guard. The mercenary soldier was half hidden in the shadows, standing with his back to a sarcophagus. He had the same body armor and really big gun as the guards outside, but he also had night goggles and kept moving his head in a slow arc, so he could cover everything in his range of vision with a minimum of movement. Daniel and Tina stood very still, concealed in their own shadows. Tina pressed her mouth against Daniel's ear.

"We have to kill every single mercenary standing guard," she said quietly. "We can't risk them sneaking up on us from behind, while we're busy dealing with the mummies."

"I didn't join Edward's war to kill people," said Daniel. "I'm only in it for the monsters."

"Some people *are* monsters," Tina said reasonably.

Daniel craned his neck, to check out the shadows around the guard. "Why can't we just go round him? We know where all the guards are stationed. It's in the file."

"Because we would have to be lucky all the time, and they'd only have to be lucky once," said Tina. "We have to kill all of them, to make sure no one gets a chance to sound the alarm." She realized her voice was starting to rise, and quickly lowered it again. "This could be our only opportunity to catch the mummies all together in one place, out in the open and vulnerable."

Daniel shook his head stubbornly. "I won't kill people just because they're inconvenient and in the way. Because they're doing their job."

"These are mercenary soldiers we're talking about," said Tina, with heavy patience. "Their whole job is based around killing people who got in the way of their employers."

"Soldiers are like policemen," said Daniel. "Doing a job that needs doing, that no one else wants to."

"You're not a policeman anymore," said Tina. "You're a Hyde."

"As long as I remember what it means to be a cop, I'm not just a Hyde," said Daniel. "I'm still me." He wished her were as sure of this as he sounded.

Tina looked like she wanted to throw her hands in the air and then grab him by the shoulders and shake some sense into him, but she forced herself to stay calm and give reason another try.

"These guards aren't soldiers serving their country," she said. "They're here to protect monsters. To make it possible for the monsters to go on destroying lives. We can't watch our backs *and* concentrate on taking out the mummies." And then she stopped, and looked closely at him. "This isn't about them—it's about you, isn't it? What's the real problem here, Daniel?"

He met her gaze steadily. "I can't kill people in cold blood. That would make me a monster. Just like Edward."

Tina shook her head slowly. "How many times do I have to tell you this? You are nothing like Edward."

Daniel smiled briefly. "Because you know him so well."

"Exactly. All right . . . Try this. These guards are professional killers. According to the mission file, which I'm assuming you didn't finish, they've hired out to every trouble spot there is, specializing in protecting the really bad apples. Because that's where the money is. Every single one of them has innocent blood on their hands; people whose only crime was to live in the wrong place. And now the mercenaries have come here, to protect the mummies, who between them have probably destroyed more lives than all the soldiers put together. Just think of all the victims who've suffered at their hands . . . and see if your blood is still cold."

"It's not that simple," said Daniel.

"Sometimes, it really is," said Tina. "We have to do this, Daniel, if we're to get to the mummies. You didn't have any problem disposing of the vampires in the Underground, because you saw what they did to people. Trust me, the mummies are just as bad. It's still all about addiction, and what it does to people."

Daniel thought about that for a moment, and then nodded slowly.

"How do you want to do this?"

"Sneak up on them from behind," Tina said briskly. "Go for a stranglehold or a broken neck, and then lower the body carefully to the floor so it won't make a noise."

"How can we get behind this one, when he has his back pressed right up against that sarcophagus?"

"I'll go out front and distract him."

"You'll be making yourself a clear target. Better I do it."

Tina smiled. "I'm more distracting."

Daniel couldn't argue with that. They moved cautiously from one piece of cover to the next until they were close enough, and then Tina stepped out into the light. The guard stepped forward, his gun whipping round to cover her, and Tina smiled and waved happily at him. While the guard was busy deciding what to do about that, Daniel moved in behind him, slipped an arm round his throat, and broke his neck. It was all over very quickly. Daniel lowered the body to the floor, and then quickly let go of it. Tina came over to join him, still smiling cheerfully.

"I thought Hydes didn't sneak?" said Daniel, to avoid having to say anything else.

"Except for when they do," said Tina. "But you're right. It did seem a little unsporting. Never mind! Once we've taken care of the mummies, I'm sure we can find some time to go head-to-head with the other guards. Just for the fun of it."

Daniel shook his head. "You and I have very different ideas about fun."

"That's not what you said at my place."

They moved off through the Egyptian Room and fell silently on the guards, one after the other, like predators in the night. None of the mercenaries even got a chance to put up a fight. Once Daniel and Tina were sure there weren't any more guards than those detailed in the file, they dumped all the bodies in a convenient storage room.

Daniel was surprised to find he was enjoying himself. The thrill of the hunt, of testing his skills against men who would quite definitely kill him if he failed . . . and it did help that he'd decided he was only killing men who deserved to die. Because of what they'd done, and because of what they served. But when it was all over, he stood in the doorway to the storage room and spent some time staring at the piled-up bodies. Tina came over to join him, but he didn't look at her.

"Killing shouldn't be this easy," he said. "Or so satisfying."

"You're entitled to take pride in your work," said Tina. "You enjoyed killing the crocodiles."

"That was different."

"Not really," said Tina. "A threat is a threat. You think too much, Daniel."

"And sometimes, you don't think enough."

She shrugged. "It gets in the way."

Daniel shook his head slowly. "This might have been necessary, but it was still wrong to enjoy it."

"You're a Hyde now," said Tina.

And Daniel had no answer to that.

When they finally got to the room where the mummies were holding their annual get-together, they couldn't even see their targets for all the ancient artifacts that had been brought in from other parts of the Museum. They had to ease their way through a forest of exhibits, using the larger pieces for cover, until they reached an open space surrounded by a circle of standing sarcophagi that immediately reminded Daniel of Stonehenge. Nine small figures were sitting in a semicircle, engulfed in comfortable chairs that were far too big for them. Daniel and Tina crept closer, silent as ghosts among the memories of the past, until they stood watching the mummies from a deep dark shadow between two of the sarcophagi.

"The mummies must have ordered all of this moved here so they could feel at home," Tina said quietly.

"Why so many sarcophagi?" said Daniel.

"Maybe they're having a few old friends round."

"Either that, or it's a family affair."

They moved a little closer, pressing right up to the edge of the shadow.

The short and stocky figures were wrapped from head to toe in grubby, discolored bandages. Most wore simple robes, but one had a dressing gown and another a bathrobe. They spoke slowly, in dry, dusty voices, in a language Daniel didn't recognize. Only their heads moved, turning slowly to follow the conversation as it moved around the circle. There was no hurry in anything they said or did, as though they had all the time in the world.

Daniel put his head next to Tina's. "Is that ancient Egyptian they're speaking?"

"How would I know?" Tina murmured. "But what else would they speak among themselves?" She shook her head slowly. "You know their biggest crime? Being so selfish in keeping everything they know to themselves. Think of all the forgotten knowledge they could have shared with the world. All the things they could have told us about the beginnings of human civilization that modern scholars couldn't even guess at. A society so far removed from ours as to be almost alien. These mummies are time travelers from the distant past, hoarding secrets of unimaginable value—because all they care about is dominating and destroying other people."

"Maybe all those years trapped in the dark really did drive them mad," said Daniel. "Or it could be like the old story, about the genie imprisoned in the bottle. At first he swore he'd reward whoever set him free, but after being a prisoner for centuries he swore to destroy whoever released him, for taking so long. It could be that all they want now is revenge on the modern world for having replaced the world they knew."

"You're overcomplicating things," said Tina. "They're monsters, responsible for generations of death and suffering just so they could profit from it. That's all that matters."

"Can't argue with that," said Daniel. "I wonder what they're saying. Memories of a world only they remember... or just sad thoughts of how it used to feel, to be human? Do you suppose they can even remember what that was like, after so long?"

And then all nine figures suddenly turned their heads, to look right at the spot where Daniel and Tina were hiding. One of the mummies raised a bandaged hand, and beckoned to them.

"No need to skulk in the shadows. Come out into the light, and join us."

The voice was flavored with an entirely unfamiliar accent. Daniel looked at Tina, who shrugged, and they stepped out from between the two sarcophagi and moved forward into the open circle, to face the mummies in their comfortable chairs. None of them moved, but their eyes burned brightly in their bandaged faces. Up close, the mummies smelled strongly of spices and other preservatives.

"How did you know we were there?" said Daniel.

"The sewers are still with you," the mummy said dryly. "How did you evade our guardians?"

"They're all dead," said Daniel. "We have no time for hired killers."

"But they do make the best guards," said the mummy. "Did you kill the crocodiles, as well? Such a pity. One of the few things that haven't changed at all since our time."

"Were they your gods?" said Tina.

"They were our pets. We used to race them through the sewers, when we could find people brave enough to sit in the saddles."

There was a brief hissing murmur from the other mummies, and it took Daniel a moment to realize they were laughing.

"Who are you?" he said.

"Our names would mean nothing to you," said the mummy. "Anyone who might have recognized them disappeared into the sands long ago. If you wish, you can call me Lord."

"That's not going to happen," said Daniel.

He started to introduce himself and Tina, but the mummy waved his words aside.

"We know what you are. Edward's malformed children. Stranded halfway between men and gods. Did you know your precious Elixir was derived from our original work? But then, so much is. We were the first scientists, back in the morning of the world, tearing secrets from an uncaring universe because we needed them to survive."

"Why are you still alive?" Tina said bluntly. "What quality of life can you have?"

"All the years we have known, and all the things we have done, and it still isn't *enough*," said the mummy. "We must go on, until we have a drug that will bring us all the way back. And then we shall be gods, and live eternally."

"And do what?" said Daniel.

"Rule!" said the mummy, and the others slowly nodded their bandaged heads.

"Why?" said Daniel.

"Because anything less would be unworthy of us." The mummy looked steadily at Daniel and Tina. "Edward sent you here to kill us. Because he's scared."

"I don't think Edward does scared," said Daniel.

"We understand the Elixir," said the mummy. "And he doesn't. Did you know he asked us to manufacture it, in our laboratories? We refused, of course. Because he isn't worthy of it." The mummy shook his head slowly. "You think we are monsters, but if you knew some of the things he has planned, you would never sleep again."

"I haven't heard a single good reason yet as to why we shouldn't kill you," said Tina.

The mummy laughed—a dry sound that was more like a cough, clearing the dust of ages from a withered throat.

"You can't kill us, but it would please us to make you ours, and send you back to kill Edward. So kneel and bow your heads, swear your lives to us and enter our service, and we will give you years beyond your wildest imagination."

He stopped, because Daniel was already shaking his head.

"Everything you have was bought with the suffering and death of others."

"That is the way of the world," said the mummy.

"But it doesn't have to be," said Daniel. "That's what life is for—a chance to change things for the better. And I've spent my life fighting things like you."

The mummy who wanted to be called Lord got up out of his chair, and walked over to stand before Daniel and Tina. He only came up to their chests, but there was still a power and authority in his ancient form. The eyes watching from out of the bandaged face were cold and unblinking.

"Edward is the real monster. Agree to serve us, and we will teach you the mysteries of the universe."

"Even if you could, which I rather doubt," said Tina, "there's nothing you can offer that's as much fun as being a Hyde."

The mummy backhanded her across the face. There was a terrible vicious strength in the blow, and Tina's head rocked under the impact. But she didn't fall back a step, and after a moment she turned her head back to face the mummy, and smiled slowly. Daniel decided he was going to stay right where he was. Because he was just dying to see what Tina was going to do next.

The mummy stared blankly at Tina. "You dare defy us?"

"It's what I live for," said Tina. "Mummy dearest."

She punched him so hard in the face that dust flew from the mummy's head, and some of the bandages broke and fell away. He staggered backward, crying out loudly with shock as much as anything else. The other mummies rose up out of their chairs. Tina's mummy quickly regained his balance and turned angrily to face her. Daniel aimed his flare pistol at the mummy he would never call Lord, and pulled the trigger.

The flare shot toward the mummy, and he snatched it out of midair at the last moment. The mummy examined the flare curiously, and then cried out again as the flare suddenly exploded, splashing flames all over the bandaged chest and face. The mummy screamed and staggered blindly round the circle, struggling to beat out the flames with his hands. The bandaged arms immediately caught alight, and flames from the burning body leapt even higher. A flaring orange red light filled the circle, sending shadows dancing madly. The burning shape turned to face the other mummies, reaching out to them with imploring arms, but they were all frozen in place, unable to believe what they were seeing. One did finally take a step forward, but couldn't force itself any closer. The awful heat just pushed it back. The burning mummy staggered away, stumbling blindly around the circle, as though trying to find some place where the flames weren't destroying it.

The other mummies turned their heads away, ignoring the burning figure. They fixed their gazes on Daniel and Tina and then headed straight for them, their bandaged feet slapping softly against the floor.

Tina aimed her flare gun at the nearest mummy, but it moved quickly to avoid her, no matter how fast she changed her aim. Tina scowled, as she realized her only real hope was to shoot the mummy at point-blank range. She walked straight at it, her extended arm perfectly steady, closing in until there was nowhere left for the mummy to go. And then the mummy suddenly reached out and slapped the flare gun out of Tina's hand with contemptuous ease. The gun skidded away across the floor and disappeared into the shadows. Tina took a step after it and the mummy was immediately standing before her, blocking her way. Tina snarled at him, and dropped back to stand with Daniel.

A fierce crimson light leapt and flared in the circle as the burning mummy was consumed by rising flames. Every bit of it was alight now, and it was hard to make out a human shape inside the flames; just a column of fire that reached almost to the ceiling. Normally, so much heat would have set off the automatic sprinklers and put the figure out, but the mummies had turned off all the power earlier. The burning figure fell to its knees, no longer screaming, no longer moving, just burning steadily in the middle of the circle like some ancient beacon. The other mummies ignored it, giving all their attention to the Hydes. They closed in, slowly and inexorably, as though they carried with them the force of ages and the inevitability of history.

Daniel had already put his flare gun away. There didn't seem any point in reloading. He'd caught the first mummy off guard, but after what happened with Tina it was clear that wasn't going to happen again. He looked at Tina, and she shot him her usual reckless grin. He grinned back, and they raised their fists and went to meet the mummies, putting their faith in the Hyde strength and power that had never failed them before.

Daniel strode right up to the nearest mummy and punched it in the face with all his strength. But his fist just glanced away, and the mummy's head didn't even rock under the impact. Daniel tried again, slamming his fist into the bandaged throat, but all he did was hurt his hand. Whatever drugs the mummies had taken in the distant past to protect them from the ravages of time had made them unstoppable. Daniel kept lashing out, even as he was forced to back away, but the mummy took no damage and felt no pain. Daniel's thoughts spun helplessly as he realized he didn't have a backup plan. This wasn't like the vampires, where he'd had several weapons to choose from. Everyone had thought the flare guns would be enough.

Daniel frowned, and made himself concentrate. How do you kill something that's already dead? That thought reminded Daniel of what he'd done at the Frankenstein gathering. He darted forward and grabbed hold of the mummy's head with both hands. But even though he wrenched at it with all his strength, he couldn't tear the mummy's head off. Bandaged hands shot up and closed on his arms, the fingers tightening with hideous strength as they crushed his muscles. Daniel cried out despite himself, as an unbearable pain filled his arms. He pulled himself free with an almost hysterical effort, and stumbled backward. His arms fell to hang limply at his sides, screaming with an agony that wouldn't let him think and only slowly died away as the torn muscles fought to repair themselves. The mummy came after him, and all Daniel could do was keep backing away around the circle, while doing his best to stay out of reach of the other mummies.

Tina was keeping their attention fixed on her, laughing mockingly as she danced among them, moving too quickly for them to keep up with her. She struck out at them with swift blows and vicious kicks, knocking the mummies off-balance and then darting back out of reach before they could react. Until a bandaged hand shot out with inhuman speed and grabbed Tina by the arm. She fought to break free and found she couldn't, and the mummy threw her across the circle as though she weighed nothing at all. Tina turned end over end as she flew through the air, and then slammed into one of the standing sarcophagi, almost overturning it. She dropped limply to the floor and lay there, facedown, struggling to get her breath back. The sarcophagus rocked slowly back and forth, until finally it overbalanced and collapsed on top of her. It crashed down on her like the wrath of the ancient gods, and the sheer weight of it pinned her to the floor. Tina fought to get out from under it, her hands scrabbling helplessly on the waxed floor, but she couldn't find any leverage. The mummies headed toward her, not bothering to hurry, their bandaged hands opening and closing with simple menace. Tina's movements became even more frantic as she realized she was trapped—and helpless.

Daniel started forward, forcing his aching hands into fists, but the mummies were already between him and Tina. His head raced as he tried to think of something he could do, and then he saw one of the mummies flinch away as it got too close to the motionless burning mummy. As though just the heat it was giving off was a danger.

And just like that, Daniel knew what he had to do. The thought appalled him, so he moved quickly forward before he could think better of it. He drove himself forward into the awful heat, even as it seared his face, and grabbed hold of the blazing figure with both hands. He gritted his teeth as the flames burned him, but somehow made himself tighten his grip. He raised up the burning mummy, spun around, and used it as a flail to strike down the other mummies. The same way Tina had used one crocodile against the others. One of the other mummies immediately burst into flames, just from sheer proximity to the blazing heat, and rippling fires shot all over his body.

Daniel sobbed in pain as his hands blackened and crisped from the terrible heat. Flames shot up his sleeves, but he wouldn't let go. He had to save Tina. He turned to face the other mummies, and they started to back away. Daniel showed them his teeth in a merciless grin, and went after them. He swung the burning figure back and forth, and in just a few moments all the other mummies were on fire. They went staggering blindly round the circle, slamming into one another and crying out in their forgotten language, blazing more and more fiercely as the ancient chemicals in their bodies fueled the flames.

The circle was full of a terrible hellish light. Shadows danced madly across the watching faces of the standing sarcophagi. One by one the mummies stopped screaming and fell to their knees, slowly bowing their burning heads as death finally caught up with them. In the end all that remained were so many motionless forms, burning steadily like funeral pyres.

Daniel tried to drop the burning thing he was holding, and found he couldn't. His blackened hands wouldn't open. Horrible pains shot up his arms as he shook them hard, but the burning shape seemed to cling to him. As though determined to bring him down too, whatever it took. Flames shot up Daniel's shirtfront and licked at his face, and he cried out miserably.

There was a great crash from the other side of the circle, as Tina finally threw the sarcophagus to one side. She lurched to her feet and raced across the circle, darting past the burning shapes to rip the blazing mummy out of Daniel's grip. Thick smoke rose up from his blackened arms and hands. Tina threw the burning thing to one side, and then beat out Daniel's flames with her bare hands, not flinching once. And when it was done, they both dropped to their knees and breathed heavily as they waited for their burns to heal.

It took a while, but eventually Dr. Jekyll's marvelous Elixir brought them back from the brink, one more time. Daniel's breathing gradually slowed and steadied as the pain died away. He held his hands up before him, though it took him a moment before he could bring himself to look at them. The blackened, twisted things that had held on to the burning mummy despite everything were now completely back to normal, and Daniel let out a long, slow sigh of relief. He leaned against Tina, and she leaned on him. Though neither of them would ever admit it, taking down the mummies had turned out to be a closer-run thing than either of them had expected. They rose slowly to their feet, and looked round the circle at the burning shapes.

"It's a pity we didn't think to bring a few marshmallows," Daniel said finally.

"Or some sausages," said Tina.

Daniel winced. "I don't think I'm in the mood for burnt meat, just at the moment."

"Time we were leaving," said Tina. "Someone must have heard something by now. A small army of heavily armed mercenaries is almost certainly heading in our direction, even as we speak. And loath though I am to admit it, I do have limits."

Daniel nodded quickly. "Back to the sewers, then."

Tina smiled. "But if we can find the time ... I always did fancy a pair of crocodile hide boots."

Chapter Eight
WHERE THE WILD THINGS ARE

✣ ✣ ✣

WHEN DANIEL AND TINA ENTERED the Jekyll & Hyde Inc. building a few days later, they didn't even get as far as the secretary's office. A message board had been planted in the center of the lobby, with a handwritten message instructing them to go down to the cellar.

"Well," said Tina. "That isn't at all foreboding."

"I am getting really tired of being led around by the nose, just so he can give me a grand tour of his building," said Daniel. "This had better not be tiger-related."

"Oh I don't know," said Tina. "I am feeling a bit peckish."

Daniel sniffed. "I didn't know this building even had a cellar."

"There are stairs at the back of the lobby."

"And what's in this cellar?"

"Beats me," said Tina. "It's always been Edward's private domain."

"More so than his playroom?"

"Definitely. I don't know anyone who's ever been allowed in the cellar before this."

"Then how do you know how to get there?"

Tina smiled. "People tell me things."

"Whether they want to or not?"

"Pretty much."

Tina led the way to the back of the lobby, and a concealed door that opened onto bare stone steps falling away under a series of softly glowing lights. Tina started down the steps, and then stopped when she realized Daniel wasn't following her.

"What's wrong?"

"I really don't like cellars these days."

"You're going to have to put that behind you one day," said Tina. "Why not now?"

"Because it's still too recent," said Daniel, not moving.

"But that was months ago," said Tina.

"No," said Daniel. "That was yesterday."

"You're a Hyde. Nothing can hurt you anymore."

"There are all kinds of hurt. And I have to wonder whether Edward knew what effect meeting in a cellar would have on me..."

"You think he's messing with your head? Why would he want to do that?"

"You tell me. You know him better."

"I don't think anyone really knows Edward Hyde," said Tina. "He keeps everyone at a distance—and most people prefer it that way. What reason could he have to mess with you? You're his new golden boy, his very own killer of monsters."

"Perhaps I've been too successful," said Daniel. "And now he sees me as a threat to his position as head of Jekyll & Hyde Inc."

Tina smiled. "It's about time somebody was. Come on, Daniel, don't let him get to you. You're the one who finished off the monster Clans when he couldn't."

Daniel moved slowly down the steps to stand beside her. "I couldn't have done it without you."

"I know that. I was just being supportive. This is probably only about reminding you who's boss."

"Wouldn't surprise me," said Daniel.

"Want me to hold your hand?"

"Maybe later."

When they reached the bottom of the stairs, they found a door standing slightly ajar, as though inviting them in. Daniel kicked the door open and barged straight in, with Tina at his side.

The cellar was filled from wall to wall with a perfect recreation of a Victorian laboratory. Gas lighting shed a cheerful glow over the very best scientific equipment from the period: test tubes and retorts, jars full of herbs and acids and strange compounds, Bunsen burners with dancing flames, and any number of things that were rarely seen outside a museum. Dark liquids pulsed through long glass tubes and distilled off into waiting beakers, while brightly colored chemicals bubbled ominously in the background. There was a definite sense of purpose to it all, even if Daniel didn't have a clue as to what that might be.

Standing before it all, smiling unpleasantly at Daniel and Tina like the lord of his chemical domain, was Edward Hyde.

"Welcome to Dr. Jekyll's laboratory, where he first created his famous potion. I came down early to set everything in motion for you, just so you could appreciate it."

"Why are we meeting here?" Tina said bluntly.

"Because I told you to," said Edward.

"There will come a time when that's not enough," said Tina.

"But until then," said Edward, still smiling his unsettling smile, "you'll do as you're told—won't you, Tina?"

Daniel was quietly relieved to discover that the cellar was so different from the Frankenstein chop shop, that it was having no effect on him at all. He made a point of studying everything with cheerful interest, and Edward made a point of not noticing.

"Everything you see came from the original lab," he said fondly. "I had it all transferred here when I first moved in."

"How were you able to keep something like that secret?" said Daniel.

"Did you have everyone involved in the move killed?" said Tina. "The way the old pharaohs used to kill off all their slaves, to keep their final resting place a secret?"

"You spent too much time talking to those mummies, when you should have been killing them," said Edward.

"Lighten up," said Tina. "Anyone would think you were worried they might have told us something you didn't want us to know."

"So young, to be so paranoid," Edward said sadly.

"I notice you haven't answered Tina's question about the movers," said Daniel. "Did you have them killed, to protect your secret?"

Edward smiled easily. "No need. I just gave them a nice bonus, and had them all sign an NDA. Oh, and I had Montague use a bit of magic to wipe their short-term memories. Because not even monsters are monsters all the time. You should be grateful I'm letting you see my little den. The only quiet place I can retire to, to escape the pressures of the modern world. There's no Wi-Fi down here, no phones, and no one to bother me."

Daniel remembered the mummies, surrounding themselves with ancient Egyptian artifacts so they could feel at home.

"I thought the police destroyed Dr. Jekyll's laboratory," he said. Just to show an interest.

"What they found was just a decoy," said Edward. "I knew I'd have to leave them something or they'd never stop looking."

"Why are we here?" said Tina.

"I wanted you to see where I came from," said Edward. "Where all Hydes come from. Everyone should cherish their roots."

Something about Edward's carefully chosen words made Daniel suspicious. Edward was telling him something important, and he was missing it. Edward's smile widened as he gestured grandly about him.

"This is where I was born—not in blood and suffering, but in chemicals and transformation. One man's dream, given shape and form."

"Is this where you brew new batches of the Elixir?" said Tina.

Edward seemed thrown for a moment, as though he hadn't been expecting that question, but he recovered quickly.

"My real lab is far more advanced. It amazes me Jekyll was able to achieve anything in a primitive setting like this."

"Then what are we supposed to be celebrating?" said Daniel.

"That Jekyll could do so much, with so little," said Edward. "He may not have had a lot to work with, but he did have an incredible mind."

He stood there for a long moment, looking out over the equipment and back into the past.

"Why are we here?" Tina said loudly.

"Because I wanted you to see how far I've come," said Edward.

"From where you were made into a monster?" said Daniel.

Edward smiled crookedly. "I wasn't 'made' anything. This is what I always was, on the inside. Buried in the depths of a small man's mind. The potion just let me out. Like the two of you: a minor police officer and a degenerate party girl . . . But I saw greatness in you, and unleashed it on the world."

"You made me strong," said Daniel. "But I have done questionable things with that strength."

Edward looked at Tina. "Is that how you feel?"

She met his gaze steadily. "Sometimes."

"You never used to feel that way," said Edward. "I think Daniel is a bad influence on you. O my children . . . small emotions are for small people. I freed you from your cages so you could lead bigger lives. Don't let your future be undermined by your past. I made you strong so you could glory in it!"

"Tell us what we're doing here or we're leaving," said Daniel.

"We're here to celebrate!" said Edward. "The three main monster Clans have been destroyed, their few surviving members scattered and broken, no threat to anyone. We can always hunt them down later, for the sport of it."

"Crime isn't going to go away," said Daniel, "just because the monsters are dead and gone. Someone will always step forward to take over."

Edward shrugged impatiently. "But they won't have the strength or the imagination to do what the monster Clans did. I'm surprised you're not more pleased, policeman. This is what you wanted, isn't it? Revenge on those who hurt you and your friends, and a world free from monsters."

Daniel couldn't help feeling that Edward was only saying what he thought Daniel wanted to hear. To keep him from thinking about something else.

"I can't believe it's all over," he said finally.

Edward turned to Tina. "Are you about to tell me you're not satisfied either?"

She shrugged quickly. "I'm sure you'll find something else for me to fight."

"Exactly! It's what you live for; I know that. There is one surviving clan . . . the werewolves."

Daniel frowned. "I thought you said they weren't a real clan? That the wolves were just muscle, to keep everyone in line."

"Perhaps I should have used the word *pack*, instead," said Edward. "At heart the wolves are just animals, driven by needs and instincts. Which made it easy for the greater monsters to put them to work. The other Clans never accepted the werewolves as equals, because they were human part of the time."

"The Frankensteins were human," said Daniel.

"Not after everything they'd done to themselves," said Edward.

"Is that why the Clans never accepted you?" said Tina. "Because you were Jekyll as well as Hyde?"

Edward glared at her coldly. "I haven't been merely human in a long time. What matters is that now the monster Clans are gone, the werewolves are free." He smiled suddenly. "What do you suppose they'll do, now the other Clans aren't here to hold them back? Can't you just see them, in their fur . . . running through city streets at night and howling at the moon? Hunting down men, women, and children and tearing them to pieces, and feasting on the remains . . . because wolves have always preyed on people."

"And reveal their existence to the modern world, after all these years?" said Daniel. "I mean, we've all seen the movies. These days everyone knows about silver bullets."

"But would people believe?" said Edward. "How many would have to die, or be bitten and changed, before the authorities could bring themselves to do what was necessary? To put aside arrests and trials in favor of a silver bullet through the head? It's been a long time since Humanity knew for a fact that monsters were real. People have got soft. The wolves will take advantage of that, now they're free. We need to stop them while we still can."

"You don't have to convince me," said Tina. "Just point me at them."

Daniel nodded in agreement, glad to be back on familiar ground again.

"It's really just a mopping-up operation," said Edward. "To make sure the wolves don't move into the gap left by the other monsters."

"But the werewolves have dropped out of sight," said Daniel.

"You said there was an internal power struggle going on," said Tina.

"All down to me, I'm afraid," said Edward. "When the wolves learned I was finally ready to destroy the monster Clans, they started to get ideas above their station. They removed themselves from the battleground so they could emerge when the danger was over and all their rivals were gone."

"But you only launched your attack a few days ago," said Tina. "And the wolves have been missing in action for weeks."

"I'm not the only one with inside men," said Edward. "All the

Clans knew I was planning something—but only the wolves believed I could do it."

"What made them so sure?" said Daniel.

"Because I've had dealings with them. They know what I'm capable of."

"What kind of dealings?" said Tina.

Edward grinned. "The profitable kind. Right now there's an argument going on among the leaders of the pack, the alpha wolves. Over what the clan should do, now there's no one left to stop them. You can't blame them for getting a bit excited; the other Clans kept them on a very short leash. And wolves have always been very good at scenting which way the wind is blowing."

"What about the ghouls?" said Daniel.

Edward stared at him. "What?"

"They're a clan too . . . aren't they?"

"Well yes, but they're just creatures with appetites." Edward glowered at Daniel, irritated at being driven off message. "They're no threat. They'll work for anyone who'll hide them from the public gaze. The wolves are the real danger, and my people have discovered where the alpha males will be meeting tonight."

"They're going ahead with a gathering?" said Daniel. "After everything that's happened?"

"Nothing so organized," said Edward. "The alphas are meeting to fight it out for control of the pack. Whichever one comes out on top, the rest of the pack will follow unquestioningly."

"How many alphas are we talking about?" said Tina.

"Maybe twenty," said Edward. "Nothing you can't handle."

"Where do we look for them?" said Daniel.

"Elstree Park," said Edward. "The nearest thing to a wild place left in London."

"What about witnesses?" said Daniel. "There are bound to be some, no matter how late it is. People go to a park for all kinds of reasons."

"You don't have to worry about that," said Edward. "People's instincts will be enough to keep them out of the park tonight."

"How are we supposed to kill the alpha males?" said Tina. "Load up with silver bullets and shoot anything that goes furry in the moonlight?"

"Pretty much," said Edward. "Except . . . you can't simply open fire the moment you see them. When threatened, the wolves attack as a pack. You might pick off a few, but the rest would be sure to bring you down. You need to stand back and let the alpha wolves fight each other to the death, and then move in to finish off the survivors. Without leaders, the pack will turn on each other. It'll be a bloodbath, and by the time they're done there won't be enough of them left to pose a real threat. We can put on our hunting pink, and chase them through the streets at night." Edward laughed softly. "Perhaps I'll make a killing, supplying wolf skins to the fur trade."

And then they all looked round as Miss Montague entered quietly through the open door. The nice little old lady in charge of the armory smiled sweetly as she moved forward to join them, carrying a heavy leather case. Edward laughed softly, his eyes sparkling with malice.

"Come in, my dear Esme! It's not often you grace me with your presence."

"There's a reason for that," said Miss Montague. "But now the war against the monsters is finally reaching its conclusion, I thought I'd bring your people the appropriate weapons in person. Because there are things they need to know."

She gave Edward a look that Daniel didn't understand at all. Edward stared calmly back at her.

"It's been a long time," said Miss Montague.

"You were the one who walked away," said Edward.

"I'm still embarrassed at how long it took me to realize you were never going to care about me," said Miss Montague.

He grinned at her. "Did you care, as long as we ended up in bed?"

The little old lady smiled briefly. "It's always the bad boy who makes the good girl's heart beat that little bit faster."

"You saw yourself as a good girl?" said Edward. "After all the missions we worked together? And all the things you did for me?"

"I was good compared to you," said Miss Montague. "And in the end, I walked away to save my soul."

Edward shrugged. "But you still stuck around, making yourself useful. I like that in a woman."

"You haven't changed a bit," said Miss Montague.

"You have," said Edward. "You got old. It's your own fault. I did offer you the Elixir."

"I never wanted it," said Miss Montague. "I saw what it did to people. They stopped being those people, and turned into Hydes."

Edward turned abruptly to face Daniel and Tina, who didn't even try to conceal how much they were enjoying the situation. Edward smiled sardonically.

"You'll have to give me a moment. It seems Esme and I have some old history to deal with, before we can move on."

"Of course," Daniel said lightly. "Take all the time you need. I'm sure Tina and I can find something to keep us occupied, while you and Miss Montague admire the scenery down memory lane."

He would have said more, but Edward's gaze was getting colder by the moment, and Daniel decided this would be a good time to put some space between him and Edward. He set off for the far side of the lab, and after one last searching look at Edward and Miss Montague, Tina went after him. They pretended to take an interest in some particularly complex glass tubing, while keeping their hearing focused on Edward Hyde and Miss Montague. Distance was no object to Hyde senses. Daniel was pretty sure Edward knew that; he was just making a point about privacy.

Daniel frowned a little as he thought about that. Edward couldn't be protecting Miss Montague's feelings, because he didn't care about things like that. And it couldn't be guilt about their past relationship, because he wouldn't give a damn about that either . . . unless there was some old scandal that Edward didn't want to acknowledge. Daniel and Tina looked at each other, smiled briefly, and then strained their hearing to pick up every word Edward and Miss Montague said.

"You know I never loved you," Edward said bluntly. "And I never promised you anything."

"Of course I knew," said Miss Montague. "You told me often enough. But I loved you. I'd never felt anything like the way you made me feel. A heat in my heart, so great it still warms me after all these years."

"Please don't tell me you came all the way down here in the hope of rekindling an old passion," said Edward. He smiled slowly, his eyes sparkling with simple malice. "I don't do nostalgia. And even if I did, I don't think there's enough fire in your scrawny little body to survive it."

"You always have to be so cruel," said Miss Montague. "I think that's one of the things I liked most about you."

Edward's smile widened. "I remember."

Miss Montague didn't smile back at him.

Edward shrugged, and his smile disappeared as though he'd lost interest.

"Why are you here, Esme, taking up my valuable time?"

Miss Montague turned her head suddenly, to look at Daniel and Tina. Caught off guard, Daniel felt like he should at least pretend to avert his gaze, but he didn't. Something important was happening here, he could feel it. Miss Montague turned her head back to Edward.

"I heard about your protégé, Tina. How you trained her personally to kill monsters. I thought at first she was just another of your dalliances, because after all, there's been so many of them . . . but instead you kept her as a resource, waiting for just the right moment. And now the monster Clans are finally falling, because of her and this new Hyde: Daniel."

"Get to the point, Esme."

"When they finally came to see me in my armory, I got a chance to see them in action. And now I know what you saw in them. They're not quite like you and me, but they do remind me of what I hoped we'd become: partners in the dance, us against the world; doing great things, just because we could."

"But you wouldn't take the Elixir," said Edward.

"I want Daniel and Tina to stand a fair chance against the werewolves," said Miss Montague.

"They're Hydes," said Edward. "They can take care of themselves."

"They'll stand a better chance with what I've brought them."

Edward's eyes narrowed. "I do hope you haven't exceeded your authority, Esme. I'd hate to have to discipline you."

She smiled briefly. "As I recall, you used to enjoy it. And, of course, so did I. Our relationship was so deliciously uncomplicated. But I have followed your conditions to the letter. Everything you asked for, no more, and no less. I just want to make sure that Daniel and Tina understand what they're getting into."

"Getting bored now," said Edward. "Don't interfere, Esme. This is none of your business."

"Wouldn't dream of it, Edward," Miss Montague said brightly. "But I won't let you throw these nice young people to the wolves."

Edward looked at her. "I could throw you out."

"Of course you could," said Miss Montague. "But then you'd have to explain why to Daniel and Tina. Make them suspicious enough, and they might decide not to follow your orders this time."

Edward laughed suddenly, a surprisingly good-natured sound. "You always wanted to be my conscience. I knew there was a good reason why I let you walk away."

Miss Montague studied him carefully, with her bird-bright eyes. "All these years, and you've barely changed at all. Except that now it's easier to see the monster in you."

"I never kept anything from you," said Edward.

"Perhaps I didn't want to see it, then."

"I never lied to you."

"No," said Miss Montague. "I lied to myself—about who and what you really were. So I could have what I wanted from you."

Edward nodded slowly, considering the matter. "Was it worth it?"

"I never felt the same about anyone else," Miss Montague said steadily. "You were my one great passion, and my greatest mistake. But I got what I wanted, for a while. And that's all that matters."

She turned away from him, to smile brightly at Daniel and Tina. "You can come back now, dears, and see the lovely toys I've brought for you."

They moved quickly out from behind the glass tubing, and hurried over to see what Miss Montague had in her leather case. She worked the combination lock carefully with her arthritic fingers, and raised the lid. Daniel and Tina stared respectfully at the contents.

"Those are Peacemakers," said Daniel, sounding almost reverent. "Long-barreled revolvers from the Old West. Wyatt Earp used them in Tombstone. He said if you ran out of bullets, you could always hit people over the head with the barrel."

"The length of the barrel also helps with range and accuracy," said Miss Montague.

"Are those really silver bullets?" said Tina. "I thought they'd be shinier. Where did you get them from—the Lone Ranger Museum?"

"I never did understand why silver bullets were so important to him," said Daniel.

"Maybe the Old West was secretly overrun with outlaw werewolves," said Tina. And then she stopped and looked at Miss Montague. "Why are there only six bullets for each gun?"

"Because they're really expensive," said Edward.

"And not at all easy to manufacture," said Miss Montague. "The calculations on the ballistics alone are enough to drive anyone crazy. Still, not to worry, dears. After you've used up all your silver bullets, you still have your silver knives."

Daniel and Tina reached into the case and took out two hand-tooled doe-skin scabbards. When drawn, the silver knives turned out to be large and blocky, with a serrated edge. More like butcher's tools than weapons. The blades flashed brightly in the gaslight as Daniel and Tina turned them back and forth, getting a feel for the balance.

"You'd have to get in really close, to stab a werewolf with one of these," Daniel said dubiously.

"Fun!" said Tina. She elbowed him in the ribs, and flashed him a grin that had a lot of wolf in it.

Daniel looked at her, and then at Edward. "What happens if a Hyde gets bitten by a werewolf? Would the Elixir provide any immunity to the werewolf curse?"

"I have no idea," said Edward. "It might turn you into something never seen before—and even more dangerous."

"Cool!" said Tina.

"What are we supposed to do if we do get bitten?" said Daniel.

"Get back here as quick as you can, so I can watch!" said Edward.

Tina looked at Daniel. "Being a wolf does have its appeal. Haven't you ever dreamed of running wild in the night?"

"You'd have to take orders from an alpha male," said Daniel.

"Forget I said anything."

They sheathed the silver knives and holstered the heavy pistols, and then settled the weapons as comfortably as possible about their persons. The silver bullets went into their pockets. Edward rubbed his hands together briskly.

"Find something to keep you busy till tonight, and then it's off to Elstree Park with you."

"What time?" said Daniel.

"When the moon is out, they'll be there," said Edward.

"Don't we get a mission file?" said Tina.

"Find them and kill them," said Edward. "What more do you need? Once the alpha wolves are dead, that will be it for the Clans. No more monsters."

"Apart from us," said Daniel.

Edward smiled broadly, and Daniel knew he'd really missed something.

Daniel and Tina left Miss Montague with Edward. Daniel frowned thoughtfully as they headed back up the steps.

"Did you see the way those two were looking at each other? What do you suppose they're talking about?"

"I don't think I want to know," said Tina.

"It's hard to think of a sweet old thing like her having a fling with the likes of Edward Hyde."

"We tend to forget just how old Edward really is," said Tina. "Though it does help to explain how a little old lady ends up running an armory full of staggeringly unpleasant weapons and devices."

"Edward is a bad influence," said Daniel.

"We should know," said Tina.

When they left the building it was barely afternoon, and a long way from night. Daniel watched as people passed by, with no idea of all the terrible things they shared the world with, and couldn't help seeing them as sheep that didn't have enough sense to look out for wolves.

"We've got hours yet," said Tina. "Want to go back to my place and help me break what's left of the bedroom furniture? Or, I know this halfway decent bar not far from here..."

"I'd prefer something a little more restful," said Daniel. "We're going to need all our strength tonight."

Tina shrugged. "There's a nice little tearoom, just round the corner..."

Daniel looked at her. "Really?"

"I am large, and contain multitudes," Tina said calmly. "Even if most of them aren't talking to each other."

And that was when a familiar voice called Daniel by name, from the depths of a side alley. Daniel and Tina stared into the gloom beyond the alley mouth, but even their Hyde eyes couldn't make out anything. Daniel started forward, and Tina grabbed him by the arm.

"Not a good idea. We've made a lot of enemies in the past few days, and not all the monsters are dead."

"I thought Hydes weren't afraid of anything?" said Daniel.

"I'm just being cautious. If someone's ready to invite a Hyde into a back alley, they must have a good reason. If it looks like a trap and smells like a trap, the odds are someone's found a weapon they think can really mess up a Hyde's day."

"Whoever that is, they know my name," said Daniel. "You can stay out here, if you want."

"And miss out on a chance to say *I told you so*?"

They entered the narrow alley side by side. Daniel's eyes quickly adapted to the gloom, showing him grimy brickwork and all kinds of rubbish on the ground. An unpleasant smell hung heavily on the air, and Daniel's hackles stirred. There was something in that smell... something rank and foul. Light reflecting off a third-story window dropped down into the alley like a spotlight, and when Daniel and Tina were close enough a single figure stepped forward to take center stage. Daniel's heart lurched in his chest, and he slammed to a halt as he recognized his old friend Nigel Rutherford.

Tina looked quickly back and forth between the two of them. Shock closed Daniel's throat, preventing him from saying anything. It had been bad enough when Paul turned up at his flat, having survived a broken back by being made into a vampire, but Daniel had seen the young Frankenstein woman crush Nigel's heart with a single blow. It couldn't be him...but Daniel wanted so badly for at least one of his friends to have survived what happened in that cellar.

Nigel's air of aristocratic grace was gone. He seemed to crouch as much as stand, as though just waiting to launch himself at some unseen enemy. Instead of his usual elegant suit he wore a black leather motorcycle jacket over distressed jeans and heavy boots. His once immaculate hair had grown out long and shaggy, and his features seemed leaner and sharper. He smiled easily at Daniel, but his cool, steady gaze had nothing of friendship in it.

"Hello, Daniel," said Nigel. "Miss me?"

"What happened to you?" said Daniel. His voice sounded harsh, even to him. "I saw you die!"

"And now I'm back," said Nigel. "I thought you'd be pleased."

"Daniel!" Tina said sharply. "Who is he?"

"This is my old friend Nigel," Daniel said steadily. "We started out in the police together. He was with me in the Frankenstein chop shop when it all went to hell. This new look really isn't you, Nigel. Did you join the Hell's Angels?"

"No," said Nigel. "Something worse."

"I was so sure you died," said Daniel.

"Not the first time a girl broke my heart," said Nigel. "I got over it."

"She's dead now," said Daniel. "I killed her at the Frankenstein gathering."

"I suppose I should express my gratitude," said Nigel.

"I didn't do it for you," said Daniel. "I did it because it was necessary."

"You always were a Boy Scout," said Nigel. "I would have tracked her down myself, but I've been busy."

There was something off about the way Nigel was speaking. As though he was only saying the things he thought Daniel expected him to say, so he could get them out of the way and move on to something more important.

"How did you survive?" said Daniel.

"Are you really so surprised?" said Nigel. "Paul beat the odds as well . . . until he sought you out. He really should have known better."

"You know what happened to Paul?" said Daniel.

"Word gets around," said Nigel. "We need to talk."

"Fine," said Daniel. "There's a bar not far from here . . ."

"No," said Nigel. "I don't do that anymore."

Daniel looked at him sharply. The old friend he remembered would never have turned down the chance for a drink. Nigel spent half his life in bars, boring people rigid with his family's extensive knowledge of fine wines.

"You've changed," said Daniel.

"You have no idea," said Nigel. "They made Paul into a vampire—but they made me into a werewolf."

Daniel remembered Paul talking about Nigel, saying *He's with someone else now. We don't talk.* Nigel took Daniel's silence for disbelief, and held his left hand up before him. Thick gray fur swept over the hand as vicious claws appeared. There was no sense of pain or struggle; it was more like one image being replaced by another.

As the human gave way to the wolf. Nigel clawed slowly at the air between them, reminding Daniel of what he could do, if he chose.

Tina stirred dangerously at Daniel's side, and he dropped a hand onto her arm to hold her in place. Nigel glanced at Tina and his mouth twitched in something that might have been a smile, before dismissing her contemptuously and turning back to Daniel. And that disturbed Daniel more than anything, because the Nigel he remembered had always been a gentleman of the old school.

"You were right, Nigel," said Daniel. "We do need to talk."

"And we have so much to talk about," said Nigel. "Something's going on but you don't know what it is, do you, Daniel?"

His hand was suddenly normal again, and he let it drop back to his side. As though he'd just shown Daniel a gun he hadn't had to use.

"I thought you needed a full moon to change?" said Daniel.

"You always did watch too many movies," said Nigel. "We can turn wolf whenever we want to, and we do."

"What does it feel like?" said Daniel.

"Humans walk through the world like they're dreaming," said Nigel. "Deaf and blind to all its wonders. Becoming a wolf is like waking up, and coming fully alive."

"So you enjoy being a wolf?" said Tina.

He looked at her properly for the first time. "Surprisingly, no." He turned back to Daniel. "Remember all the petty rules and regulations we hated so much, when we were training to be policemen? Being part of the pack is actually worse. I cannot disobey any order an alpha male gives me, and as a newcomer I'm right at the bottom of the heap. And on top of all that, I'm constantly at the mercy of my animal side, driven by the needs and instincts of the beast."

"Can't you just leave?" said Daniel.

"The moon would follow me wherever I went."

"What happened to you, after the chop shop?"

"The werewolves were sent in to clean up, before the bookshop was torched," said Nigel. "The Frankenstein doctors had already taken Oscar's head for a souvenir. Paul's broken body had been sent to the Vampire Clan so it could be turned and made to answer questions. The werewolves took me just so they wouldn't be left out. I was more dead than alive when they dragged me from the ruins—

but the werewolf bite brought me back. And at first . . . I enjoyed it. I had come so close to dying that a second chance felt like more than I deserved. To be strong and free, running wild in the moonlight . . . I thought I'd hit the jackpot. Until I realized what had been taken from me.

"I come from a long-established family. Raised to enjoy and appreciate the very best of everything. I was a gentleman, with the most refined of tastes. But the beast in me drove all that out. I don't care about the arts anymore, about style or elegance. Fine foods and wines mean nothing to me. All I have is the thrill of the hunt, the delight in a fresh kill, and rutting in the night. No matter what shape I hold, I'm someone else now."

"There's a lot of that going around," said Daniel. "The Frankensteins used Oscar's head to complete one of their creations. I put a stop to that."

"Good for you," said Nigel. "That makes two of us you've killed."

"Paul asked me to destroy him," Daniel said steadily. "To drive a stake through his heart and set him free. Is that why you came to see me, Nigel? Do you need my help to put you out of your misery?"

"No," said Nigel. "I'm here because there's something you need to know."

"I think I'm pretty much up to speed on the secrets of the monster Clans," said Daniel.

"You only think you are," said Nigel. "Edward has secrets of his own."

"Secrets?" said Daniel.

Nigel's smile widened mockingly. "You have no idea . . ."

"If you're not here for old times' sake, then just tell me what I need to know," said Daniel.

Nigel's gaze was sharp and cold, and his smile grew wolfish, as though delighting in the bad news he brought.

"Edward only got rid of the Clans so he could take control of the criminal underworld. To be king of it all, with no one left to challenge him. I'm telling you this in the hope you still care enough about right and wrong to do something about that."

Hearing the truth at last should have come as a shock to Daniel—but it didn't. He just nodded slowly.

"It does sound like something Edward would do," said Tina.

"And it would explain why he's been so keen for his organization to take over the vampire nightclubs and the mummies' drug business," said Daniel.

"Tip of the iceberg," said Nigel. "You have no idea what some of the Clans were into."

Tina fixed him with her best hard stare. "How do you know about Edward's plans?"

"Because you weren't his first choice to take down the Clans," said Nigel. "Before he settled on you he wanted to use the werewolf clan to attack the other monsters. This was when he was planning for open war instead of assassins. The alpha wolves held a special secret meeting just to hear his proposal. It had to be secret, because if the other Clans had found out there would have been serious reprisals. But the wolves saw a chance to be free at last, and that's why they were prepared to listen to the one monster all the others hated and despised.

"There's no doubt the wolves were tempted when Edward offered them a chance for revenge on the Clans who'd held them down for so long. But in the end they said no. Because they didn't trust Edward; because they didn't think his plans would work; and because open war would have meant too many dead wolves. But I think mostly... because he's the only one who *wants* to be a monster. The wolves are just what the world made them, but Edward Hyde is a self-made abomination."

Daniel gestured for Nigel to stop, so he could have a moment to think. He stared at the ground for a long moment, and then turned to Tina.

"Every time I think I'm getting my head around what's really going on, someone comes along and kicks my feet out from under me."

"What he's saying would explain a lot," said Tina.

"It would mean that we've been used," said Daniel.

"I'm used to it," said Tina. "What do you think we should do?"

"Listen some more," said Daniel. He turned back to Nigel, who met his gaze steadily.

"The wolves don't want to run the criminal underground," said Nigel. "They just want to be free to run wild, like they did in the old days. To leave civilization, get back to the untamed places of the earth, and be left to themselves."

"Are there any places like that left?" said Daniel.

"You'd be surprised," said Nigel.

"What is it you want us to do?" said Tina.

Nigel kept his gaze fixed on Daniel. "Stop Edward—because the wolves can't. He's too well defended. But you can get close to him."

"And kill him?" said Daniel.

"Don't you want to?" said Nigel. "Everyone else does, who's met him."

"I'm not sure we could take Edward Hyde," said Tina. "He might actually be stronger than both of us together. He's been a Hyde for so long..." And then she stopped, and grinned suddenly. "Be fun to try, though."

"What about the other Hydes?" said Daniel. "Could we get them to side with us, against Edward? If we told them the truth?"

"Who's to say they don't already know?" said Tina. "We were set up to do Edward's dirty work for him, and then be discarded afterward. The moment he didn't need us, he could just throw us to the other Hydes..."

"Would they kill their own kind?" said Daniel.

"They're Hydes," said Tina.

Daniel nodded reluctantly. "You know them better than me."

Tina frowned. "Not really. I was never a part of Jekyll & Hyde Inc. Until Edward put us together, I'd never met another Hyde."

"There's a reason for that," said Nigel.

Daniel and Tina looked at him sharply, and he smiled slowly.

"And so we come at last to the great secret at the heart of Jekyll & Hyde Inc. There *are* no other Hydes. There used to be ... but Edward killed them all, one by one. You two are the only Hydes left, apart from him."

Daniel and Tina looked at each other, and for a long moment they were both too shocked to say anything.

"But ... I used to go drinking and fighting with them!" said Tina.

"Hope you have good memories of that," said Nigel.

"Why would Edward kill all the other Hydes?" said Daniel.

"Because he felt threatened by them. He wanted to replace them with new and weaker Hydes, created by a diluted version of the Elixir. But he couldn't make any more. I don't know why. Perhaps some important ingredient isn't available any more. The only way he could get more Elixir was to kill the existing Hydes and harvest what remained of the potion from their corpses. Apparently a lot of it gets lost during the extraction process." Nigel smiled coldly at Daniel. "You drank the very last dose in existence."

"Of course!" said Daniel. He turned to Tina. "That's why he made such a point of showing us that lab this morning. It was all misdirection, to make us believe he still had control of the Elixir."

"It would explain why the attacks on the Clans were left to us," said Tina. "He didn't have anyone else. We were his last chance."

Daniel nodded quickly. "Remember when the mummies said Edward asked them if they would help manufacture the Elixir? That's why he was concerned about what they might have said: because it might have led us to the truth."

"That's why Edward had to launch his war against the Clans," said Tina. "He had to destroy them before they found out how weak he really is."

"It was never about waiting for the right person, after all," said Daniel. "He had to go with me because I was all he had."

"So," said Nigel, raising his voice to draw their attention back to him. "You have to take care of Edward, to stop him building a new power base from the criminal underworld . . . and save the humans and the wolves from the last real monster in the world."

Daniel's gaze was still fixed on Tina. "There's no way we could persuade Edward to step down, or change his plans."

"He'd fight us to the death," said Tina. "But can we take him? You saw what he did to the tiger."

"I'm starting to think he arranged that deliberately," said Daniel. "To warn us not to mess with him."

"We could always visit the armory and load up with really big guns," said Tina.

"You think Miss Montague would just hand them over? She'd be bound to suspect something, and get word to Edward. Our only real chance is to hit him without warning."

"You're ready to do that?" said Tina.

"Why not?" said Daniel.

Tina grinned brightly. "You know how to show a girl a good time!"

"But could you kill him?" said Daniel. "After everything he did for you?"

"He saved you too," said Tina.

"But at heart, I'm still a copper," said Daniel. "I didn't go through all of this just to see the monster Clans replaced by something worse. If you'd known what he was planning, would you have gone through with it?"

"Probably," said Tina. "I spent a lot of time learning how to kill monsters; and I wasn't about to be cheated out of the experience. But ... he could have trusted me with the truth and he didn't. So to hell with him. What about you, mister policeman? Could you kill Edward?"

Daniel smiled suddenly. "I signed on to kill monsters. All of them."

"I never liked the man," said Tina.

"Does this mean you'll do it?" said Nigel, breaking in impatiently.

"Yes," said Daniel. And then he turned slowly, and fixed his old friend with a thoughtful stare. "But what about you?"

"What about me?" said Nigel.

"Paul knew he'd gone too far," said Daniel. "That he'd become something his old self would have hated. So I have to ask: Have you killed people?"

Nigel met his gaze steadily. There was no guilt in his face, nothing to suggest Daniel's question meant anything to him.

"When the moonlight fills my head I run with the pack, and kill whatever they chase. We're predators—and everything else that lives is our prey."

"It must have driven the wolves crazy," said Daniel. "To be forced into a subservient role all these years, only allowed to kill on the Clans' orders."

"You have no idea," said Nigel.

"That's why they can't wait to get back to the old ways, and hunt like they used to."

"This is their time, come round again," said Nigel.

"But even when you're a wolf, you still have human intelligence," said Daniel. "You could choose not to kill."

Nigel shook his head impatiently. "When I'm a wolf, I do as a wolf does. The hunt and the kill are in the blood."

"You told me you hated what you'd become," said Daniel. "Losing all the rarefied tastes that defined the man you used to be. But while your human self might regret what it's lost, he's not in the driving seat—is he? The wolf has taken over."

"None of this matters," said Nigel. "Edward is the real threat."

"But he's not here, and you are," said Daniel. "And I have to deal with what's in front of me."

Nigel's smile looked suddenly more like a snarl. "Are you threatening me, old friend?"

"You said it yourself, Nigel: You're not the man I used to know. The wolf has eaten him. At least Paul had the courage to ask me to kill him."

"Paul always *was* weak."

Daniel met his gaze steadily. "I really wanted to believe you, when you said the werewolves intended to leave civilization and go away from Humanity. That they just wanted to run free. But there really isn't anywhere for you to go, is there? I don't doubt that Edward is everything you say he is, but that's not why you want us to kill him. The werewolves want him dead because he and his organization are all that's left to protect Humanity from the wolf pack."

"You can't stop us, Daniel," said Nigel.

"Why did they send you?" said Daniel. "Did the alpha wolves think I would believe everything you said, just because you and I used to be friends?"

"Something like that," said Nigel. "I volunteered for this because I always could talk you into anything."

"You're a wolf now," said Daniel. "And you love it."

"What does it matter?" said Nigel. "You have to stop Edward and his plans, or everything you've endured will have been for nothing. And without Edward and what's left of his organization . . . you can't stop us."

"There's more to Jekyll & Hyde Inc. than just Edward," said Daniel. "There's Tina, and there's me."

"You think his people will follow you, after you've killed their leader?"

"Why not?" said Tina. "Nobody likes Edward Hyde. And if we can take him, we can take care of the werewolf clan. Just like we did the Frankensteins, the vampires, and the mummies. Because we're smarter than you and we fight dirty."

"Because we're Hydes," said Daniel.

"You only beat the others because they didn't see you coming," said Nigel. "Thanks to Edward, we've been preparing for an attack. You come at us and we'll eat you alive."

"Good thing that's not the plan," said Daniel.

For the first time Nigel looked at him uncertainly, and then he shook his head as though dismissing Daniel's words.

"Don't think you can make me choose between you and the pack. All I can offer you is the chance to walk away."

Daniel looked at him steadily. "I'm sorry, Nigel. I can't do that. I have to kill you, here and now. Because I owe it to the man you used to be."

Nigel disappeared, replaced in a moment by a huge humanoid wolf. The massive gray-furred figure towered over the Hydes—a lean and powerful killer with a barrel chest and a narrow waist, built for the hunt and the kill. The large hands ended in vicious claws, the long muzzle was crammed full of teeth, and the burning yellow eyes were smart and crafty. The rank smell of the beast was almost overpowering. It stank of hate and hunger and sudden death. The werewolf smiled slowly, savoring the carnage to come. And Daniel smiled right back at it.

"Very impressive, Nigel. But unfortunately you're just a wolf. While Tina and I are so much more."

The werewolf surged forward, its great teeth straining for Daniel's throat. But he saw the attack forming in the werewolf's muscles, and by the time it launched itself he was already somewhere else. The great beast shot through the space where Daniel had been, and he slammed a fist into its side as it passed. Ribs shattered as his fist sank into the gray hide, all the way up to the wrist. The wolf howled loudly, in shock as much as pain, and Daniel jerked his hand out. The werewolf spun round with dizzying speed, and the broken ribs repaired themselves in a series of low popping noises.

The werewolf went to leap again, but while its attention was fixed on Daniel, Tina jumped high into the air and brought her fist slamming down on the werewolf's head. The skull caved in, and Tina's hand sank in so far she was able to grab a handful of brains and rip them out. The werewolf howled miserably, and lurched back and forth in the narrow alley, clutching at its head with both hands.

Tina studied the pulpy pink-and-gray mass in her hand, took a mouthful, and chewed thoughtfully.

"I've never munched on a mind before. Could use some salt."

And then she broke off, because the werewolf was straightening up again. The skull had already repaired itself, and the yellow eyes were sharp and clear. Tina threw her handful of brains aside, and moved quickly to stand beside Daniel.

"I say we get out our guns and fill him full of silver."

"Good idea," said Daniel. "Unfortunately, we never did get around to loading them."

"There's always something..." said Tina. "If you have any other ideas, I'm ready to listen."

"I'll draw my knife. While he's focused on that you get in behind him and restrain him, and I'll stab him in the heart."

"I can hear you, you know," said the werewolf. Its voice was a low growl, and sounded nothing like Nigel. "You even try to stick me and I'll bite your hand off."

Daniel's skin crawled at the sound of an animal talking like a man, but he made himself smile easily at the massive creature.

"I'm going to cut your heart out, Nigel. If you still have one."

He drew the knife from its hidden scabbard in one swift movement, and the werewolf went for him. The bared teeth had almost closed on Daniel's face when Tina jumped the werewolf from behind. Her weight almost drove the creature to its knees, and while it was caught off-balance she slipped an arm around its throat and pulled back hard. The werewolf bucked and reared, trying to throw her off, but she clung on grimly, tightening her hold until the werewolf's head was forced up. The beast raked at Tina's arm with its claws, and blood spurted. She hissed with pain, but wouldn't loosen her grip. And then Daniel stepped forward and pressed the tip of his silver knife against the taut skin just below the werewolf's breastbone. The huge creature held very still.

"You know the touch of silver, don't you, Nigel?" said Daniel.

"Stab him!" said Tina. "I can't hold him forever!"

But Daniel was looking into the yellow eyes of the werewolf. He thought he saw someone he knew looking back.

"Do it!" yelled Tina. "If he gets away he'll warn the others."

"You're still in there, Nigel," said Daniel, holding the werewolf's eyes with his own. "Remember the man you used to be. Think of how much the wolf has taken from you. All the things that defined who and what you were. A gentleman of the old school. Don't let the wolf make you nothing but an animal, grubbing around in the guts of your latest kill. Please, let me help you. Let me free you from the curse of the werewolf."

Suddenly the wolf was gone, and Tina had her arm around the throat of a man.

"Just do it," said Nigel.

Daniel stabbed his old friend through the heart, and the light went out of Nigel's eyes. Daniel jerked the blade back, and Nigel slumped in Tina's grasp. She let him collapse to the alley floor, and then stepped back and nodded slowly to Daniel.

"That was a brave thing you did."

"It was a brave thing *he* did," said Daniel. "Are you hurt?"

Tina didn't even glance at her arm. "Werewolves aren't the only ones that heal quickly."

"This war has been very hard on my friends," said Daniel. "Oscar, Paul, and now Nigel."

"You still have me," said Tina.

"And you have me," said Daniel.

They shared a smile.

"The alpha wolves won't appear till the moon's out," said Daniel. "We've got time for a few drinks first."

"Or a lot of drinks."

"Even better."

Tina looked at him steadily. "When all the alpha wolves are dead, are we going to kill Edward?"

"Why not?" said Daniel. "I promised him I'd kill all the monsters."

"What will we do, once he's dead?" said Tina. "When all the monsters are gone?"

"We'll think of something," said Daniel.

They left Nigel's body lying in the alleyway, and went looking for a bar to drink in and wreck. Until it was time to go to Elstree Park and hunt wolves.

Night fell over London. The full moon did its best to shine through the pollution, its light cold and distant as a broken promise.

A bitter wind blew from out of the east, pushing the clouds around. Traffic still roared in the city streets, but it was only a murmur deep in the heart of Elstree Park. Daniel and Tina quietly made their way through a copse of trees that bordered on an open clearing. They hadn't passed a single other person so far, as though everyone else had stayed away because they could sense something bad was loose in the night. Edward had been right about that.

Daniel and Tina moved on through the copse, sticking to the deepest and darkest of the shadows. The whole place was eerily silent, as though they'd crossed over into another world. Parks usually had a tame feel to them—of nature brought under control, to provide a safe setting for people to relax in. Somewhere they could sit and rest, picnic and sunbathe. But on this night, Elstree Park felt very different. As though just the presence of the alpha wolves had made it a wild place, where nature still followed the old ways . . . red in tooth and claw.

"The wolves are right ahead," Daniel said quietly. "Listen—you can hear them."

"Hell with that," said Tina. "I can smell them. Like a fur rug that's gone feral."

"That's why I was careful to approach downwind," said Daniel. "So the breeze wouldn't carry our scent to them."

"Good for you, Boy Scout," said Tina.

"Do you want me to start a fire by rubbing two werewolves together?"

"I think I would pay good money to see that."

They stopped at the edge of the trees, careful to remain hidden in the shadows. Out in the clearing, sleek, gray-furred figures were running in the moonlight and jumping high in the air just for the joy of it. Some were fighting, in a relaxed sort of way, though the biting and clawing looked real enough. There was a splendor to the wolves, of wild things running free in a way humans had long forgotten.

"I count twenty of them," said Tina. "Just like Edward said. Do we have a plan, as such?"

"If we open fire from a distance the survivors will scatter," Daniel said thoughtfully. "And we'll never catch them all. We have to get close enough to hold their attention, so they'll think they have a chance of bringing us down. Then they'll attack as a pack."

"So your great idea is: show ourselves to the werewolves and hope they charge us?"

"We have silver bullets, and silver knives."

"I'm starting to think we might have been better off with a silver bomb and a really long fuse," said Tina. "Your friend Nigel took a lot of punishment, and he wasn't even an alpha."

Daniel smiled at her. "Isn't this when you usually say, *But we're Hydes?*"

"I'm all for a good scrap," said Tina, "but werewolves are harder to kill than cockroaches. A little strategy wouldn't go amiss here."

"Leave the trees and walk straight at them."

"Okay..." said Tina. "If nothing else, that should confuse them. It confuses the hell out of me."

"Hold your fire until we're almost upon them," said Daniel. "We only have twelve bullets."

"Won't the survivors run off?" said Tina.

"I don't think so. Once they realize we're out of bullets, all they'll be able to think of is revenge. And that's when we go to the silver knives."

"Twelve bullets," said Tina. "Even if we never miss, that still leaves eight really angry werewolves coming right at us."

"Isn't this where you usually say, *Fun?*"

"It is just possible that we could be pushing our luck here," said Tina.

"This is our only chance to take out all the alpha wolves," said Daniel. "And finally put an end to the monster Clans."

They looked out into the clearing, where the werewolves had stopped playing and formed a circle. If they were saying anything, the sound didn't carry.

"Edward said they'd tear each other apart," said Tina. "And we'd just have to mop up the survivors."

"No plan survives contact with the enemy."

"Now you tell me."

They broke off as the alpha werewolves suddenly went for each other's throats. No warnings, no howled challenges, they just slammed into one another with bared fangs and slashing claws. Blood flew on the moonlit air. The fighting was so savage Daniel thought the alpha werewolves really might wipe each other out, but it quickly became clear that although the wolves were tearing away with vicious intent, none of them were dying. Their wounds closed almost immediately, the blood stopped spurting, and they went right back to ripping the guts out of each other.

Until, one by one, a wolf would just give up and bare its throat submissively to the victor and the loser would be allowed to retreat, leaving the fight to go on without them. It wasn't long before it was all over, and one huge wolf stood alone in the shimmering moonlight. And all the other wolves bowed their heads, to the new leader of the pack.

The one who would lead them against Humanity.

"All right," said Daniel. "Let's get this show on the road."

"It has been a while since we had a real challenge," said Tina.

"Looking forward to it, after all?"

"You know I am."

"You know more about guns than I do," said Daniel. "Any advice?"

"Don't miss." Tina stopped, as a thought struck her. "Do you suppose Edward deliberately only gave us twelve bullets to make it less likely we'd come back alive to challenge him?"

"Wouldn't surprise me one bit," said Daniel. "Ready?"

"Always."

"Bet I kill more than you do," said Daniel.

"You're on. What are we betting?"

"We can sort that out later."

Side by side they left the cover of the trees and walked out into the clearing. Holding their guns down by their legs so they wouldn't be immediately visible. All the werewolves' heads snapped round to look at them, eyes glowing golden in the moonlight. And then they raced forward across the open clearing at incredible speed, hoping their prey would break and run so they could have the fun of chasing them down.

Daniel and Tina kept walking, even though every instinct was screaming at them to do something. They made themselves wait until the werewolves were close enough to see what they had in their hands, and then they both raised their long-barreled pistols and took aim. The alpha wolves slammed to a halt, crouching low as they studied the Hydes and their guns. Daniel kept his hand steady, even as he wondered whether the wolves realized what kind of ammunition they were facing. And if so, whether they would do the sensible thing, and turn and run. If they did, Daniel wasn't sure he'd be able to shoot them in the back.

The werewolf clan wasn't supposed to be in the same league as the other monster Clans. More pressed into the service of evil, rather than evil themselves. But then Daniel remembered Nigel talking about the hunt and the kill, and how the wolves saw all of humanity as nothing more than prey, and he kept his aim steady.

The whole pack suddenly surged forward, crossing the intervening space at incredible speed, and Daniel discovered he didn't feel quite as confident as he had just a few moments before. Death was coming right at him, with huge bared teeth and vicious claws. Daniel suddenly wondered whether the silver bullets would be enough to do the job on their own, or whether he had to hit the heart every time. Like staking a vampire. He wasn't even sure exactly where a werewolf kept its heart. But once he looked, he had no trouble spotting the wide and prominent breastbone on each wolf, so he just exchanged a glance with Tina, and then they opened fire together.

Twelve silver bullets slammed home in swift succession, and twelve alpha werewolves crashed to the ground as though they'd just run into an invisible wall. Daniel and Tina emptied their guns so quickly, all twelve were dead before the other wolves even realized what was happening.

The dead wolves turned into dead men. Just so many naked corpses with great wounds in their chests, lying still and steaming in the cool night air, on blood-soaked grass. The other wolves crashed to a halt, so they could study the dead bodies. They sniffed at them and licked their faces, and even pawed at them in a hopeful way, but they didn't whine or howl. They just turned their heads to stare at Daniel and Tina with brightly shining eyes, gray lips pulled back to show the savage teeth. Their hatred burned on the cool night air like a living presence. Daniel and Tina met their gaze steadily, and waited for the last of the alpha wolves to come to them.

"All those bodies are male," said Daniel as he holstered his empty gun. "Not a single alpha female in the pack."

"Werewolves are sexist," said Tina as she put her own gun away. "Who knew?"

"Maybe they're just strong on tradition."

"Same thing."

They drew their silver knives and showed them to the wolves. Their heads came up, but they didn't howl. They didn't even growl. The surviving alphas just charged straight at the Hydes, their shining eyes full of murder and revenge. Heavily clawed paws sent divots of grass flying as they hurled themselves forward. Daniel was sure they recognized the silver in the blades, shimmering in the moonlight, but it didn't slow them down.

Daniel and Tina waited till the wolves were almost upon them, taking up a ready stance and holding their knives held out before them. Daniel could see the wolves' paws slamming into the ground, hear their heavy breathing, and the thick musky scent of them was heavy on the air. He could feel the tension in Tina's arm as it pressed against his. That steadied him a little, to know she felt as uncertain as he did. Even after all the unnatural creatures they'd fought, and triumphed over, it seemed to Daniel that there was something horribly primal and basic in the wolves' threat. As though fear of the wolf was written into his genes, an inherited knowledge and a warning from his primitive ancestors.

But that was then, and this was now. And Daniel was a Hyde now.

The werewolves threw themselves at Daniel and Tina, bared fangs straining for an extended arm or an undefended gut. The first wolf to reach them suddenly leapt high, going for Daniel's throat. He grabbed a handful of its gray fur with his free hand, and slammed the wolf to the ground at his feet with enough force to drive all the breath from its body. And then he thrust his knife into the wolf's eye, and twisted it. The wolf shuddered and stopped moving, changing back into a man as though it was shrugging off a fur coat.

Another wolf had leapt at Tina, and she ducked underneath it, her knife thrusting up to gut it as it passed. The wolf howled horribly, but it was a man by the time it hit the grass in a flurry of bloody intestines.

The remaining wolves hit the Hydes low, going for the groin or an exposed leg muscle. Daniel and Tina stood their ground and hacked and stabbed at everything that came within range. The gray-furred shapes surrounded them, coming at them from every side at once, but never making a sound. Silver knives backed by Hyde muscles plunged in and out of the lean wolf bodies, forced all the way in till they slammed to a halt against the heavy hilts. The blades were sharp enough to cut like razors, and heavy enough to shear through bones as well as flesh. Dark blood spurted on the night air and rained down onto the grass, and the werewolves finally howled in pain and fury as they realized the wounds they took from the silver blades weren't healing. The pack circled Daniel and Tina, darting in to bite and claw before pulling back again, evading the silver blades and doing their utmost to keep the Hydes off-balance.

Daniel and Tina moved quickly to stand back-to-back, lashing about them with undiminished strength and speed. The wolves were moving so quickly now they were just a gray blur in the moonlight, changing direction so suddenly the Hydes were never sure where the snapping teeth and tearing claws were coming from, and it took everything Daniel and Tina had, just to keep up with them.

Daniel plunged his silver blade deep into gray-furred sides, searching for the heart, while Tina's blade flashed fiercely as it cut the throats of wolves that got too close. Werewolves fell dying to the blood-soaked grass in a sprawl of gray fur and clawed paws, but were pitifully human by the time they lay still. The last of the wolves gave up all thought of tactics and threw themselves bodily at the Hydes, desperate to drag them down and finish them.

Huge fangs tore through Daniel's jacket and savaged the flesh beneath, while terrible claws raked bloody furrows in Tina's bare arms. The Hydes laughed in the wolves' faces and kept on fighting. Hate and stubbornness kept them going, long after strength and courage might have failed them. Hyde blood rained down onto the grass, to mingle with that of the wolves, and sometimes Daniel or Tina would cry out from shock or pain, but their silver knives never slowed or faltered as they killed one alpha wolf after another. This was their last fight, the end of their war against the monster Clans, and they were damned if they'd lose now after having come so far.

In the end the wolves lost because they were all attack and no defense. They were too used to surviving whatever wounds they took, as long as that brought them to the kill. It had been a really long time since they'd had to face silver knives in the hands of those who knew how to use them and had the guts to go head to head with werewolves. And it did help that the Hydes' wounds closed and healed when the wolves' didn't. The werewolves threw themselves at Daniel and Tina again and again with increasing desperation, a raging storm of teeth and claws—but the Hydes stood firm and met them with cold silver and colder determination. They were beyond hot blood; they were in the killing place now. And for all the wolves' strength and speed and fury, they were the ones who died, while the Hydes didn't.

One last wolf finally got close enough to hit Daniel square in the chest and bowl him over. The two of them went sprawling on the blood-soaked grass, and the werewolf locked its jaws on Daniel's shoulder and shook him like a dog shakes a rat. Daniel gritted his teeth and plunged his knife into the werewolf's ribs again and again, until finally he pierced its heart and a dead human body collapsed on top of him. Daniel heaved it off and lurched to his feet, blood streaming down from his savaged shoulder. He looked round just in time to see Tina thrust her silver knife deep into a werewolf's throat, almost cutting its head off before it finally collapsed.

And that was the end of the alpha wolves. Daniel saw the blood dripping from Tina's many wounds and stumbled over to hold her; it was a sign of how exhausted she was that she let him. They leaned heavily on each other, breathing hard. Blood from their injuries dripped down onto the trampled grass, but already the wounds were closing and their heads were clearing. Tina pushed Daniel away and checked him over carefully, searching for any wound that hadn't closed, any sign that the werewolves might have infected him with their change . . . but all the wounds were gone, even the deep bite on Daniel's shoulder. He looked Tina over too, and then they both smiled and relaxed, as it became clear they felt no fire in their blood, no fury in the soul, and that the moonlight was just moonlight. Daniel sighed, and stretched slowly.

"It seems Hydes are immune."

"Well," said Tina. "That's good to know."

They looked at the human bodies piled up around them. The last alphas of the werewolf clan, come to a very final end on the blood-soaked grass. Daniel and Tina looked at each other, and laughed out loud.

It sounded like the howling of wolves in the night.

Chapter Nine
IT'S IN THE BLOOD
✥ ✥ ✥

IN THE COLD AND QUIET of the early morning, Daniel and Tina headed back to the Jekyll & Hyde Inc. building. There was no traffic and no one about to see them return in triumph from a mission that should have killed them. It occurred to Daniel that this was probably a good thing, given that the werewolves had made a real mess of their clothes. He looked at the ragged remains of his jacket, and then glanced sideways at Tina and winced. She caught Daniel looking at her, and raised an eyebrow.

"What's the matter? See something you don't like?"

"We look like we've been dragged through a threshing machine backward," Daniel said solemnly. "And then beaten with sticks by people who really didn't like us. Of course, on you, it looks good."

"Nice save," said Tina. "You, on the other hand, look like crap."

Daniel checked himself out. The alpha werewolves had savaged him from head to foot, but as far as he could tell all his wounds had healed.

"No," said Tina. "I mean, you look tired."

"We've done a lot, and been through a lot," said Daniel. "And it isn't over yet."

"I know," said Tina. "Edward will be waiting to see if we survived the trap he set for us."

Daniel looked down the empty street to their destination. "Do we have a plan, as such?"

"March straight into his office and tell him the game is over," said Tina. "And that we've come back to deal with the worst monster of them all."

Daniel frowned. "You're still set on killing him?"

"He deserves it," said Tina.

"Of course he does. But ... we do owe him a lot. Think what our lives were like before we drank the Elixir. He gave us hope and new purpose."

"But he didn't do it for us," said Tina. "He just needed pawns to do his dirty work. And once we'd won his war for him, he threw us to the wolves. We don't owe that man a thing."

Daniel nodded at the Jekyll & Hyde Inc. building. A few lights were showing, here and there.

"Looks like someone's still up ... What makes you so sure Edward will be in his office? Why wouldn't he have gone home?"

"Because he doesn't have one," said Tina. "Think about it: Can you really see Edward Hyde taking it easy in a comfy chair, watching television with his feet up? You've seen what he does for fun; I don't think that man ever relaxes. I'm not even sure he sleeps anymore. It's hard to think of him doing anything that weak—or vulnerable."

"But why would he choose to live here?" said Daniel.

"Because it's the only place he feels safe," said Tina. "He doesn't fear his enemies; I think he glories in them. But he knows only major layers of protection can keep him secure." She smiled briefly. "From anyone but us."

"*Can* we kill him?" said Daniel. "I mean, do you think it's physically possible? We haven't been Hydes long, and we just survived a mauling by a whole pack of werewolves. He is the original Mr. Hyde, the embodiment of evil, and he's grown impossibly strong down the years. It could be there isn't a weapon that can kill him."

"We can take him if we work together," said Tina. "All we have to do is knock him down, rip his head off, and throw it out the window. Let's see him survive that."

"But—"

"I don't want to hear any buts!"

"We can't kill him until we've got some answers," said Daniel.

"We know all we need to know," Tina said bluntly. "We were played! We should have known. He told us, right to our faces, that we were just part of a scheme he'd been working on for years."

"But what's his endgame?" said Daniel. "Would control of the criminal underworld be enough, for someone like him?"

"Why not?" said Tina. "This way, he has his revenge on the monsters who never respected him *and* gets to keep everything that was theirs."

"But can you honestly see Edward Hyde resting on his laurels? We're talking about a man driven by hate and evil."

"Given a choice, between keeping him alive for answers or killing the most dangerous man in the world . . . I vote we concentrate on the killing," said Tina. "Or bits of us could end up scattered all around his office."

"Good point," said Daniel.

They came to a halt outside the main entrance. Light shone dimly through the tinted lobby windows, but there was no way of seeing in. No way of telling what kind of welcome Edward might have arranged for them. Daniel tried the door. It wasn't locked. He took his hand away.

"What?" said Tina.

"I'm just wondering if there might be a tiger or two waiting," said Daniel. "That does strike me as the kind of thing Edward would find funny."

"If we can handle werewolves, we can handle tigers," said Tina.

"This is true," said Daniel.

"It doesn't matter what's waiting in there," said Tina. "We just plow right through it, because we can't afford to be distracted. There's always the chance Edward might run, rather than face us openly."

"No," Daniel said immediately. "That would make him look weak, or scared, and he couldn't bear that. He always has to be the most dangerous thing in the room. His pride won't stand for anything else."

"I'm putting my money on some kind of ambush," said Tina. "Something to slow us down and wear us out before we get to him."

"Who'd still be in the building at this hour?" said Daniel. "Are we going to end up fighting the janitors?"

"Whoever it is, knock them down and walk right over them," said Tina. "Because good people don't come to work for Jekyll & Hyde Inc."

Daniel looked at her. "You did."

She met his gaze steadily. "I wasn't a good person when Edward found me. If I have mellowed since then, it's because of you."

"*Mellow* is not a word I would ever use to describe you," said Daniel.

She flashed him a quick smile. "You say the nicest things."

Daniel went back to staring at the door. "Given that we have killed Frankensteins, vampires, mummies, and werewolves to get to this point, I'm hard-pressed to think what Edward could have waiting in there that might stand a hope in hell of stopping us."

"He'll have thought of something," said Tina. "Edward lives to put the boot into his enemies, in new and inventive ways."

"I'm past being impressed," said Daniel. "I just want this to be over."

He kicked the door open and strode into the lobby, with Tina right beside him—and then they crashed to a halt. Because for the first time in Daniel's experience, the lobby wasn't empty. It was crammed from wall to wall with all kinds of people aiming all kinds of guns. Daniel and Tina looked thoughtfully at the massed gunmen, and a series of soft clicks traveled through the crowd as some of them remembered about safety catches. Daniel and Tina glared unwaveringly at the gunmen, refusing to be intimidated.

"People with guns?" Tina said loudly. "I think we've just been insulted."

"There are an awful lot of them," said Daniel.

"It's the principle of the thing!" said Tina.

Daniel studied the crowd carefully.

"I'm seeing automatic weapons and all kinds of handguns, but nothing to suggest these people have any experience in using them. They're just suits, office workers, maybe lower management. Security must have had the good sense to do a runner, rather than face us. If you ask me, most of these people would jump out of their socks if I shouted *Boo!* at them. Shall I try?"

"That would be cruel," said Tina.

"Is that a yes, or a no?"

"They're just office drones," said Tina. "I know some of them. We used to go drinking together." She raised her voice. "Johnny, Frank, Nathan . . . what the hell is going on here?"

The three gunmen named had the grace to seem a little abashed. They all looked at one another, hoping someone else would go first.

"Why are you pointing guns at me?" Tina said loudly.

"And me," said Daniel, just to make it clear he wasn't going to be left out.

Under the pressure of Tina's gaze, Nathan cleared his throat uncomfortably. "We're here because Mr. Hyde told us we had to be. And because we're more afraid of him than we are of you."

There was a general murmur of agreement that died quickly away when Tina scowled around her.

"But he's not here, and I am. Feel free to wet yourself now, and avoid the rush." She glanced at Daniel. "I can't believe Edward set his office staff on us."

"Not everyone's here," said Daniel.

Tina looked quickly round the crowd. "Who's missing?"

"I'm not seeing the two tailors," said Daniel. "Which is just as well, given that they always creeped the hell out of me."

"Really?" said Tina. "I thought they were sweet."

"That's because you're weird."

"And you love it," said Tina. "I don't see Miss Montague. And no one here seems to be armed with any of the really nasty things we saw in her armory."

"Now that is odd," said Daniel. "Maybe Miss Montague decided she didn't want any part of this, and barricaded herself inside the armory."

"Let's hope so," said Tina. "Because I saw a few things in there that could punch a hole through a mountain and make it apologize for being in the way." She turned back to Nathan, who looked like he was trying to pretend he was hiding behind someone else. "Do you know why Edward only gave you ordinary guns?"

"Because he wants your bodies as intact as possible," Nathan said miserably.

"How considerate," said Tina.

"Not really," said Daniel. "He has a use for them."

"Okay..." said Tina. "My head is now full of appalling images and I really wish it wasn't."

"I'm wondering why no one's opened fire yet," said Daniel.

"Ask them," said Tina. "No, let me do it. I can be more menacing."

"I can do menacing," said Daniel. "I used to be a policeman."

"Mr. Hyde said he didn't want your bodies destroyed," Nathan said quickly. "He did say he was prepared to accept damaged, if you didn't obey orders."

"We're not good at obeying orders," said Daniel.

"We're really not," said Tina.

"We're Hydes," said Daniel.

"Damn right," said Tina.

Nathan did his best to stand up straight and sound like he was in charge.

"You must see you're massively outnumbered! And that we have lots of really big guns. There's no way you could hope to survive massed firepower like this. So . . . please surrender, and let us take you to see Mr. Hyde in his office. Who knows? Maybe he just wants to talk to you."

"Does that even sound likely?" said Daniel.

"Not really, no," said Nathan. "But it has to beat dying here in a hail of bullets. Please come along . . . and then we can all go home and hide under our beds till this is over."

"Oh sure," said Tina. "Because this is all about you." She turned to Daniel. "I get it now. Edward wants our bodies as undamaged as possible, so he can use them to make more Elixir."

"And I'm pretty sure he can't do that while we're still alive," said Daniel. "So the most likely scenario is . . . we'll be ushered into his office, where Edward will be all smiles and apologies, and say there's been a terrible misunderstanding; and would we care for a nice drugged drink? Once we're under the influence he can just carve us up, and squeeze what's left of the Elixir out of our systems."

"That does sound like Edward," said Tina.

"Couldn't you cooperate just a little?" Nathan said desperately.

Daniel looked at Tina. "Do you feel like cooperating? It might get us to Edward's office a bit quicker."

"Really not in my nature," said Tina.

"Or mine," said Daniel.

Tina stretched slowly, in an anticipatory sort of way, and the whole crowd flinched.

"I think it's time we got to work," said Tina. "Beating up a whole crowd of gunmen isn't going to happen on its own."

"Sounds like a plan to me," said Daniel. "Tallest pile of bodies wins?"

"Now you're talking," said Tina.

They threw themselves at the massed gunmen, and before any of them could react the two Hydes were in and among them, moving too quickly for anyone to draw a bead. They punched people out, kicked their feet out from under them and trampled them underfoot, or just picked them up and threw them at the nearest wall. And laughed out loud while they did it.

At first, the gunmen hesitated to open fire for fear of hitting one of their own, but as more and more of them crashed bleeding or unconscious to the floor, it was inevitable that someone would panic. A man Daniel and Tina hadn't even got close to suddenly started screaming and opened fire with his machine pistol, shooting through everyone else to get to the Hydes. And once he started, everyone else joined in.

The noise of so many guns firing at once was deafening. Some people were blown off their feet, while others dropped their guns and threw themselves to the floor, praying for it all to be over. Heads disintegrated, and flesh exploded in bloody clouds. People were screaming everywhere, but no one could hear them for all the gunfire. Daniel and Tina darted back and forth, slapping guns out of hands and punching out those who tried to hang on to them, but as more and more people were cut down there was less and less cover. Daniel suddenly found himself facing a man with an automatic weapon, and nowhere left to go. Daniel hesitated, and the gunman opened fire at point-blank range.

The gun seemed to keep on firing forever. Bullet after bullet slammed into Daniel, but though his body rocked from the impacts, he stood his ground and stared defiantly back at the gunman. His body soaked up the bullets, and stopped them before they could penetrate far enough to do any real damage. It hurt like hell, but Daniel had known worse.

Everyone else stopped what they were doing, so they could stand and watch. Eventually the weapon ran out of ammunition, and a sudden hush fell across the lobby. The man slowly lowered his gun and stared, wide eyed, as one by one the bullets slowly emerged from Daniel's body and fell in a soft metal rain to the floor. Daniel looked down at his wounds, to reassure himself they were already healing—and then looked up again to stare coldly at the man with the empty gun.

The gunman threw his weapon away and sprinted for the exit. In a moment the rest of the crowd had thrown away their weapons and were hot on his heels, fighting one another as they struggled to force their way through the only door. It wasn't long before the lobby was empty, apart from all the bodies lying scattered across the floor. Most were dead or unconscious, and the rest had enough sense to pretend to be. Tina moved over to stand before Daniel and ran her fingers gently over his healed wounds.

"I didn't know you could do that," she said quietly.

"Neither did I," said Daniel. "But if I can do it, so can you."

Tina grinned. "Good to know."

"Edward made us better than he knew," said Daniel. "Let's go talk to the man and show him how appreciative we are."

"Can't wait," said Tina.

They headed for the elevators at the rear of the lobby. The air was thick with slowly dispersing gunsmoke and the hot copper smell of freshly spilled blood. Daniel and Tina breathed it in like fine wine as they stepped casually over the fallen bodies. It was all very quiet now, though not necessarily peaceful. Daniel stopped before the elevator doors, and Tina looked at him impatiently.

"You're frowning again."

"I think it might be best if we took the stairs," he said thoughtfully. "Edward could have sabotaged the elevators."

"That is what I would have done," said Tina. "Come on, I know where the door to the stairwell is."

"Of course you do," said Daniel, following her off to one side. "You know where everything is."

"Somebody has to," said Tina.

She led the way to the door, tucked away in a far corner of the lobby, but when she went to open it Daniel stopped her.

"Edward could have anticipated that we'd avoid the elevators, and booby-trapped the entrance to the stairwell."

"What if there is a bomb?" said Tina. "By now we're probably strong enough to shrug off an explosion."

"Probably," Daniel said carefully, in a way that suggested he wasn't really agreeing. "Do you want to bet your life on it?"

He leaned forward to examine the door, but Tina just barged right past him and slammed the door open with her shoulder. She strode into the stairwell and nothing bad happened, so Daniel sighed quietly and followed her.

"Will you stop being cautious?" Tina said over her shoulder as she started up the stairs. "You're a Hyde!"

"And I'd rather like to go on being a Hyde," said Daniel, moving up alongside her.

"You just shrugged off a whole magazine of high-velocity bullets!"

"Everyone has their limits," said Daniel.

"And I can't wait to find out what Edward's are," said Tina.

In the end, they ran all the way up the stairs to the top of the building, and when they finally stepped out onto Edward's floor they weren't even breathing hard. Daniel felt energized, like he'd just warmed up for the main event. He bounced up and down on his toes as he studied the corridor before him, and smiled at Tina.

"I can't believe how strong we're getting . . . Do you suppose this is how Edward feels all the time?"

"He's been a Hyde much longer than us," said Tina. "I'm wondering if there are things he's learned to do that we can't."

"I think we're about to find out," said Daniel.

"Are you clear on the plan?" said Tina.

"Hit him fast, hit him hard."

"We can do this. We outnumber him."

"But he's Edward Hyde," said Daniel.

"Not for long."

The corridor was completely empty, the only sounds their soft footsteps on the thick carpeting. Daniel kept a cautious eye on every door they passed, but they all remained firmly closed, as though they didn't want to get involved.

"Edward must know we're on our way," he said quietly. "Why would he still be waiting for us in his office?"

"Maybe he's got one last deal to offer us," said Tina.

"What could he possibly have that we'd want?"

"I don't know," said Tina. "But it's worth thinking about."

Daniel shot her a quick look. "Are you going off the idea of killing him?"

"No. I'm saying we should take what he has to offer—and *then* kill him."

"It has to be a trap," said Daniel. "And he's just sitting there, like a spider in his web, waiting for us to walk into it."

"Spiders get stepped on," said Tina.

They'd almost reached Edward's office when a small figure stepped suddenly out of a side door to block their way. Daniel and Tina stared blankly at the sweet little old lady in her nice sweater with puppies on. The woman in charge of the most dangerous part of Jekyll & Hyde Inc. There was something determined and implacable about her, even though she wasn't carrying any kind of weapon.

"What are you doing here, Miss Montague?" said Tina.

The old lady smiled easily. "I can't let you hurt my Edward." Her smile widened. "You wouldn't think I could still carry a torch for that man after all these years, would you? Especially after the way he's treated me. But what can I say? I knew I wanted him from the moment I set eyes on him."

"You must know he doesn't love you," said Daniel.

"I don't think Edward ever loved anybody," said Miss Montague. "I doubt he's capable of it. Perhaps that's part of the attraction—to love someone you know will never love you."

"Did he ask you to come here and defend him?" said Tina.

"Oh no, dear. I went to him and told him what I had in mind. I made it clear that I was ready to die for him, and he just shrugged and told me to get on with it. I'm pretty sure he thought it was funny . . . But that doesn't matter. I'm doing this for me, as much as for him."

"I'm not seeing anything nasty from your armory," Daniel said carefully. "So how do you propose to stop us?"

"With this," said Miss Montague. She produced a vial of dark liquid, and held it up before her. "The final dose of Dr. Jekyll's Elixir."

Daniel frowned. "I thought I drank the last one."

"Well, yes, technically you did," said Miss Montague. "This is the dregs, the leftovers. I was supposed to destroy them, but I decided to hang on to them for the armory. I had a feeling they might come in handy some day. I never thought I'd end up drinking this muck myself."

"Don't do it!" Tina said urgently. "The Elixir kills far more people than it transforms."

"I know, dear," Miss Montague said calmly. "But this is my chance to be like Edward. Perhaps he'll feel differently about me, when I'm more like him. And having seen so many Hydes come and go down the years I am curious as to what it will feel like, to be more than human.

"And ... I am so very tired of being old. Of having to struggle to do the things I used to take for granted. I'm ready to risk the potion, just for a chance to be young again. To feel like myself ... instead of a useless bag of bones."

She smiled happily at Daniel and Tina. "So, you just stand where you are while I drink this. And then I'll kick both your arses."

She took the cap off the vial and knocked the whole dose back in one. She threw away the vial, pulled a face, and shook her head vigorously.

"Oh, that tasted *vile*..."

Her back snapped straight and her head came up, her face filled with shock and wonder. Her body bulged as new muscles formed and youth swept through her like a cleansing wind, driving out old age. All the wrinkles disappeared from her face, leaving her looking like the woman who first fell in love with Edward Hyde. She blazed with fierce intensity, like a living goddess, and smiled dazzlingly at Daniel and Tina.

But even as they braced themselves for a fight, Miss Montague frowned ... as though something was happening that she didn't understand. Her muscles suddenly became even larger, bulging out until she couldn't stand straight anymore. Her back hunched, and one shoulder rose higher than the other. Miss Montague opened her mouth to say something, and blood poured out. She fell to her knees, twitching and shuddering, and then fell backward, staring in horror at something only she could see. Daniel and Tina rushed forward, feeling the need to do something even though Miss Montague had been ready to kill both of them just moments before. They knelt by her side but already she was growing older, shrinking in on herself, as though her own energies were burning her up. She became small and fragile, and her face collapsed into a maze of wrinkles. When she finally let out her last rattling breath, she looked like an ancient mummy.

Daniel and Tina slowly got to their feet again.

"I did warn her," said Tina.

"I don't think she cared," said Daniel. "She said she was ready to die for Edward."

"He wasn't worthy of her," said Tina.

"No," said Daniel. "He wasn't. Let's go visit the old monster—and make him pay."

"Sounds like a plan to me," said Tina.

When they finally burst into Edward's outer office, it was empty, with no sign anywhere of the determinedly glamorous secretary. Daniel looked quickly around in search of hidden traps or ambushes, but everything seemed normal. He frowned, and sniffed the air.

"Can you smell something?"

"Something..." said Daniel. "What is that?"

"Nothing good," said Tina.

They cautiously approached the door to Edward's office. Daniel placed one hand flat against the door and pushed it open, and when nothing bad happened, he led the way into the office. Where Edward Hyde was sitting happily behind his antique mahogany desk, waiting to greet them.

His secretary lay sprawled across the desk, her throat cut from ear to ear. Blood had streamed down the sides of the desk and pooled thickly on the floor. The secretary's face was a mask of horror, and her clothes had been ripped open so Edward could get at the flesh. There was a great hole in her side, with the ribs showing. Edward put a hand into the hole, pulled out a piece of meat and popped it into his mouth. He chewed thoughtfully, savoring the flavor, and blood ran down his chin as he smiled at Daniel and Tina.

"I got a bit peckish while I was waiting to see if you'd come back."

"I always knew you had no heart," said Tina.

"Neither does she, now," said Edward.

"How could you?" said Daniel.

Edward shrugged. "She served a purpose, which is all I've ever asked of anyone. I told her she could go, but she insisted on staying in case there was anything she could do for me. And as it turned out, there was. Did you happen to bump into Esme Montague, on your way here?"

"She wanted to protect you," said Daniel. "Because she loved you."

Edward shrugged again. "I never asked her to. Where is she?"

"She drank what was left of the Elixir," said Tina. "It killed her. And you don't give a damn—do you?"

"I never have," said Edward. "One of the great secrets of life, if you want to be free." He smiled easily. "And the other great secret? You're all just here for me to play with."

He paused, to wipe the secretary's blood off his mouth with the back of his hand. "Oh, don't look at me like that...It's not like you knew her. Or are you going to tell me you give a damn?"

"Just enough to make killing you that much easier," said Daniel. "We know about your plan to take control of the criminal underworld."

Edward sat back in his chair, and nodded happily. "I was wondering how long it would take you to work that out. And come on...Is it really such a surprise? I am the original Mr. Hyde! All the evil in a man, let loose on the world by Jekyll's marvelous Elixir."

"No," said Daniel. "I don't believe that's what the Elixir does. Tina and I took it, and we're not evil."

"A bit extreme, sometimes," said Tina. "But I like to think of that as just achieving my potential."

"The Elixir brings out what's inside someone," said Daniel. "And all you had in you was evil."

"You say that like it's a bad thing," said Edward. "But see how far it's brought me."

"You weren't sure whether we'd be coming back from the werewolves, were you?" said Tina.

"Either you'd kill them or they'd kill you," said Edward. "Whatever the result, I would come out ahead. Oh, don't look so outraged...I created you, o my children. I meddled in your lives to shape you, to make you what you are, just so I could turn you loose on my enemies. And look at what you've achieved! But now I'm wondering whether I really need you anymore."

He rose to his feet, and came out from behind the desk. Squat and powerful, broad shouldered and barrel chested, a living engine of destruction. Driven by hate, powered by evil. He smiled at them, like the devil looking on his works and finding them fair.

"You've both come so much farther than I ever thought possible. I feel a sort of paternal pride in you...And I suppose it is always possible that I might need your assistance in the future, as I use the criminal underworld to prey on Humanity and bring every last one of them under my control. So, I'll give you one last chance to rise above human weakness, and be real Hydes. Work for me, be my second-in-commands, and we will trample the whole world under our feet."

"I became a Hyde to kill monsters," said Daniel. "To make sure they couldn't hurt people anymore."

"And I got into this because I could feel free from addiction again, and have fun," said Tina. "Well guess what, Edward? You're no fun anymore."

Edward looked at her with mock sorrowful eyes. "How sharper than a serpent's tooth it is, to have raised an ungrateful child."

"I was never your child," said Tina. "Just something you could use. Without properly asking."

Edward smiled. "There's a difference?"

"You never did anything for us," said Daniel. "It was always all about making us into your soldiers, to fight your war for you. Because you didn't have the guts to go out and finish off the monster Clans yourself."

Edward's eyes narrowed dangerously. "I've killed any number of monsters."

"Only the ones who came to you," said Tina. "You hid yourself away in your own little fortress, behind layers of protection, and waited for the Clan's assassins to come to you. On your home ground, where you'd have the advantage . . . so you could have fun killing them, just like the tiger."

"I had so many enemies I couldn't risk taking them on openly," said Edward. "All the monster Clans wanted me dead! I had a war to fight, and generals don't put themselves in the front ranks."

"Everyone in Jekyll & Hyde Inc. was just cannon fodder," said Daniel. "More warm bodies to be thrust into the meat grinder, to give you a moment's advantage."

"That's what war is," said Edward.

"You even killed off your best soldiers," said Tina. "All the other Hydes. Because you were scared they might turn on you."

"Just like you turned on us," said Daniel. "You didn't really expect us to come back from the alpha wolves, did you? Not after everything you'd done to stack the odds in their favor."

"Lying about the situation, giving us misleading information about the alpha wolves—and carefully not providing enough silver bullets," said Tina.

"But just in case we made it back, you arranged a nice little welcome for us in the lobby," said Daniel. "You armed the night crew and put them in our way, so you could retrieve the Elixir from our corpses."

"You were supposed to die, but you couldn't even get that right," said Edward. "Why couldn't you just die for me, after everything I did for you?"

"We were always the patsies in the deal," said Daniel. "We don't owe you anything, because you never gave us anything that wasn't meant to serve you."

"The monster Clans are dead and broken," said Edward. "And you have your revenge. Haven't I delivered everything I promised?"

"All that time you spent training me," said Tina. "You made me think I was special, that I mattered. Did you ever feel anything for me?"

Edward looked at her for a long moment. "Did you want me to?"

"Tell me the truth," said Tina. "For once in your life."

"I would have cared for you, if I could," said Edward. "But that's not me. Hydes don't do family."

"You're just another monster," said Daniel.

"Now that's where you're wrong," said Edward. "I was never *just* another monster. Should I tell you the truth . . . ? I always wanted to tell someone the real story of Dr. Jekyll and Mr. Hyde. Well, why not? Tell the truth and shame the devil. Listen closely, my children. I never was Henry Jekyll. I was his friend: the lawyer, Gabriel John Utterson."

He gestured at the framed photo on his desk, and for the first time Daniel saw a vague resemblance to Edward Hyde in the man smiling out of the faded image.

"A lawyer," said Daniel. "Makes sense."

"You said it yourself, Daniel," Edward said happily. "Why would the good and saintly Dr. Jekyll want to take a potion that would release all the evil in a man? But the repressed and frustrated Utterson . . . he couldn't wait to take the potion, and do all the things he'd dreamed of. And then murder and frame his old friend Henry Jekyll for the sins he committed."

"You bastard!" said Daniel.

Edward Hyde put back his great head and laughed heartily, savoring the memories.

"You really are a monster," said Tina.

"And proud of it," said Edward.

"Is that why you never took the potion again, to change back?" said Daniel.

Edward hesitated, as though he hadn't expected that question. He glanced at the man in the photo and frowned, as though he didn't recognize him.

"He was such a weak man," he said finally. "Why would I want to go back to being something that small?"

"Why are you still here?" Daniel said bluntly. "You must have known those gunmen wouldn't be enough to stop us. You had to know we'd come for you."

"Of course I knew," said Edward. "But I just couldn't resist the challenge."

"You should have run," said Tina.

"I'm Edward Hyde!"

"So what?" said Tina.

Edward snarled like a cornered animal and launched himself at Daniel. He punched him in the face, and the sheer force of it sent Daniel staggering backward. Tina cried out angrily and went for Edward. Without turning round he back-elbowed her in the throat, stopping her dead in her tracks. By then Daniel had recovered from Edward's blow, and he lunged forward and punched Edward in the side of the head.

The sheer force of the blow drove Edward down onto one knee, but when Daniel moved in to pursue his advantage, Edward's fist came flying up from the floor and buried itself in Daniel's groin. A red flood of agony bent Daniel in half, and his eyes squeezed shut. Edward rose to his feet again, laughing breathlessly, just in time to face a new attack from Tina.

She lashed out at him with deadly force, and he didn't even try to avoid the blow. He just stood his ground and took it, absorbing the impact without even blinking. The two Hydes went at each other hammer and tongs, taking punches that would have killed any ordinary human being. Neither of them tried to defend themselves, or dodge or deflect a blow. They just threw themselves at each other with single-minded ferocity, snarling into each other's faces.

Daniel forced himself back onto his feet and went to join the fight, giving everything he had to every blow, but Edward just soaked up every attack Daniel and Tina could deliver, taking no damage and feeling no pain. His eyes danced merrily and he grinned like a shark, revelling in the moment as he finally unleashed his hatred on the two young Hydes who thought they were ready to replace him. He struck out at them again and again, with vicious strength and speed, but they stood their ground too, taking all the punishment he could hand out. Together Daniel and Tina piled on the pressure and drove Edward Hyde back, step by step.

The sounds of fists slamming into flesh were sickeningly loud, accompanied by harsh grunts from all three of them as they packed all their strength and emotion into every blow, calling on every resource they had to get the job done. Daniel and Tina pounded away at Edward, forcing him back toward his desk, and Daniel thought he saw the first flicker of fear in Edward's eyes as he realized that, for the first time in his extended life, sheer brute force wasn't going to be enough.

And that if he didn't win this fight, he was going to die.

Edward stopped laughing, and lowered his fists a little, as though the strength was going out of him. Tina took the bait and moved in, but the moment she came within range Edward spat into her eyes. Temporarily blinded, Tina cried out and fell back, shaking her head as she fought to clear her sight. And while Daniel looked at her, distracted, Edward seized the chance to back away. Daniel thought he would make a rush for the door, and moved quickly to block his way. But Edward went for his desk.

Daniel assumed Edward had some kind of special weapon stashed away there, and went after him. Instead Edward scooped up the body of his dead secretary, spun around, and threw her right into Daniel's face. His arms came up automatically to catch the secretary, cradling her in his arms. He never doubted she was dead, but he couldn't help feeling she deserved to be treated properly, after everything Edward had done to her.

And while Daniel was preoccupied with that, Edward went after Tina. She'd only just got her sight back, but even as she raised her fists to defend herself, Edward thrust his arms past hers and locked his huge hands around her throat. She grabbed his wrists with both hands and fought to break his hold, only to find that she couldn't. Edward's arms were thick with great cables of muscles, and her hands couldn't make any impression on them. She let go and punched him hard in the face, but he didn't flinch. She slammed a vicious blow into his side, and was sure she felt ribs crack and break, but he didn't react. He just piled on the pressure, forcing Tina's throat shut while he grinned fiercely. She fought for air, and started to panic when she found there wasn't any. Edward moved in close, pushing his face right into hers, so he could savor her growing fear . . . and watch the life go out of her.

Daniel forgot about treating the dead secretary respectfully. He threw her to one side, and rushed to help Tina. He slammed a punch into Edward's back, so hard he felt he must have destroyed one of the man's kidneys, but Edward didn't flinch or look back. Daniel hit him again and again, bruising his hands against the heavy muscles, but Edward just ignored him. Daniel saw Tina struggling helplessly, her face flushed crimson and her eyes bulging, as she fought for breath that wouldn't come. And Daniel knew that if he didn't do something quickly, she was going to die.

He lowered his fists, and thought furiously. There had to be a way to stop Edward. And then he smiled coldly as he realized it wasn't how hard you hit your enemy, but where. Everyone, no matter how strong, had the same weak spots. Daniel stepped forward and punched Edward on the back of his neck.

Daniel could feel the vertebrae break and shatter, and Edward's hands leapt open in a reflex action. For a moment Edward was helpless as the broken neck repaired itself, and Tina planted a foot against his massive chest and shoved him away with all her strength. Edward went stumbling backward to where Daniel was waiting. He rabbit-punched Edward again, putting all his strength into the blow, and drove him to his knees.

Daniel and Tina took a moment to look at each other over Edward's bent back. They knew they had to kill Edward while they had the chance. But Edward was a Hyde, just like them, and they had already survived everything the monster Clans could throw at them. What could they do to Edward that the Frankensteins, the vampires, the mummies, and the werewolves hadn't already tried?

And then Daniel realized he was looking at Tina as she stood behind Edward, just as she'd stood behind Nigel in the alleyway.

"Grab him, Tina!" Daniel yelled. "Hold him in place, like you did Nigel!"

Tina lunged forward, air still rasping painfully in her crushed throat. Her face twisted with the need for revenge, but her gaze was steady as she thrust an arm around Edward's throat. She pulled back hard and hauled him upright, holding him in place with his chest thrust out. Edward threw all his strength against her, struggling to break Tina's hold and throw her away, but he couldn't. Tina held him firmly, and glared at Daniel over Edward's shoulder.

"Do it!" she said, the harsh words only just understandable.

Daniel drew his silver knife, and stabbed Edward in the heart. Slamming the blade home with all his strength, until the hilt jarred against Edward's chest. But Edward didn't die. Even with his heart cut in two, Dr. Jekyll's Elixir wouldn't let Edward die. Daniel jerked the knife out. No blood spurted, and the gaping wound in Edward's chest healed in a moment. Edward snarled at Daniel mockingly as he struggled to break Tina's grip. She clung on determinedly, raking at Edward's face with her free hand. Blood ran down his cheeks, but he didn't care.

"Do something!" Tina yelled to Daniel, her words clearer now her throat was healing. "I can't hold him much longer!"

Daniel knew he had to think of something. He looked quickly round the office, searching for inspiration, for something he could use. His gaze fell on the two sepia photographs in their silver frames, still standing on the desk. They'd been pushed right to the back by the secretary's body, but now that was gone they both stood revealed again. Ancient images of Dr. Henry Jekyll and his old friend, the lawyer Utterson—who was now Edward Hyde. And a sudden cold certainty rushed through Daniel as the answer came to him. It was all about the Elixir. It had always been all about the Elixir. Why didn't Edward drink all of it once he'd turned? Why save it for decades?

Was the poison also the antidote?

Daniel wondered where could he get more of it.

He set the edge of the silver knife against his opposite wrist, gritted his teeth and pressed down hard, shearing through the great veins with one swift motion. Blood started to spurt, but before the wound could heal itself, Daniel surged forward and pressed it against Edward's open mouth. Caught off guard, Edward didn't have time to react before the pressure of the jetting blood forced itself down his throat. He swallowed despite himself, and then bent suddenly forward with such force that he threw Tina over his shoulder. She tucked and rolled and was quickly back on her feet, ready to grab Edward again, but stopped as Daniel shook his head. He pressed his hand over his cut wrist, and felt the wound heal. Edward straightened up, shaking and shuddering, his eyes full of a terrible foreshadowing.

Tina moved over to Daniel, and put an arm round his shoulders. They watched silently as Edward dropped to his knees, and then fell over onto his side. His convulsions were so powerful now they shook his whole body like a dog shakes a rat. He began to shrink on himself, in sudden fits and starts, his massive frame disappearing as though consumed by some inner fire, until at last he looked once again like the man in the sepia photograph. But the change didn't stop there. His face grew steadily older, shrinking back to reveal the skull beneath, as the years he'd defied for so long finally caught up with him. And when he finally stopped breathing and lay still, the withered thing curled up on the floor had nothing of Edward Hyde left in him.

Tina made sure Daniel could stand on his own, and then she went over to the body and looked down at it, her face completely unreadable.

"What did you do to him?"

"Our blood contains the Elixir," he said steadily. "The one thing that could turn Edward back into who he used to be."

"Good thinking," said Tina.

She turned to look back at him, and they stared at each other for a long moment.

"So," said Tina. "What do we do now?"

"We're Hydes," said Daniel. "The only ones left. Which makes us heirs to Jekyll & Hyde Inc., and all it controls."

"And what do you think we should do with all of that?" said Tina.

"Make the organization something to be proud of," said Daniel. "Turn it loose on all the monsters that are still out there."

"Typical policeman," said Tina. "We could own this city! Make everyone in it do what we want!"

"And become monsters, just like Edward."

"Are we going to have to fight over who takes charge?" said Tina.

"That would have to be a fight to the death," said Daniel.

"Yes," said Tina. "It would."

They stepped forward and put their hands on each other, and then they slow danced around Edward's office. They looked into each other's eyes, and smiled.

"What happens when we stop dancing?" said Tina.

"Oh," said Daniel, "I'm sure we'll think of something."